THE ELIZABETH STORIES

Isabel Huggan's short fiction has appeared in a variety of publications, including *Best Canadian Stories: 83*. Her stories have been read on CBC Radio, and one of them, "Jack of Hearts," was recently made into a television film. The recipient of several grants from the Canada Council and the Ontario Arts Council, Isabel Huggan has taught creative writing at the University of Ottawa and is now working on her next book. She currently lives in Nairobi, Kenya, with her husband and daughter.

THE
ELIZABETH
STORIES

ISABEL HUGGAN

A KING PENGUIN
PUBLISHED BY
PENGUIN BOOKS

PENGUIN BOOKS
Published by the Penguin Group
Viking Penguin Inc., 40 West 23rd Street,
New York, New York 10010, U.S.A.
Penguin Books Ltd, 27 Wrights Lane, London W8 5TZ, England
Penguin Books Australia Ltd, Ringwood,
Victoria, Australia
Penguin Books Canada Limited, 2801 John Street,
Markham, Ontario, Canada L3R 1B4
Penguin Books (N.Z.) Ltd, 182–190 Wairau Road,
Auckland 10, New Zealand

Penguin Books Ltd, Registered Offices: Harmondsworth,
Middlesex, England

First published in Canada by Oberon Press 1984
First published in the United States of America by
Viking Penguin Inc. 1987
Published in Penguin Books 1988

Some of the stories in this book first appeared in *Grain* magazine,
First Impressions, and *Best Canadian Stories:83*.

Grateful acknowledgment is made for permission to reprint
an excerpt from "Who's Sorry Now?" by Burt Kalmar,
Harry Ruby, and Ted Snyder. Copyright © 1923 by Mills Music, Inc.,
Ted Snyder Music, and Harry Ruby Music. Copyright © renewed.
Used by permission. All rights reserved.

LIBRARY OF CONGRESS CATALOGING IN PUBLICATION DATA
Huggan, Isabel, 1943–
The Elizabeth stories.
Reprint. Originally published: 1st American ed. New York:
Viking, 1987.
I. Title.
[PR9199.3.H757E4 1988] 813'.54 87-25782
ISBN 0 14 01.0199 3

Printed in the United States of America by
R. R. Donnelley & Sons Company, Harrisonburg, Virginia
Set in Garamond

For my sister and my daughter

THE
ELIZABETH
STORIES

Celia Behind Me

There was a little girl with large smooth cheeks and very thick glasses who lived up the street when I was in public school. Her name was Celia. It was far too rare and grown-up a name, so we always laughed at it. And we laughed at her because she was a chubby, diabetic child, made peevish by our teasing.

My mother always said, "You must be nice to Celia, she won't live forever," and even as early as seven I could see the unfairness of that position. Everybody died sooner or later, I'd die too, but that didn't mean everybody was nice to me or to each other. I already knew about mortality and was prepared to go to heaven with my two aunts who had died together in a car crash with their heads smashed like overripe melons. I overheard the bit about the melons when my mother was on the telephone, repeating that phrase and sobbing. I used to think about it often, repeating the words to myself as I did other things so that I got a nice rhythm: "Their heads smashed like melons, like melons, like melons." I imagined the pulpy insides of muskmelons and watermelons all over the road.

I often thought about the melons when I saw Celia because her head was so round and she seemed so bland and stupid and fruitlike. All rosy and vulnerable at the same time as being the most *awful* pain. She'd follow us home from school, whining if we walked faster than she did. Everybody always walked faster than Celia because her short little legs wouldn't keep up. And she was bundled in long stockings and heavy underwear, summer and winter, so that even her clothes held her back from our sturdy, leaping pace over and under hedges and across backyards and, when it was dry, or when it was frozen, down the stream bed and through the drainage pipe beneath the bridge on Church Street.

Celia, by the year I turned nine in December, had failed once and was behind us in school, which was a relief because at least in class there wasn't someone telling you to be nice to Celia. But she'd always be in the playground at recess, her pleading eyes magnified behind those ugly lenses so that you couldn't look at her when you told her she couldn't play skipping unless she was an ender. "Because you can't skip worth a fart," we'd whisper in her ear. "Fart, fart, fart," and watch her round pink face crumple as she stood there, turning, turning, turning the rope over and over.

As the fall turned to winter, the five of us who lived on

Brubacher Street and went back and forth to school together got meaner and meaner to Celia. And, after the brief diversions of Christmas, we returned with a vengeance to our running and hiding and scaring games that kept Celia in a state of terror all the way home.

My mother said, one day when I'd come into the kitchen and she'd just turned away from the window so I could see she'd been watching us coming down the street, "You'll be sorry, Elizabeth. I see how you're treating that poor child, and it makes me sick. You wait, young lady. Some day you'll see how it feels yourself. Now you be nice to her, d'you hear?"

"But it's not just me," I protested. "I'm nicer to her than anybody else, and I don't see why I have to be. She's nobody special, she's just a pain. She's really dumb and she can't do anything. Why can't I just play with the other kids like everybody else?"

"You just remember I'm watching," she said, ignoring every word I'd said. "And if I see one more snowball thrown in her direction, by you or by anybody else, I'm coming right out there and spanking you in front of them all. Now you remember that!"

I knew my mother, and knew this was no idle threat. The awesome responsibility of now making sure the other kids stopped snowballing Celia made me weep with rage and despair, and I was locked in my room after supper to "think things over."

I thought things over. I hated Celia with a dreadful and absolute passion. Her round guileless face floated in the air above me as I finally fell asleep, taunting me: "You have to be nice to me because I'm going to die."

I did as my mother bid me, out of fear and the thought of the shame that a public spanking would bring. I imagined my mother could see much farther up the street than she really could, and it prevented me from throwing snowballs or teasing Celia for the last four blocks of our homeward journey. And then came the stomach-wrenching task of making the others quit.

"You'd better stop," I'd say. "If my mother sees you she's going to thrash us all."

Terror of terrors that they wouldn't be sufficiently scared of her strap-wielding hand; gut-knotting fear that they'd find out or guess what she'd really said and throw millions of snowballs just for the joy of seeing me whipped, pants down in the snowbank, screaming. I visualized that scene all winter, and felt a shock of relief when March brought such a cold spell that the snow was too crisp for packing. It meant a temporary safety for Celia, and respite for me. For I knew, deep in my wretched heart, that were it not for Celia I was next in line for humiliation. I was kind of chunky and wore glasses too, and had sucked my thumb so openly in kindergarten that "Sucky" had stuck with me all the way to Grade 3 where I now balanced at a hazardous point, nearly accepted by the amorphous Other Kids and always at the brink of being laughed at, ignored or teased. I cried very easily, and prayed during those years—not to become pretty or smart or popular, all aims too far out of my or God's reach, but simply to be strong enough not to cry when I got called Sucky.

During that cold snap, we were all bundled up by our mothers as much as poor Celia ever was. Our comings and goings were hampered by layers of flannel bloomers and undershirts and ribbed stockings and itchy wool against us no matter which way we turned; mitts, sweaters, scarves and hats, heavy and wet-smelling when the snot from our dripping noses mixed with the melting snow on our collars and we wiped, in frigid resignation, our sore red faces with rough sleeves knobbed over with icy pellets.

Trudging, turgid little beasts we were, making our way along slippery streets, breaking the crusts on those few

8

front yards we'd not yet stepped all over in glee to hear the glorious snapping sound of boot through hard snow. Celia, her glasses steamed up even worse than mine, would scuffle and trip a few yards behind us, and I walked along wishing that some time I'd look back and she wouldn't be there. But she always was, and I was always conscious of the abiding hatred that had built up during the winter, in conflict with other emotions that gave me no peace at all. I felt pity, and a rising urge within me to cry as hard as I could so that Celia would cry too, and somehow realize how bad she made me feel, and ask my forgiveness.

It was the last day before the thaw when the tension broke, like northern lights exploding in the frozen air. We were all a little wingy after days of switching between the extremes of bitter cold outdoors and the heat of our homes and school. Thermostats had been turned up in a desperate attempt to combat the arctic air, so that we children suffered scratchy, tingly torment in our faces, hands and feet as the blood in our bodies roared in confusion, first freezing, then boiling. At school we had to go outside at recess—only an act of God would have ever prevented recess, the teachers had to have their cigarettes and tea—and in bad weather we huddled in a shed where the bicycles and the janitor's outdoor equipment were stored.

During the afternoon recess of the day I'm remembering, at the end of the shed where the girls stood, a sudden commotion broke out when Sandra, a rich big girl from Grade 4, brought forth a huge milk-chocolate bar from her pocket. It was brittle in the icy air, and snapped into little bits in its foil wrapper, to be divided among the chosen. I made my way cautiously to the fringe of her group, where many of my classmates were receiving their smidgens of sweet chocolate, letting it melt on their tongues like dark communion wafers. Behind me hung Celia, who had mistaken my earlier cries of "Stop throwing snowballs at Celia!" for kindness. She'd been mooning behind me for days, it seemed to me, as I stepped a little farther forward to see that there were only a few pieces left. Happily, though, most mouths were full and the air hummed with the murmuring sound of chocolate being pressed between tongue and palate.

Made bold by cold and desire, I spoke up. "Could I have a bit, Sandra?" She turned to where Celia and I stood, holding the precious foil in her mittened hand. Wrapping it in a ball, she pushed it over at Celia. Act of kindness, act of spite, vicious bitch or richness seeking expiation? She gave the chocolate to Celia and smiled at her. "This last bit is for Celia," she said to me.

"But I can't eat it," whispered Celia, her round red face aflame with the sensation of being singled out for a gift. "I've got di-a-beet-is." The word. Said so carefully. As if it were a talisman, a charm to protect her against our rough healthiness.

I knew it was a trick. I knew she was watching me out of the corner of her eye, that Sandra, but I was driven. "Then could I have it, eh?" The duress under which I acted prompted my chin to quiver and a tear to start down my cheek before I could wipe it away.

"No, no, no!" jeered Sandra then. "Suckybabies can't have sweets either. Di-a-beet-ics and Suck-y-ba-bies can't eat chocolate. Give it back, you little fart, Celia! That's the last time I ever give you anything!"

Wild, appreciative laughter from the chocolate-tongued mob, and they turned their backs on us, Celia and me, and waited while Sandra crushed the remaining bits into minuscule slivers. They had to take off their mitts and lick their fingers to pick up the last fragments from the foil. I stood there and prayed: "Dear God and Jesus, I would please like very much not to cry. Please help me. Amen." And with that the clanging recess bell clanked through the playground noise, and we all lined up, girls and boys in straight, straight rows, to go inside.

After school there was the usual bunch of us walking home and, of course, Celia trailing behind us. The cold of the past few days had been making us hurry, taking the shortest routes on our way to steaming cups of Ovaltine and cocoa. But this day we were all full of that peculiar energy that swells up before a turn in the weather and, as one body, we turned down the street that meant the long way home. Past the feed store where the Mennonites tied their horses, out the back of the town hall parking-lot and then down a ridge to the ice-covered stream and through the Church Street culvert to come out in the unused field behind the Front Street stores; the forbidden adventure we indulged in as a gesture of defiance against the parental "come right home."

We slid down the snowy slope at the mouth of the pipe that seemed immense then but was really only five feet in diameter. Part of its attraction was the tremendous racket you could make by scraping a stick along the corrugated sides as you went through. It was also long enough to echo very nicely if you made good booming noises, and we occasionally titillated each other by saying bad words at one end that grew as they bounced along the pipe and became wonderfully shocking in their magnitude . . . poopy, Poopy, POOpy, POOOOPy, POOOOPPYYY!

I was last because I had dropped my schoolbag in the snow and stopped to brush it off. And when I looked up, down at the far end, where the white plate of daylight lay stark in the darkness, the figures of my four friends were silhouetted as they emerged into the brightness. As I started making great sliding steps to catch up, I heard Celia behind me, and her plaintive, high voice: "Elizabeth! Wait for me, okay? I'm scared to go through alone. Elizabeth?"

And of course I slid faster and faster, unable to stand the

thought of being the only one in the culvert with Celia. Then we would come out together and we'd really be paired up. What if they always ran on ahead and left us to walk together? What would I ever do? And behind me I heard the rising call of Celia, who had ventured as far as a few yards into the pipe, calling my name to come back and walk with her. I got right to the end, when I heard another noise and looked up. There they all were, on the bridge looking down, and as soon as they saw my face began to chant, "Better wait for Celia, Sucky. Better get Celia, Sucky."

The sky was very pale and lifeless, and I looked up in the air at my breath curling in spirals and felt, I remember this very well, an exhilarating, clear-headed instant of understanding. And with that, raced back into the tunnel where Celia stood whimpering half-way along.

"You little fart!" I screamed at her, my voice breaking and tearing at the words. "You little diabetic fart! I hate you! I hate you! Stop it, stop crying, I hate you! I could bash your head in I hate you so much, you fart, you fart! I'll smash your head like a melon! And it'll go in pieces all over and you'll die. You'll die, you diabetic. You're going to die!" Shaking her, shaking her and banging her against the cold, ribbed metal, crying and sobbing for grief and gasping with the exertion of pure hatred. And then there were the others, pulling at me, yanking me away, and in the moral tones of those who don't actually take part, warning me that they were going to tell, that Celia probably was going to die now, that I was really evil, they would tell what I said.

And there, slumped in a little heap, was Celia, her round head in its furry bonnet all dirty at the back where it had hit against the pipe, and she was hiccupping with fear. And for a wild, terrible moment I thought I had killed her, that the movements and noises her body made were part of dying.

I ran.

I ran as fast as I could back out the way we had come, and all the way back to the schoolyard. I didn't think about where I was going, it simply seemed the only bulwark to turn to when I knew I couldn't go home. There were a few kids still in the yard but they were older and ignored me as I tried the handle of the side door and found it open. I'd never been in the school after hours, and was stricken with another kind of terror that it might be a strappable offence. But no-one saw me, even the janitor was blessedly in another part of the building, so I was able to creep down to the girls' washroom and quickly hide in one of the cubicles. Furtive, criminal, condemned.

I was so filled with horror I couldn't even cry. I just sat on the toilet seat, reading all the things that were written in pencil on the green, wooden walls. *G.R. loves M.H.* and *Y.F. hates W.S. for double double sure. Mr. Becker wears ladies pants.* Thinking that I might die myself, die right here, and then it wouldn't matter if they told on me that I had killed Celia.

But the inevitable footsteps of retribution came down the stone steps before I had been there very long. I heard the janitor's voice explaining he hadn't seen any children come in and then my father's voice saying that the others were sure this is where Elizabeth would be. And they called my name, and then came in, and I guess saw my boots beneath the door because I suddenly thought it was too late to scrunch them up on the seat and my father was looking down at me and grabbed my arm, hurting it, pulling me, saying "Get in the car, Elizabeth."

Both my mother and my father spanked me that night. At first I tried not to cry, and tried to defend myself against their diatribe, tried to tell them when they asked, "But whatever possessed you to do such a terrible thing?" But whatever I said seemed to make them more angry and they became so soured by their own shame that they slapped my stinging buttocks for personal revenge as much as for any rehabilitative purposes.

"I'll never be able to lift my head on this street again!" my mother cried, and it struck me then, as it still does now, as a marvellous turn of phrase. I thought about her head on the street as she hit me, and wondered what Celia's head looked like, and if I had dented it at all.

Celia hadn't died, of course. She'd been half-carried, half-dragged home by the heroic others, and given pills and attention and love, and the doctor had come to look at her head but she didn't have so much as a bruise. She had a dirty hat, and a bad case of hiccups all night, but she survived.

Celia forgave me, all too soon. Within weeks her mother allowed her to walk back and forth to school with me again. But, in all the years before she finally died at seventeen, I was never able to forgive her. She made me discover a darkness far more frightening than the echoing culvert, far more enduring than her smooth, pink face.

Sawdust

I've had warm, tingling feelings between my legs for as long as I can remember. One of my earliest, most vivid memories is being made to stand penitent at my grandmother's knee, made to tell her what awful indignities I had performed upon the teddy she'd given me only months before for my third birthday. It was Easter, and her front parlour was cold with damp April chill. There was a pot of lilies on a lace-covered table by the lace-covered window and I could smell their perfume as I waited for her wrath.

"You rub it? Where?" She glared down at me, having

been coached in the questions to this catechism by my parents. "We've simply got to get her to stop," they must have said. "Maybe if *you* shame her."

"There, Nana," I remember saying, and pointed quickly to my plump little crotch, hidden away beneath layers of cotton and velvet. Hoping that, somehow, she would smile. Maybe she did this secret thing too, and would say, "Oh, how nice. I'm sure teddy doesn't mind." But no such luck. There were white-faced intakes of breath, there were slappings and scoldings and tears, and the forbidding of any candy eggs, before or after supper.

The withholding of candy was old hat to my grandmother. She would always proffer her tray of Black Magic with the reminder, as my hand hovered by the liquid cherry, "You may have any but the soft centres. Your Nana loves the soft centres." And my resigned teeth would fasten on some terrible toffee she'd offer me, or clamp down on a chewy nougat for what seemed hours. I still hate hard centres, and find them, with their dreadful inedible interiors concealed beneath sweet chocolate, a shock and a cheat.

Teddy was confiscated as punishment and replaced in my private activities by other furry dolls. I knew now it was a bad thing I did, yet oddly enough my name for the rubbing and ensuing sensation was a particularly open and public one. I called it "greeting," and I have no idea what series of connective leaps my mind must have made to arrive at that. But greeting it was, and I would greet myself before sleep, my loneliness temporarily allayed.

By the time I turned five, greeting was no longer a solitary pursuit but involved either the observation or participation of Joyce and Sharon and Dennis and Dieter and Rudy. In those months before kindergarten, we'd be put in our yards to play during the mornings, and eventually there'd be a gathering in one spot or another and then a trek to the large vacant lot that backed onto my side of Brubacher Street. Along one edge of the field stood a row of poplars whose heavy low branches afforded easy access to more lofty places from which scouts could look out for mothers. Beside the trees lay the collapsed remains of a wooden bread waggon, abandoned by old man Kenny once he got rid of his horse and bought himself a real delivery truck. The waggon was dark brown with BREAD painted in gold on each side and with gilt scrolling around the edges. A square box of a waggon, not unlike a loaf itself. Inside there were three rows of shelves on either side of the door where the hot loaves would sit on their trip from bakery to table. There was just enough room on a shelf for one child to lie down, and so there we'd lie, stacked like loaves, greeting ourselves and giggling.

It was dark in the waggon except for the shaft of light cut by the door, and there was a heavy yeasty smell that must have engrained itself in the wood over the years. It was a comforting smell, not unlike the smell of life itself, sweat and skin and breathing.

There was a security and safety in that companionable place, as if by playing like this together we achieved mass absolution for our sins. God only knows who first suggested the activity or how we all came to trust each other. I can't remember. But it was Rudy and I who first took off our clothes and felt each other's bodies with exploring fingers. Once, at the end of the summer before we went off to school for the first time, I took off my cotton sundress and he his shorts and shirt, and we lay together on one of the shelves, first squeezed side by side and then with him on top of me. I can feel the heat inside the waggon, and the weight of his body on mine, and how we just lay very still.

Our mothers must have assumed that we played "store" or "house" inside the bread waggon, and so could not understand our dismay the following spring when the trees were chopped down and the waggon removed and the field cleared to make way for the new Pentecostal church. They were upset themselves, but about the noise and dirt of construction, and about the threat to the neighbourhood's tone. Except for the Roman Catholic Falconers on the corner, everyone on Brubacher Street was United Church or Lutheran, and the prospect of fundamentalist fervour on their doorstep made them nervous. My father, who had been chief among those trying to block the land sale by tightening the zoning laws, ranted for weeks. "Just one hallelujah," he'd say. "Just one hallelujah comes floating out one window and I go to council. Disturbing the peace."

What most infuriated my father was that he had been powerless to stop the deal in the first place, because there had been no need for the Pentecostals to go through his bank or any bank—they had paid Mr. Myers, who owned the land, cash. "Cash, Mavis," he'd say to my mother at dinner during those trying days. "Where have those holyrollers got that kind of money from? Nobody has cash these days." I listened to these conversations intently, my mind a guilty welter of questions. What would happen to a church built on such a wicked spot?

My father was manager of the Imperial, which was the only bank in Garten if you didn't count the trust company or the farmers' co-op. And my father certainly didn't count them. He had a pride and dignity that came from his absolute assurance that his was the only game in town. In all but wet and snowy weather he walked to and from the bank each day, and I think his motivation rose not from love of exercise but of being viewed. He had the idea that people should respect him, and so strong was his notion that there came a kind of validity on the heels of his vanity. He dressed in navy and his heavy tubular body filled out his suits so exactly that there was never excess fabric to make a wrinkle or unwanted crease. Even in the way his brown hair was clipped close to his bullet-shaped head there was a precision

that seemed evidence of his profession. His stance, his measured speech all said, "Yes, I am a man who deals with
money. I cannot afford to make mistakes. Banking is not a
career for the careless."

Rudy's father, on the other hand, didn't look like what
he was at all. Butchers in nursery rhyme pictures are slightly
porcine in build, with suety fingers and bright beefy cheeks.
But Mr. Shantz was small and pale and dry, with a sharp,
ferrety face. He wore a white apron with long string ties
that wound around him twice and knotted at the front, and
he seemed able to slice and saw through hunks of meat and
bone without ever spattering himself for he was always
clean, pristine. Only when I found a row of fresh aprons,
hanging on nails just inside the back room, was the mystery
of his marvellous neatness solved. The day of that discovery
was to change his life, and mine, forever.

The church was built within a year of the land sale, and
the field of tall grass was replaced by the plainest of low
brick buildings. The bread waggon would probably have
lain unused even if it had been there, for once we entered
civilized society we became self-conscious beings. Now we
learned to jeer and sneer at each other's sex and, by the end
of Grade 1, joined the other children in the playground
game of Girls After Boys, or Boys After Girls.

The game was simply a variety of tag, in which opposing
teams took turns chasing each other, the object being to
catch and drag prisoners to a base, the enormous sandbox
in the middle of the yard. Years ago pines had been planted
at each corner of the box, and now stood at least 30 feet
high, shading the sand so that the centre was always cool
and damp and dark. Prisoners were guarded there by the
less swift members of the offensive side until the recess bell
rang. Then there would be a counting and marking down of
the number on the side of the box. Then, in the next recess,
there'd be a switching of position, and the chasing and

catching would have an extra zest springing from revenge. Day after week after month it went on, wavering only now and again for skipping and baseball or skating and snow-forts. It was a merciless game with only the most unpleasant sexual overtones—kisses were given as the gravest humiliation, and retaliation was inevitable. The kisser's face would be pushed down into the sandbox during the following recess.

Rudy and I played with as much vigour as any, and if we caught each other were as rough and mean as the rules demanded. Yet periodically we would play with each other after school, returning to our touching and feeling games of the bread waggon days. It was a secret thing now, to which we never invited the other children.

It was at his house we played this way because his mother was often down at the shop tending the cash register. She was just as small and dry and neat as her husband, as unlikely a butcher's wife as she was the mother of four boys. Rudy was the youngest, and shared a bedroom with his eldest brother who was seven years older and never home after school. The other brothers had a room down the hall where they built model train sets and made engine noises. They were a couple of grades ahead of us and treated us with disdain, knowing that there was nothing we could ever think of to do that would interest them.

What we thought of to do was to take off our clothes and stand before the enormous oval mirror on the dressing-table, and examine our nakedness together. My body was smooth and round, heavy and thickened from waist to knees like all the women in my father's family. But I had the creamy skin of my mother, and her heart-shaped face and surprising blue eyes. Mine were magnified by my glasses, which I had to keep on during this game or else our reflections blurred into unrecognizable beige.

Rudy was thin and dark with lovely moles dotting his

skin all over. He had a long, thoughtful face and heavy straight hair that fell forward over his forehead. He would place his finger between the folds of my vulva and I would feel the bunchy, ruffled skin of his scrotum and we'd laugh when his penis would nod its approval. It was a strange, disembodied curiosity we felt, quite divorced from the clothed selves we ordinarily were. Sometimes we would return to the greeting of our early explorations, and sit, each on a separate bed, touching our own bodies until there were small explosions of pleasure leaping up from our hands.

Once Otto, the brother who shared the room, came home unexpectedly. We heard his entry, and his feet landing heavily on the stairs as he came up three steps at a time. Rudy always locked the door when we were there, and within seconds Otto was rattling the handle, saying, "Look, you little bugger, let me in!" Rushing, rushing, pulling on our clothes, all the while Rudy arguing back. "It's my room too, you know" and "I can lock the door if I want" and "just cause you're older doesn't mean I have to do what you say." Rudy holding the door handle until I had my ribbed stockings fastened in their garters, and had scattered a few comic books around to make it look as if we'd been reading. Feeling scared, and amazed at my own guile. Otto, when the door opened, looked suspiciously around and said, "What are you two little buggers up to?" but was too intent on his own business to care.

But that frightened us, and we stopped. And even in the closed world of Brubacher Street there began to be an unease between us. We were growing older and guilt, even shared guilt, made us awkward instead of intimate. Our childhood was passing, but all we knew was that there was no more safety, anywhere. In the game of Boys After Girls, Rudy would purposely bang my head on the wooden sides of the sandbox whenever he'd drag me in, prisoner. And when it was my turn, if I could grab him, which was rare

because I was seldom fast enough, I would dig my finger-
nails into his arm, trying to bruise or mark him in some
way. He had forsaken me and I would get him back if I
could.

By the time we were ten, Rudy always played with boys
after school and we hardly ever walked home together. But
in the spring we were both on the class spelling team, and
often had to stay late for drills. On those days we'd go along
together and sometimes stop by the meat store to get a few
slices of summer sausage from Mr. Shantz to eat on the
way home.

One afternoon in April, two or three weeks before the
big spelling contest, we left the school together and Rudy
said, "We have to go by downtown. I have to go to the
shop." And I said, "But it's Wednesday, stupid," since
Wednesday was half-day closing in Garten.

"I know, dummy," he said, "but my Dad is going to pay
me 50¢ every week if I go in and do a cleaning. If you want
to come, you can help."

"Do I get half then?" I asked, knowing I'd go whether
or not he ever gave me a quarter. I had a deep sense of
loyalty to Rudy, and a belief that our lives would be connected forever. Because we had begun our lives together, I
thought we would probably marry when we grew up. We
were perfectly matched, the same age and height, and were
equally good in school, although sometimes he was a better
speller. Just that afternoon he had spelled "interregnum"
right after I missed it.

When we reached the store we ran down the side alley
and around the back, and Rudy drew a key out of his shoe
and unlocked the door. Something in that action made my
heart race with excitement. He'd had that key in his shoe
all day long and I hadn't even known. What else might he
have hidden I couldn't see?

Inside, the smell of sawdust and blood filled our nostrils.

I had never been in the back before and the odour was stronger there. Rudy showed me the cold locker where sides of beef and pork hung on large hooks, and a freezer where pale plucked chickens were mounded in rows. On the walls there were all kinds of calendars, pink girls in low dresses holding red roses, fluffy dogs on blue velvet cushions, autumn wildernesses and smiling babies. Wonderful photographs that kept me walking around the room looking at them all. And then I came to the six hooks by the door, and the clean white aprons hanging there. I turned to tell Rudy I'd always wondered how his father kept so spotless, but he had had enough of my wandering. "You do the shelves in the shop," he ordered, "and I'll do the floor."

I went out round the glass-faced counter to where cans of stew and jars of horseradish were arranged on side shelves along the walls. I dusted and stacked, and shone up the cash register. The room was a shady green colour because the front blinds were down and I felt the kind of calm you do in a summer forest. I could hear Rudy sweeping in the back, and it seemed such a cheerful sound. We were working together, just like his mother and father did.

He came into the shop then, cleaning the floor behind the counter, gathering up the old sawdust and sprinkling fragrant new shavings everywhere. All the enamel trays of shiny purple kidneys and liver, of fat-speckled chuck and repulsive sweetbreads, had been put away in the refrigerator at noon when Mr. Shantz closed up. All that was left in the display case was sausage. Rudy slid open the door and reached in for a large salami. With a daring I envied, he turned on the slicing machine and held the hard sausage up to the blade until there was a pile of mottled slices on the metal plate.

I came round to where he stood without invitation and he divided the pile so we each had a handful of the spicy meat. It was foreign and exciting, the kind of food I never had at home. For although my father's background was German, as it was for many of the people in town, my mother's was English, and she deplored garlic and anything the least bit European as being not quite clean. Still, she shopped at Shantz's store for her weekly roast and bacon, and simply avoided looking at any of the sausages. I, on the other hand, loved those meats with so many flavours you couldn't tell what it was you were tasting as it moved around in your mouth. I stood there chewing the salami, smiling as Rudy put the rest back in the display, fully and completely happy. He turned back toward me then, with an odd smile.

"Do you want to greet?" he said, and the colour rose in his face.

"I don't do that any more," I lied.

"I mean with each other," he said. "Here, on the floor, here. Nobody will ever know. C'mon, Elizabeth, let's." He reached out and touched my waist and such shudders ran through my legs I felt as if he had lifted me up. I didn't know what he meant to do, but the sudden old memory of his soft, hot body on top of mine in the yeasty dark made me want more than anything to capture again that closeness, that secret time.

"Okay," I said, and quickly went down on my knees behind the counter, waiting for what his next move would be.

"Take off your pants," he said, and he began pulling down his own trousers. From under my skirt I took off my pants and bunched them in my hand. "Now lie down," he said, and I lay back in the fresh sawdust, not minding at all that it would coat my clothes and hair. He lay down on me immediately, as if he were shy that I should see his partly naked body. I, who knew his shape and size as well as my own. And yet, it did seem different, not the same at all when he lay on me, and I felt the jutting of his penis against my bare skin. There was an urgency to his squirming on top of me that had never been part of the game before. I felt the first shreddings of female dread, the coming apart of the dream.

"Don't greet so hard," I whispered, and tried to push him away a little bit. All the warm feelings I'd been having had dissipated with the discomfort of being pressed down so heavily. But he wouldn't stop, he kept moving rhythmically on top of me, saying, "Shut up, Elizabeth, shut up."

And of course, no sooner had I begun to wish for some way to stop him than his father came through from the back room. In a suit, without his apron on, he looked even smaller and drier, and his face broke into a bright, angular rage at the sight of his son's naked buttocks. "What are you doing?" he asked, in a voice that was only a throaty gasp. Then, in a shout that sent Rudy reeling against the far wall, "Get up! Get off her! Get up!"

I stayed on the floor and pulled down my skirt, hoping that maybe he hadn't seen there were no pants beneath. I kept the bunched-up pants in my hand behind me. Mr. Shantz was looking at me with a wildness in his eyes like hatred, and I realized afterward how much he must have guessed at that moment what the sequence of events would be. But all I knew then was that I was as guilty as Rudy, and as frightened, but that somehow I was safer than he. I was safer because I was the girl, because he was the boy and had been on top.

Mr. Shantz moved with quick steps across the sawdust toward his shaking son, and raised his arm as he spoke. "Scum!" he rasped, and brought his hand down on the side of Rudy's head. "Scum, worse than scum!" and he hit him again and again. "Put your clothes on, you, you. . . ." Words failed him, and he turned again to me. "You too, Elizabeth, get up, put those panties on."

Humiliation, anger that he had seen all, knew all, made me want to cry and cry. But at my first tremulous sob he reached out and wrenched my arm, pushing me toward the door. "You're okay," he said. "No crying. Get in the truck." I heard Rudy behind me, still pulling his trousers on. "You're going home now, both of you," said Mr. Shantz, and he sounded tired and sad instead of raging the way he had been.

We walked through the cool back room, past the butcher blocks and wrapping-table, slowly, all wishing we could go backwards in time. He must have been wishing, even more than we were, that he had never come back to the shop to see how Rudy was doing with his chores.

He drove us to Brubacher Street in the delivery truck, the three of us crowded together on the narrow bench seat. Afraid to speak or look at each other, Rudy and I stared straight ahead. My mind was busy with detail, wondering how I could possibly turn the events to my advantage once my parents were told. And I had no doubt that Mr. Shantz intended to tell.

But I knew in my heart that no matter what version my parents were given by anyone, it would all be my fault. My mother's view of the universe excluded chance and no matter what tragedy happened to whom, her final statement on the subject would be that they had brought it on themselves. I had an amazing capacity for sins that had the ability to bring on disaster—carelessness, showing off, selfishness, arrogance and what can only be described as innate badness. "Why are you such a bad girl?" my mother would cry. "What have I done to bring this on myself?"

But strangely, this time she had almost nothing to say. She stood at the door untying her flowered apron and folding it into a very small parcel as Mr. Shantz told her, in his harsh, dry voice, that he had found his son attempting to perform an indignity upon my body. He was sure he had prevented anything from actually happening, she was to understand, but nevertheless he thought it was his duty to tell her. Of course there must be no more contact between the children, and he and Mrs. Shantz would deal with Rudy in a severe fashion. Perhaps she and Mr. Kessler would also reprimand Elizabeth since, from what he had seen, she had not been unwilling. I was sent to my room as they finished their conversation in low tones, and told to wait until my father came home.

It was nearly five o'clock and as he always arrived promptly at twenty past, I knew there wasn't long. I was far too terrified now to cry, and stood instead at my dresser, arranging my dolls from many lands into neat rows. I heard the front door close; that was Mr. Shantz going. I wondered if he was going to hit Rudy some more. What frightened me then was what Rudy might say to defend himself. He might tell about all the other times, even the waggon times, and if he did, then there'd be no hope for me. I knew I would be locked in my room forever.

Then I heard the door open again and it was my father. I heard the rush of muttering voices as my mother met him and I heard his growing anger in the way he said "Disgusting!" three times as they were coming up the stairs. Her voice was a constant fret beneath his, supplying the details that brought on his vehemence. My father's skin, when he was really angry, always took on a bluish, nearly metallic cast, and when he entered my room I knew from the heavy, dull glow of his face I was in for a bad time. I began lying immediately, without really meaning to. I said that I had never wanted to lie down, that Rudy had made me, that he had taken off my panties and been very mean to me. I said I didn't understand what he wanted to do, and that no, of course we had never done anything like that before.

"But you must have done something to bring it on," my mother said, the planes of her face focused to an accusing point. "Good girls don't get themselves in situations like this."

27

"I didn't, I didn't, Mommy! Honestly, it wasn't me, it's not my fault." I cried and whimpered, and lied and lied.

My father seemed much more willing to believe me than my mother did, and he turned his outrage toward the Shantzes.

"And that bastard had the nerve to sit in my office this afternoon and ask for a loan. While his son was...My God! He thinks he'll expand and get into groceries, does he? Well, I'll teach him a lesson, the little weasel."

My mother suddenly shed her harping tone and took on the voice of reason. "Now really Frank, it's hardly Elvin Shantz's fault if his son. . . ." I could feel her still blaming me, and I hated her with a furious hatred, even as I was constricting with fear that a chain of events had been begun that I would be helpless to ever unlink.

"Like father, like son," he said, with a kind of weightiness, secure in aphorism the way he was with interest rates and mortgages. "It must come from somewhere, Mavis."

"And where did your daughter get it then?" she asked, flushed and bitter and oddly aggressive.

"You heard what the child said, it had nothing to do with her. It's all the boy, he's a menace. They've done something wrong in his upbringing, the last child, who knows. I want that family out of town, I want them out." His body seemed to be ballooning, a navy serge sausage filling the doorway of my room. "Leave it to me, Mavis, you tend to Elizabeth here. Leave it to me."

I was taken to the bathroom and told to take a bath, while my mother sat on the toilet seat looking tired and hurt. "I just feel crushed, Elizabeth," she said. "I had really thought you were starting to be a good girl, and now this. Look at the shame you have brought on us, think what you have done." She raised her head and looked at me with the sorrow I knew so well, with eyes that had seen countless disappointments because of me. "Wash between your legs,

Elizabeth," she said. "Get yourself clean. Oh, people will hear about this, I know they will. How will I be able to hold my head up in this town again?"

I was made to go to bed then, but was given a fresh flannelette nightgown to wear even though it was the middle of the week and we didn't ordinarily change except on Saturdays. I lay and watched the spring twilight flicker through the venetian blinds, sucking my thumb quietly, with my other hand tucked in my crotch, the way I liked best to go to sleep. I always remembered to remove both hands from their comfortable places just at the moment I felt the most sleepy so there would be no chance of my falling asleep and getting caught. I had never felt so lonely or so unable to soothe myself, and long after my parents had looked in and then gone to bed. I lay in the dark and heard Rudy's voice. "Shut up, Elizabeth, shut up."

In the days that followed I gathered from my parents' coded consultations that revenge was rearing its head and preparing to strike at the Shantzes. My father refused the loan. I heard him tell my mother that "I just said, 'Elvin, we've had a look at your assets and we don't think this is the time for you to expand. It's a tight money situation for everyone now, not only here at the Imperial, if you see what I mean, Elvin.' He saw what I meant, all right. He won't go anywhere else in town for the money."

I didn't really grasp the implications of that conversation until later. What I had to think about at the moment was how to endure the torment of each day at school. My mother had been right—somehow, everyone knew. I think what happened was that my parents spoke to the principal who told our teacher, Miss Cracken, that Rudy and I were no longer to sit near each other in class, and were not to be seen together at recess. Of course, human being that she was, Miss Cracken must have rushed to the staffroom with the news that the Shantz boy had done something indecent to the Kessler girl. And there were probably speculations about what exactly we had done, and some laughter, and in a matter of hours it had all filtered through the school.

By the end of the week there was a rhyme in the playground:

Rudy, Rudy, Rudy Shantz
He took off Elizabeth's pants.

And in Boys After Girls, both sides would shout, "Go after her, Rudy, let's see what you do to her!" Or they'd call to me, "C'mon, Elizabeth, lie down for Rudy!"

On the shed wall behind the school someone wrote in blue chalk "Rudy put it in Elizabeth" and beside the message made a crude drawing of massive, disembodied genitals. Many years later, travelling across North Africa, I came across these same gun-shapes and clam-shapes chalked on walls, but with exotic-looking Arabic inscriptions alongside. I viewed them with the same kind of horror I had back in Garten, unmoved by time or distance from that first awful recognition. But it wasn't like that, no, it couldn't be! The other children from our street must have remembered our shared investigations in the bread waggon, but mutual guilt kept them wisely silent. Or perhaps they really had forgotten, or didn't understand what was happening, as they later claimed.

I cried openly and deserved the taunts of "Sucky-baby" during their teasing. I think I hoped to bring on their pity and consequent kindness if I showed myself to be weak, a tactic it has taken me half a lifetime to learn doesn't pay off. Rudy, on the other hand, became ice itself, able to pass me by as if I were a ghost. I didn't exist for him; he abided by the rules to the letter, and preserved an adult kind of dignity while he did it. I think he probably hated me but there was no way of opening things up to see. I couldn't speak to him because of the rules, and also because I was so alarmed by his aloofness. Did he know how much I had lied? My parents must have repeated those denials to his parents, who would of course have accosted him with these fresh facts: "Elizabeth says you made her do it." What could I do?

Once I passed him a note on a very small piece of paper which I had folded and folded into a tiny ball. I slipped it into his fist as we came out of the classroom one morning on our way to assembly. On it I had written, "I'm sorry. I had to lie." But he took the paper and unfolded it, without reading it, and ripped it into tiny, tiny shreds. And didn't look at me. Wouldn't look at me. I would try to catch his eye in the class all day long but he would always turn away.

We were both taken off the spelling team, which lost quite badly in the school competition. My mother pointed out we had ruined things for the team, that the circles of consequence go out and out and out. Rudy was instructed to go to the butcher shop every day after school, alone. I was most often met by my mother, but occasionally walked home with Dieter and Joyce and Dennis and Celia who had all been told by their mothers not to speak to me. Or so they said.

I thought a lot about dying but no amount of concentration on the blackness in my head seemed to make it possible. Instead, that spring I discovered movie magazines, and in the pages of *Photoplay* and *Screen Lives* I lost myself. I fell in love with Jeff Chandler, whose craggy presence had already mesmerized me at Saturday matinees. I dreamed that he would find me walking alone on a long beach and ask me to come home with him and live with him forever and be a movie star. When I read a story that suggested he had a wife and two daughters, I extended the boundaries of my fantasy to include the family, and we all lived together in the forgiving California sunshine. My mother was appalled by my interest in film stars, and so I kept the magazines in

31

my closet. At night, by flashlight, I would sit beneath my pleated skirts and navy jumpers, thrilling myself with the possibility of escape.

In June, the day after school ended, the Shantz family moved. My parents must have known where they were going but there was no way I could ask. In a peculiar, almost mystic way, Rudy was now a dead person, replaced by Jeff Chandler, whose rough, tender voice now haunted my waking and sleeping life. The family who moved into the Shantz house told my mother that it was spotless, amazing when you considered they'd had four boys living there. My mother implied that they may have been clean but not entirely wholesome and there the subject of the Shantzes was stopped. The butcher shop was taken over by the IGA up the street who eventually bought out three adjoining stores and made a real supermarket.

Several years later, I got up the courage to ask Dieter, who had been Rudy's best friend besides me, whether he knew where they had gone. He said he thought they'd gone to Winnipeg where Mrs. Shantz had some relatives, but he wasn't sure. Nobody had ever heard from Rudy again, he said, not even a postcard or a Christmas card. The kids who knew the older brothers were too far out of my reach and I could never ask any of them about the family's whereabouts.

And so my father was successful and in time the town closed over the space where the Shantzes had been, and they were forgotten. But not by me. I still find Rudy in my thoughts from time to time and wonder if I am ever in his. Once, passing through Winnipeg a few years ago, I found his name in the telephone book. I put a coin in the slot of the pay phone and said, "Hello, this is Elizabeth Kessler, is this the Rudolf Shantz who used to live in Garten?" But it wasn't, or if it was he lied, and said, "No, I'm sorry, you must have the wrong number."

Jack of Hearts

People never expect me to be good at poker, probably because I have such an open face. (My mother used to say she
could read me like a book. Her mistake, my advantage.)
But what people don't know is that I've been playing poker
since I turned eleven, and I play the game very well. I may
appear flushed and agitated, but my excitement is impersonal, abstract. How can I explain this? What I love about
poker is the tension, not the actual winning or losing but
the tension between random chance and changeless numbers. Slap, slap, slap, slap, cards dealt and destiny beckons,

two-and-a-half million different hands in a deck. It's the chance to play around with fate a little, that's what draws me in. It's what you do with what you've got; in every encounter with pure, immutable kings and queens and their rough and tumble shuffle with luck, you get the chance to make it work for you. There is no certainty anywhere, but in poker that's part of the game.

Sometimes strangers, especially men, are surprised by my lack of compunction in taking their money after I've bluffed my way to the pot. But as Aunt Eadie used to say, *If you can take 'em by surprise, then take 'em for everything they've got.* It was Aunt Eadie who first taught me how to play, strengthening in me a toughness that, sadly, only shows itself at cards. But then, poker isn't life, after all. I think Aunt Eadie said that, too. And of course that's what I first loved about the game. It wasn't like life at all.

Eadie was a friend of my mother's, not really an aunt. They'd worked together in Toronto when they were young, and even when they were 45 or 46 they seemed girlish when they were together. Eadie was still a secretary there, although not just any secretary, my mother was quick to point out, but an executive secretary to one of the top brokers in the whole stock exchange. I had no idea what a stock exchange was. The only exchange I knew was the one at Medley Sports where you traded in skates.

But it was easy to see that Aunt Eadie was important from the way she held herself, as if she were much taller than she actually was, and from the glamorous clothes she brought in her matching leather luggage. In winter she'd arrive in mink or in fox, and those first hellos at the door were wonderful for the smells—sweet fur and perfume and smoke. "You bring the city with you, Ead," my mother would say, and it was true; there was a roar of traffic and glitter of lights just in the way she smelled. Beneath her coat there was bound to be something bright and silky, for

Eadie loved passionate, tropical colours. The image still lingering in my mind is of feathers and flowers, palm leaves and hibiscus, brilliant and foreign. In her lectures to me about the importance of appearance, my mother often used Eadie as an example of someone who bought the very best quality, someone whose handbag and shoes were always the same colour. But she'd usually end with a proviso such as "although Eadie does use a trifle too much rouge" or "of course, she is a little over-fond of jewellery." Nevertheless, her friend from the city had a flair for fashion that no woman in Garten could match, and she wanted me to take note. Perhaps she hoped that I might see in Eadie what she had been, before her life required only cotton house-dresses and navy crêpe for going out.

As much as my mother admired her friend, my father disparaged her. He was critical not only of the way she dressed ("flashy") and looked ("hair is never that colour in nature"), but even of the way she laughed ("she has a loose laugh, Mavis, loose!"). She was, in a word, flamboyant—the epitome of all that Frank Kessler loathed and feared.

Their mutual interest in money, rather than giving them common ground, kept them apart, for my father had such distrust of the stock market that he lumped Eadie in with "all those crooks who make their money by speculation." Banking, on the other hand, he regarded as good solid business; careful investment and guaranteed interest, twenty-year bonds and steady growth. The money in *his* bank, he said, was clean.

"She's no better than a gambler," he'd say after one of Eadie's visits in which she had described her latest killing on the market. "Never was and never will be." He'd known her nearly as long as he'd known my mother. They had all met while working on Bay Street during the thirties. Those years of Depression influenced the course of their lives not only by changing them, but by compressing and intensifying the qualities they already had. So Frank became more heavy and solid, weighed down by the metal in his soul, and Eadie hardened under the pressure to diamond-like sharpness. Mavis stayed, as she had always been, carefully in between, but when the chips were down, her money was on solidity. The house, the husband, the child.

Eadie had never married, and that too was a flaw that incurred my father's wrath. He thought that she "ran around" and that my mother oughtn't to invite her to the house in case I, his impressionable young daughter, be corrupted. Once, when they were arguing and didn't know I was listening from behind the kitchen door, he said, "She may be smart but she's still a tart!" and I nearly gave my hiding place away by laughing out loud.

"Don't worry so much, Frank," my mother would say on these occasions. "Elizabeth has no idea what Eadie's private life entails, nor need she ever. Eadie's got a lot of goodness in her, no matter what you say. I think it's just lovely to see her with a child after all she's been through. These visits are good for them both."

In fact, I was never so fond of Aunt Eadie as either of them seemed to think. After the preliminary questions about how school was going, she didn't have the slightest notion of what to talk to me about. Not until the night she taught me how to play poker did she ever give me anything of value.

It must have been sometime in early March, for there was still snow and it was the week after my disgrace at the ballet recital. Looking back I can see how lucky I was that Eadie and her cards came along when they did, offering me salvation and self-preservation. Somehow, when you're a child, you simply accept each turn of events as it comes, as if there is no other way for the world to be. And perhaps that *is* the right way to look at life. But looking back you can see how coincidence created your character, like coral atolls in the Pacific, building themselves slowly, moment upon moment.

By all odds, I should have been dragged down by the life I led as a child in Garten. I should still be there, or somewhere like it, forced under by my upbringing and all the expectations around me. But luck was with me, and small pockets of defiance multiplied beneath my surface, keeping me afloat, preparing me for that final escape.

Our ballet teacher, Mrs. Verser, always chose to hold the recital in the bleak weeks of late winter because it was then, she said, that most people needed an escape, a promise of springtime. What better harbingers of spring than the daughters of Garten leaping across the stage? Along with most of my friends, I had been enrolled in Saturday morning classes at the age of seven. We were beginning that long process of instillation, the steady drip, drip, drip of Values onto our skulls and into our brains. If our parents could only control our lives long enough, we would eventually achieve grace, tidiness and frugality.

But it wasn't for the social graces alone that Mavis Kessler sent her only child to dancing class. She hoped to combat my natural inelegance. I had inherited her face but my father's shape, with such large, heavy bones it became apparent early that I would be close to six feet when I grew up. In another time or place my body might have been prized for its usefulness in the fields. Unlucky soul, I was born generations away from where I should have been; and my sturdy peasant legs, which would have been well employed plodding down the turnip rows, were instead engaged in vain exercise at the barre. "Heels down!", Mrs. Verser would cry as we'd do our *demi-pliés*, lined up along the stage at the end of the high school gymnasium. Sharon's father was manager of the ironworks factory and had produced a portable barre of pipe for the class, to which we clung white-knuckled as we tried to bend and stretch without wobbling.

Strangely, I grew to like ballet, and looked forward to those sessions of music and movement, learning to hold my arms and legs just so, as careful of my body as if it were glass. Mrs. Verser had an assistant who gave tap lessons as well, but I was in full agreement with Mavis on this point; tap was crude and showy, ballet was *élégant*. There were no French phrases in tap, it was all just brush, brush, slide, step, hop. But in ballet there was the marvellous beauty and authority of Mrs. Verser calling out,"*Battements tendus! Maintenant, ronds de jambes! Changement de pieds!*" Across the floor we would go, obedient automatons responding to her clear high voice. "*Glissade, jeté, assemblé, entrechat royale. . . .*" She was a small woman who had been at Sadler's Wells (no-one knew for what or for how long), with a straight back and a snappy manner, and a sense of mission that made it possible for her to teach dance in Garten, year after year, without ever descending into self-pity or cynicism. She was like a small bright bird chirping "*Plus haut! Plus haut!*"

The recital we worked toward was an event that beckoned with the same inviting gleam as the annual trip to the city hockey arena to see *The Nutcracker*. My mother and I always went with her friend June, whose daughter Trudy was in my ballet class. High up in the cavernous building we'd sit on wooden benches and pass my father's field glasses back and forth. I liked the music, its easy slippery flow, and I liked the predictable patterns of the dance. But best of all I liked the costumes, and would take away with me visions of velvet and satin and sparkling lace in which to clothe my own fantasies for another year. Even in the early years of our own recitals, when the junior classes only got to dress up as tulips or bunnies, I felt my heart would burst with excitement once I was zipped and buttoned into a new being. I would become, for the duration of that dance, whatever my costume dictated and thus discovered a release from the confines of Garten, transient but intense.

Ordinarily, Mrs. Verser made a big thing out of the story in each number she choreographed for us, and exhorted us to let our faces tell the tale. She made us practise various expressions—grief, joy, anticipation—along with the corresponding arm and leg movements, which we eventually interpreted as "up is happy, down is sad." But this year she put off telling us intermediate girls what our recital piece would be about, because she wasn't sure she could get the right costumes from Malabar's, and if she had to make changes at the last minute she didn't want any of us to be disappointed. So for the first few weeks of preparation she simply put us through specific drills and we learned step after step. I liked this way of doing it, having the movement clean and devoid of meaning; the purity of *des battements dégagés, des battements tendus.* I would have preferred to dance like that always, to let my own mood determine the way I rendered the steps. Often we danced without any sort of music, just Mrs. Verser on the side, steadily counting time.

There were five of us for this number—myself and Trudy, Sharon, Amy and Janet. Trudy and I kept up the pretence of liking each other for our mothers' sakes because they seemed so pleased to see their friendship extend into the next generation. But in truth we were bitterly jealous, especially in ballet class, each convinced she was better than the other. And so it was with open exultation that I noted, as we began fitting the various steps of the dance together, I was always in the middle. Trudy said it was only because I was the tallest, but I was sure I detected Mrs. Verser's subtle plan. She had been watching us practise and now it was clear to her that it was I, Elizabeth, who would be the star. I imagined what our costumes might be, and foresaw something for myself in glistening white satin and tulle. The other girls would be my handmaidens, circling around, perhaps bringing wreaths of flowers for me to wear in my hair. Twisted silk lilies would be perfect, I decided.

Still, I felt confused by some of Mrs. Verser's directions as the weeks wore on, and it became apparent that the movements required of me were much less intricate than the other girls'. And it struck me as a little odd, if I were indeed the best, that I should not be given the most difficult steps to execute, a series of *entrechats quatres*, perhaps. Nevertheless, I was completely unprepared for the letter that Mrs. Verser waved at us, that February morning, and I could barely absorb her words.

"And Malabar's have exactly what we need for our number, and in all the right sizes, at such reasonable cost I know your parents won't mind paying a little extra so that we can give a really pro*fes*sional show. And so this morning, girls, at long last, we can begin our rehearsal for *Jack of Hearts*, and you'll see now how all our steps go together to make a story. Quickly, let's get ourselves up on stage. Come, Elizabeth! We'll have to call you Jack from now on!" A smile, a wave of the hand, a clucking noise made to gather up the other four around me.

My heart fell like a stone. I stood there blinking, hardly able to breathe or think, with Mrs. Verser holding my elbow, ready to guide me across the stage in the opening steps.

"Now we can put our expression in, as we see what is happening in the dance. You, Jack, enter with the skipping step, a one-and-two-and-one, lightly and gaily, we must see you for what you are, a rogue, a knave, a stealer of hearts. You'll have a lovely red velvet heart, here on your arm. You must make these girls think you wear your heart on your sleeve, but really, you have no heart at all, you are the fellow who loves them and leaves them." She stopped for a moment, looking at my sad and bewildered face. She took my expression for puzzlement, and gave her tinkling, ballet-mistress laugh. "But of course, you are too young to know about the cruel ways of love. Well then, you must learn about life through the dance. You will see how, in the end, because you wouldn't choose *one* you are left alone by them all, broken-hearted." She made an extravagant gesture, hand to breast, head bowed.

I heard Trudy and Janet giggling, and knew they weren't laughing at Mrs. Verser the way we usually did. They were laughing at me because I was being humiliated, and they knew it, even if silly Mrs. Verser didn't. What worse shame than to play the part of a boy? It meant you were too ugly to be a girl, that's what it meant. I dreaded the mockery and teasing I knew would come as soon as we were changing in the dressing-room.

Somehow I got through the hour of rehearsal, noting at each turn how stupid I had been not to have seen before why I needed only *promenade* behind the other girls, as each one did her *pirouettes* and *arabesques*. Of course, that's why I was left alone at the end. My body had never felt so thick and lumpish, so unable to extend itself through the air. Around me danced Trudy and Janet and Sharon and Amy, more daintily than ever, making little comments whenever they came near. When we joined hands or I had to touch them in any way, they shrank away with giggles. "Don't get fresh with me," Trudy whispered as we crossed the stage in our brief *pas de deux*. "You boy, you!"

Finally, out in the cold grey noon, I ran home by myself, able to give vent at last to pent-up tears. I was still crying when I let myself in the back door. My mother heard me and came from the kitchen, holding a saucepan by its handle. "You're late, Elizabeth, your father and I went ahead with lunch. I'll just put your soup on the tab . . . goodness' sake, Elizabeth, what's wrong?" Her forehead furrowed with sympathetic concern. That's all I needed to start a fresh flow of tears and I sobbed out my story with emphasis on the awful injustice of it all. As we so seldom met on any level where we could communicate, I think my mother entered my crisis eagerly. Here was something she could feel too. "What a shame," she kept saying, sensing only my disappointment about the costumes and not the very thing that made it unbearable. The shame, the shame. I wanted her to hold me in her arms and stroke my hair, but she just stood there with the saucepan between us, tears filling her eyes.

My noisy grief brought my father from the living-room, the Saturday *Globe* in his hand. "I have to be a boy in the recital, Daddy," I said. "I have to be a boy just because I'm the tallest." More tears, and the waiting for his sympathy to fall down around my shoulders like silk scarves, the way my mother's had. But not a chance. No coddling from Frank Kessler.

"Nothing wrong with being a boy," he said, folding the newspaper into a narrow roll. "Be proud of it. All the other girls will look the same, you'll be different. Right, Mavis? Whoever remembers the corps de ballet, eh? No sir, you be glad, Elizabeth. A chance to show character. A chance to shine. Nothing wrong with being a boy. You be glad." He tapped his open palm with the paper for emphasis and smiled down at me. I had an excruciating opening of the heart like the wrenching up of a window. I saw clearly and absolutely how much he had wanted me to be a son. And what he had was a daughter who wasn't even very good at being a girl.

I knew all about humiliation and I coped as I always did, by clenching myself in a corner of my closet, safe in the wool-smelling dark. I tried to work out for myself what meaning there might be in what had happened, but it seemed as if there were too many things to think of at once, and my mind became more and more jumbled. The conven-

42

tions of dressing up were familiar enough to me, and yet I felt so confused. What did it *mean* to be a girl or a boy, and why did I feel like such a failure? It was as if I had touched with my toe a hidden switch that suddenly made visible, as far as my eye could see, limits and lines and boundaries over which one could not transgress without great danger and pain. There it was for the first time; the minefield of sex.

The night before the recital we all met in the gymnasium for the dress rehearsal. The costumes, some made by mothers, and some ordered from Toronto, were placed on tables along the walls with crayoned signs above them. Under *Jack of Hearts* lay the Malabar boxes; I felt their unopened threat from across the room. As I crossed the floor the babble of voices around me became nightmarish, filling my head as if ten insane radio stations were screaming through at the same spot on the dial. I couldn't move, I held back as my mother went on ahead. She was determined to show me how to make the best of things.

"Ginny, stand still, the waist needs tucking." "Where are the wings, the blue wings?" "All tulips, on stage, five minutes." "Tell Susan to hitch up, her ankles are wrinkled." "Ruthie, leave Judy alone, get your slippers on." At the centre of the madness, Mrs. Verser, resplendent in sapphire silk, her small body arched with a thrilling tension. She loved the dress rehearsal, she told us, possibly even more than the actual performance night itself. This was it, the glamour of the dance in all its potential. Perhaps here she could still imagine that her girls would, with the donning of their costumes, materialize into lithe, graceful dancers. There was still a chance, there was still a hope.

Once Malabar's boxes were opened, I lost all hope. Out of the tissue paper wrappings came pastel dresses, pale green and apricot, lemon and lavender, just as Mrs. Verser had promised. And then mine; short grey velvet pants caught with an elastic band at the thigh so that they looked full and blousy, and a matching long-sleeved jacket with padded shoulders which would, as one mother noted, help to make me look "even more boyish." I was to wear high red knee socks to accent the red velvet heart, and to top it all off, a jaunty velvet hat with a red feather, to pull down over my head at one side.

"If Elizabeth's hair were just a teensie bit shorter, Mrs. Kessler, I think the whole effect would be so much more, ah, professional," suggested Mrs. Verser in that tone that implied there were no options. My hair was already bobbed at my ears, thick straight brown hair that stuck out oddly from beneath the cap. I could tell from my mother's silence, as I tried various angles, that she would have me on the high stool in the kitchen for a trim before Mrs. Verser set eyes on me again.

I went off to the dressing-room to try on the costume, and then regarded myself in the mirror above the row of sinks. I did, I looked like a big fat boy. I took off my glasses and was met by a blessed blur of grey and red. That was better. If only that was how the rest of the world would see me, I thought, a grey blur on stage. We were never allowed to wear our glasses at the recital, and dress rehearsal was usually the first time the more myopic of us danced blind. It meant there was lots of bumping and joking backstage and I could manage to avoid looking at the jeering faces of my dancing partners as we waited for our turn. But once out on the brightly lit stage, I could not help but see the glint in Trudy's eyes.

At the end of our number I was flushed with hope that once Mavis had seen her daughter being made a fool of, she would make Mrs. Verser change the dance, even at this late moment. But no, she was caught up in my father's enthusiasm for teaching me to face the challenge, and she was bound now to help me be brave. "This will help form your character," she told me on the way home, her voice all cheery. But I could tell from her expression that she was as devastated as I, and would have been much happier as the mother of Trudy, whose blond curls were perfectly set off by the apricot dress. Or Amy, who had a solo toe number to *The Surrey With the Fringe on Top* in the second half of the program. These were the daughters she should have had. For unlike Frank, she had wanted a girl; she told me she had prayed all during her pregnancy that I would be a girl.

She was 35 when I was born, as late to motherhood as she had been to marriage seven years before. She had met my father when he was starting his bank career at the Imperial's main office, long before he was near any kind of managerial level. When they wed, the Depression had the country in its grip, and perhaps they put off parenthood until they could save a little money. That's the kind of sensible move I would expect them to have made. Or perhaps they tried and tried, and I was the result of diligence and perseverance. Or perhaps she had planned to keep on working, as Eadie did, and I was a mistake that altered her expectations. I have no idea. The whole matter was so closely allied to sex that it was never possible to ask questions. It was all part of my mother's private life to which I only had secret access— rifling through her bureau drawers or eavesdropping on telephone conversations.

❋

As soon as I wake the next morning I determine I will get out of the recital if I can. I complain of stomach cramps and a headache immediately upon rising, and later tell my mother I feel feverish. I drink hot water out of the bathroom tap before asking her to take my temperature. The thermometer registers 106 degrees, and Mavis has the presence of mind to make me lie down where she can keep an eye on me for an hour before she takes it again. Then she cuts my hair. I try to find the courage to throw myself down the cellar stairs, but each time I lunge forward my hand always goes involuntarily out to the railing. It's no good, there is no way out.

After lunch my mother announces that she and I are going to go downtown and that she is going to buy me a surprise. I feel I've had enough surprises lately but she has a sprightly look that means she has decided to be nice to me and I know there's no point in resisting. In our bare feet I am as tall as Mavis, but she is wearing her high-heeled winter boots that have a ruff of black fur around the ankle, and so I feel smaller and daughter-like as we walk along. She is wearing her black Persian lamb jacket with its matching hat and she looks very smart and important. My mother always dresses to go downtown, even though the shopping district is only four blocks from our house. It is a matter of pride with her to keep up her city habits; she does not expect to be in Garten forever, she says.

She tells me repeatedly not to scuff my feet and to walk properly but I keep forgetting and let my feet slide and drag along the sandy ice on the pavement. I have begun to feel curious about what she is going to buy. I know full well that her idea of a good surprise and mine are entirely different. I would like a cream-filled long-john from Bauman's Bakery, or a *Photoplay* magazine, or a box of coloured pencils, and I expect to be disappointed. We walk the full length of the street, my mother nodding and waving to several acquaintances, until we reach my father's bank standing squarely up to the corner, like a great ship anchored in the harbour.

We turn down the side street there and stop outside The Beverly Shoppe, Lingerie and Women's Apparel. My mother and her friends always call it The Beverly Shop-pay, making fun of the pretensions of its owner, a widow with whom they all play bridge on Wednesday afternoons, her half-day closing. Her name is Beverly Mutch, and she is a tall, dry stick of a woman with whom my mother loves to talk about quality. They will stand together fingering cloth and murmuring until my skin crawls and itches as I stand before the trio of mirrors in whatever sensible outfit my mother is buying for me. I loathe this store. It is where my mother buys my navy blue jumpers and bloomers, and all my wool and cotton underwear and starchy blouses. Nothing she ever buys here is beautiful or nice, it is always just good quality, meant to last.

Mavis bends toward me at the door of the shop, her voice a low, conspiratorial whisper. "Here's where we go for the surprise," she says, smiling at me in a flushed, earnest way. "I'm going to buy you a brassière. I think it's time."

She steps back and looks at me, hoping for some reaction on my part. I am stunned. She really *has* surprised me. All the blood in my body seems to be rushing to my head and I feel very hot and red around the eyes. I am still blushing when we go into the store, hating as always the little chime that rings ding-ding-dong when the door opens and closes. I would go crazy if I worked in a place where there was a bell like that, I think. No wonder Mrs. Mutch always seems so edgy and can never settle her eyes on your face.

"Ah, Elizabeth!" She comes from behind her small counter where she has been smoking a cigarette and reading a magazine. She clasps her hands and smiles at me, intimate, benevolent. "So this is the big day."

I know right away that she does not mean the ballet recital, that my mother has phoned ahead and made an appointment. It has all been plotted behind my back. I am trapped. I do not want a brassière. Nobody else in my grade has one and I do not want to be first. If I am first I will suffer for it. I would much rather be third.

"Just take off your parka, dear, and we'll go to the back

for a fitting," says Mrs. Mutch. My mother gives me a little push with her hand on the place between my shoulder-blades that means "behave yourself" and so I obediently follow the other woman to the room separated from the rest of the shop by a heavy pink curtain. "Take off your blouse," Mrs. Mutch says, as she unrolls a frayed yellow tape measure, holding it out straight, ready to "do" me. The curtain moves aside and my mother's face appears, anxious to be involved in every step of the project.

"What do you think, Bev?" she asks, as Mrs. Mutch's thin fingers pull the tape tightly around my chest.

"Oh yes, Mavis, by all means," she says, appraising my breasts through the woven cotton undershirt. "Now, Elizabeth," she continues, turning back to me, "I'm going to bring you a number of bras to try on. I think you'd like to try them on yourself, wouldn't you?" She smiles, aware of how alert and sensitive she is being. "After you have each one on, your mother and I will come have a look. Like a little fashion show." A final cigarette-stained smile, and she ducks through the curtain, to join my mother in preserving my modesty.

I hear their whispered voices. "At the rehearsal," my mother is saying. "Just hadn't noticed before . . . bouncing up and down . . . in this costume especially . . . really kind of funny, but . . . I knew you could help, Bev . . . probably more puppy fat than anything else, but still. . . ."

I run my hands over the coarse undershirt and think how much I have always complained about wearing it, and how much now I don't want to part with it. There is nowhere to turn. Even my mother thinks I'm laughable.

The brassières are all stiff and unkind, digging into my skin along the edges. White cotton, pointy, harsh, unnatural. My discomfort grows with each attempt and with Mrs. Mutch's professional prodding and poking. She and my mother are having a lovely time, laughing and reminiscing,

48

perhaps trying to make me feel a part of their charmed circle of womanhood. I don't know.

"They really don't feel very nice," I finally say to Mrs. Mutch as she is hooking me up at the back.

"Oh dear, it's only because they're new," she says. "You'll get used to the feeling in no time. But say now, I do have a junior in satin, maybe that will be more comfy. Just a minute now."

Mutterings from behind the curtain, little murmurs and "ahs" from them both, then a blue satin brassière is thrust in. "Try this, dear," she says, and I do. It feels cool and costume-like, it is at least bearable.

"Now then, Elizabeth, isn't this a special surprise?" asks my mother as we stand at the cash register.

"Do I have to wear it all the time now?" I inquire in my most plaintive tone, hoping against hope for a no.

"Support is terribly important for big girls," Mrs. Mutch assures us, and goes on to warn of the horrors of sag and droop. "Once you get used to this one, dear, we'll get you into a nice everyday cotton and you'll feel just fine."

"You'll wear it tonight for a start," says Mavis as we head back home. She is not cross but she is very decisive. She will not have her daughter's breasts bouncing on stage, not for anything.

Right after supper I walk to the school, dreading the taunts I am sure will come. But the other girls are far too absorbed in their powdering and rouging to notice my newly short hair or the shiny blue brassière. I hunch in a corner, pulling on the heavy velvet suit. It makes me sweat before I even move. I get a little brown pancake rubbed on by one of the mothers, who tells me I look like a perfect little man, a real heartbreaker. I tell her I feel like throwing up, and she tells me to go to the washroom and be careful not to spatter the velvet. I go, but I can't make myself vomit even by sticking a finger down my throat. I wonder about falling against the porcelain toilet bowl and knocking myself out, but there's not enough room in the cubicle and I give up. I feel desperate but there are no choices. I am in a nightmare out of which I cannot wake.

Even when we have to run across the snow outside to get in the side door of the stage, the bright cold March night can't clear away the colours of the dream. We crowd together behind the curtain and make little peepholes to look out. The gymnasium is full, all of Garten seems to be there, restless on their metal folding chairs. I can't find my parents, I can't see farther than the first row where Mr. Willis, editor of the weekly *Enterprise*, sits with his camera and flash on his knee. Mrs. Verser has made him promise not to take pictures during the performance but he is there at the front just the same.

Then, lowered lights, darkness, a spotlight on Mrs. Verser introducing the junior class and *The Coming of Spring*. We mass together in the wings, waiting our turns, listening to the clatter of applause. *Spanish Dancers* follow on the heels of *Southern Belles*, and after *Anchors Aweigh* there we are, out in the warm bath of light, the phonograph needle falls down on the record and the music swells up and out of the loudspeakers and I am skipping, hands on my hips, across the stage. I think I hear a murmur from the audience but it is such an anonymous sound I have no way of judging what it means. The girls in their frothy dresses weave around me and I dance with each one, and with them all, trying to smile and wink the way Mrs. Verser showed me, putting expression in. My face is very hot from the exertion of the dance and from the effort of not crying. I am weighted down by the velvet suit, and the brassière cuts and binds along my midriff and under my arms. When I raise my arms the straps dig into my shoulders. I think no-one in the world knows how unhappy I am, and somehow that helps. There is comfort in solitude.

Before I can believe it the music is over and we are joining hands for a curtain call. Trudy smiles at me in an open
and friendly way and I know it is because our mothers are
watching. She and Sharon and Amy and Janet all make
sweeping, graceful curtsies, their heads bent low over their
pointed toes, and I give my bobbing bow, then fall to one
knee in the centre so that they can cluster around me. Suddenly, unrehearsed, Trudy jumps up and perches on my
extended knee and fluffs her skirt, and Mr. Willis springs
up and snaps a picture. The flash leaves little green explosions in my eyes, and the sound of applause is now mixed
with laughter. I am feeling very odd, as if I am swelling up.
But I get to my feet with the others, retreat back ten steps,
and see Mrs. Verser in the wings urging us forward for one
last curtain call. As we skip forward to the footlights, I can
feel it, I can feel the pressure building. The summoning of
the dark abyss. The others step back and I lean forward, on
the edge of the stage. Into the darkness, driven.

"I'm really a girl," I shout, my voice horribly high and
tinny. The noise in the gym lulls and I shout again, as loud
as I can, into the startled silence. "I'm really a girl, I'm
really a girl!"

●

My parents' scoldings that night were probably tempered
by some instinctive sympathy, but it still seemed to me that
my mother's major concern was *her* humiliation, not mine.
My father's theme was his great disappointment at the
weakness of my character. "Hysteria, Elizabeth, that's what
that was! No self-control! No call for such a display, none
at all!"

What could I say to explain myself? Nothing. I sat, red-
faced and weeping as they reproached me, unable to tell
them why I had called out, unable to understand myself

why I had done it. All I knew was that I had disgraced not only myself and our household but the entire ballet school, and the next day was made to write a letter of apology to Mrs. Verser. I didn't care, I was past caring, no further punishment could equal the dance itself.

Surprisingly, the matter was never spoken of again. Mr. Willis, whether through my father's intervention or his own kindly intuition, did not publish the photograph in the paper, and used a full-length picture of Amy *en pointe* with his recital review. I was so relieved I felt no envy of Amy at all. She and Trudy and the others no longer called me "Jack" at school; it seemed as if everyone had set about forgetting the incident. It was almost as if I had frightened them all with the intensity of my pain.

My mother might have made more of the whole thing if there had not been the lucky diversion of a visit from Eadie, who arrived on Monday for a four-day visit. Normally she only stayed one or two days, but this time, for some reason I was not allowed to know, Aunt Eadie needed a nice long rest away from the city. As usual, she brought gifts: a lacy slip for Mavis, silver cufflinks for Frank, and for me a box of discarded costume jewellery and scarves, last season's accessories but a gift that never failed to please me. Once, these things had all gone in my dressing-up box, but now they had a more immediate appeal. I found a ring of rhinestone chips set in red enamel, and put it on my fourth finger. A little loose, but spectacular.

My mother and her friend settled into a routine of secretive, girlish behaviour that produced in my father a more clipped and aloof manner than usual. He contrived to be out at meetings both Tuesday and Wednesday evenings, which suited my mother just fine. She and Aunt Eadie sat at the kitchen table, smoking Black Cat cigarettes and drinking tea and endlessly, endlessly talking. Sometimes they would laugh so hard they'd lean back in their chairs, gulping air and wiping away tears, and sometimes they seemed really to be crying, but in a soft, resigned sort of way. They'd barely notice my coming or going in the kitchen after supper, and if they did I was always told to get along up to my room. But my mother always said it nicely, and would slip her arm around my waist for a moment before giving me a little push off. She looked rosy and happy. She was always nicer when Eadie was there; the lines that had begun to pucker her small mouth into a tight purse seemed, suddenly, not to be there.

On the Thursday night there was a "coffee and dessert" meeting at the church, being given by the Couples' Club for the new minister. It was the kind of social event that neither Frank nor Mavis could resist, but it was also not the sort of thing they could take Eadie to—nor would she have gone. She waved them out the door, reassuring them that she looked forward to some time alone with me. I felt nervous and embarrassed, wondering whether I was now obliged to stay down in the living-room with her all evening.

As soon as they disappeared, Aunt Eadie said, "Well, let's get out the cards, Elizabeth, we'll pass the time with a little poker."

I was relieved that she wasn't intending to talk to me, but worried because the only card games I knew were Rummy and Fish. I found the good deck my parents used at their Bridge Club, and confessed my ignorance. She had brought down her purse from her bedroom, and opened the clasp slowly as she spoke.

"Okay, then," she said. "We'll make a deal. I'll teach you how to play poker, and you'll keep a little secret." She took from her purse a flat silver flask engraved with flowers and fancy scrollwork. "Your Aunt Eadie is going to have a drink or two. God knows after three days in Garten I deserve it. And you're not going to tell a soul. How's that for an idea?" She flashed the same kind of warm smile she gave my mother when they were whispering, and I felt a terrific pleasure spreading all through me. I nodded, speechless, watching her fingers working, undoing the lid of the flask. It was a large cap, meant to be used as a measure, and she poured the amber liquid into it with a slow, steady hand. "Whisky," she said, looking at me. "Here's to you, Elizabeth."

She put the silver jigger to her lips and drained it, then poured another. She smiled and gave an enormous, happy sigh. "I'll just set this here beside the couch. You be careful now, the last thing we want to do is spill it. Now get a little table for us while I shuffle."

I could hardly move I was so fascinated by this revelation. I had never seen anyone drink openly before, and the air seemed charged with wickedness and endless possibility. Once, I had seen my father pouring drinks for a party, but he was huddled over the kitchen counter to shield my eyes from his sinning, and I was told to leave. Alcohol was a vice, to be indulged in carefully and privately, never in front of the children. I didn't have any idea that people might carry liquor with them or drink alone, and the sheer nerve of what Aunt Eadie was doing made me quiver with excitement. What if they came home and she got caught? But she seemed not even to consider that, and with each emptying of the cap grew more relaxed and easy. I could see at last what my father really hated about her—because she didn't care, she was safe.

Her painted nails flashed as she cut the deck, all the while outlining the basic rules of the game. "Get something for us to bet with, Elizabeth," she said, and I ran to the sewing closet and brought back the button jar, pleased with myself for doing something to make her laugh. And she did, she laughed and laughed, her head thrown back, her hands still busy flicking the cards out onto the table. "Okay, look sharp now," she said. "There's a lot to learn here."

Right from that moment I loved it, loved the simplicity

54

and quickness of the game, the wonderful formality that was almost like a dance. Aunt Eadie and I were to play poker together many times in the years that followed, but I don't remember any other evening as vividly as that. I asked questions and she answered, instructing me in matters of technique and terminology. What we both sought we found in the cards—the solace of rules ("three of a kind always beats two of a kind") and the thrill of tampering with chance. Here, at last, I could exert some influence over whatever fate dealt me. My head felt as clear as if a cold wind had blown through.

By ten o'clock I had a pile of buttons in front of me and she had only a scattering. She seemed not as interested in the game as she had been, and her face had a slackness that made me feel a little uneasy. "One last hand and off to bed," she said, and dealt. I looked her straight in the eye and bluffed so that I won the whole pot, every last button she had, with a crummy pair of jacks.

"You're good," she said. "You're going to be okay, Elizabeth. Put the cards away now, and remember this is our little secret. Nighty-night." She leaned back on the couch and smiled at me, her arms spread out like wings. A bird of paradise, as out of place in that pale beige and green living-room as the joker in the deck. The wild card that meant I now had the means of escape. Even that night I began what was to become a ritual whenever I wanted to make myself feel calm. By flashlight in my closet I would lay out hand after hand, figuring out all the possibilities.

I was still in the closet when I heard my parents come in downstairs. I went to the door of my room to listen, heard a rustle of voices and then my father's heavy exclamations, and my mother's voice, all warm and forgiving. "Eadie, Eadie, what have you been doing?" And my father's, "Did the child see you like this?" Then Aunt Eadie's low laughter, and the words "bed early" and then silence. I crept away from the door and into my bed as I heard their feet on the stairs. My stomach and legs didn't stop shaking for a very long time but finally I slept, dreaming of face-cards.

At breakfast the next morning Aunt Eadie was still asleep, and all my mother said in reference to the night before was, "What time did you get to bed, Elizabeth?" And I said, "Gee, I went up to my room about 8.30, I guess. Aunt Eadie and I couldn't think of much to talk about."

When I came home for lunch she had gone. My mother's eyes were red and she let me have two bowls of fruit cocktail for dessert. At dinner that night my father told me to take off that ridiculous rhinestone ring, he didn't want to see me wearing that trash. My mother pursed her lips tightly and said, "Be a good girl, Elizabeth. Do as you're told."

Into the Green Stillness

The summer I was nine my mother and I spent nearly four weeks in Streetsville looking after my three cousins. Their mother had died the year before, along with another of my mother's sisters, in a dreadful car accident near Clappison's Corners. My Uncle Rennie was having a hard time getting over his grief. Memories of Aunt Mabel lurked in closets and kitchen cupboards, hovered over her jars of jams and jellies in the basement so that he could not bear to open and eat them. He couldn't stand the charitable offers of help from the neighbours, the sympathetic eyes of the minister each Sunday, the well-meant invitations out to bridge parties to meet new widows and divorcées. He'd rave and rage, sitting at our kitchen table with my mother, and finally they decided that what he should do was drive out west and look for work in Alberta or BC. My father agreed. "A complete change of scene, that's what I'd do," Frank said.

Uncle Rennie got a week off without pay to add to his vacation, packed up his Studebaker and left my mother, Mavis, in charge of his children. She wanted them all to come to Garten—she may not have wanted to dwell with her sister's ghostly presence any more than Rennie did—but in Streetsville my cousins had their own rooms and our house couldn't provide that. So it was decided that she and I would go there the middle of July.

I had mixed feelings, for although I liked my cousins well enough I hated giving up my swimming-lessons at the Rotary pool. On the other hand, the idea of getting out of Garten was attractive even at that age. I'd only been to my cousins' house a handful of times but I loved it—a grey brick bungalow on the farthest edge of a new development, with only a school playground between it and a maple bush. There were no trees at all on the streets, as if having the bush so near provided sufficient greenery, and something about the stripped-away bareness was appealing. I liked too the smell of fresh plaster that seemed to linger in their house over the years, and the ivory-coloured venetian blinds on the windows, and the pastel carpets covering all the floors.

Unlike my mother or uncle, I did not mind Aunt Mabel's house for fear of being reminded of her at every turn. I was not sad that she was dead and gone—I rather welcomed the chance to enjoy the house without her there always pricking sharply at us children: "Shoes off at the door! How many times have I told you?. . . No cookies in the bedrooms! Crumbs everywhere! . . . Really, Elizabeth, would you do that at *home*?" The very worst aspects of my mother, it seemed to me, were magnified and intensified in her older sister. I inevitably felt grateful for Mavis after an encounter with Mabel, just as I had always been made discontent after a visit from Rita, the younger sister who was 32 and still unmarried at the time of the accident. She had been a teacher at the school for the deaf in Milton, and would teach me and my cousins how to sign rude words, which we would then do in front of our untutored parents while she smiled and winked at us. Rita was the one I missed, I mourned—not Mabel.

My cousins, however they felt, knew a good thing when they saw it, and played up their position as motherless children during that whole year after the accident. The eldest, Ted, who'd been eleven at the time Mabel died, always took full charge of the recital of events surrounding the accident, and Charlene, two years younger, filled in details, emotional fragments that worked to flesh out the story and give it immediacy.

"Mom and Aunt Rita had gone over shopping to Hamilton," Ted would begin, and Charlene would add dramatic punch: "And Dad had told them to be real careful because of all the construction on Highway 5." Between the two of them they sorted out melody and harmony, motif and refinements, so that as their tale progressed my teeth would be on edge with anxiety even though I knew the ending.

"Dad was pacing up and down the kitchen saying 'Those dang fool women shoulda been home an hour ago,' " Ted would say. "By then rain was coming down something awful and the lightning was making us jump like crazy," Charlene would provide, giving Ted a moment to pause.

"I was looking out the window so I was the first to see it, the police cruiser," Ted would resume. "I saw the red light flashing out there in the storm and it didn't hit me till I turned around to tell Dad there were two cops getting out of their car and coming up the driveway. He was just at the doorway to the living-room when the doorbell rang then and ..."

"His face went white as white." Charlene, all breathless. "And he said 'Oh Christ, no.' Just like that."

Then would follow all the gruesome details of the accident itself, the overturned transport truck, the slippery highway, the badly marked detour, the rain, the blood, the women flung into their windshield. In all this, my cousin Grace, who was six months younger than me, never said a word. Not because she couldn't speak, but because she had the mind of a three-year-old and didn't have very much to say. "Brain-damaged" we were taught to explain if anyone ever asked about her. And so her part in the family recital was simply to weep softly, spontaneously, from the heart, for Gracie knew only that her Mom had gone forever. Her Mom, who had been told by the nurses to hang on, keep that baby in, don't push yet, the doctor will be here any minute ... and hadn't pushed, had kept that baby in its birth canal too long, had deprived it of oxygen, had stunted its poor brain forever. I wasn't told all that until I was an adult—at the time, the distinction merely was made that Gracie was not a moron, it was not a flaw that ran in families, it was only an accident at birth. She was the same as the rest of us except she was a little slow.

In fact, she was the prettiest of us all, and but for a vacancy in the eyes, and a kind of slackness that came to her mouth and cheek muscles in later years, hers was the sort of appearance that would have been the conventional ticket to success, had life turned out a little differently. Her fair wavy hair, her even features and wide-set grey eyes would have made her a teacher's pet, a prom queen, a heartbreaker. I loved the way she looked, the pretty ruffled dresses she was allowed to wear even though she was chubbier than I was—Mavis always said chubby girls shouldn't wear ruffles. I think once it became clear to Aunt Mabel what the score was she allowed Gracie to wear anything she liked and to eat all she wanted, either to allow her some small pleasures in life or, as likely, to minimize the chances of her growing up to be so attractive that she "got in trouble."

My mother really wasn't comfortable with Gracie. Slowness of any kind made her impatient, and I think she sometimes thought the child was "just putting it on to get attention." Ted, the first-born, was very much her favourite, and could do no wrong in her eyes; but Charlene she found sneaky. "She's a little too nicey-nice to be trusted," I heard her say in conversation with my father the night before we left for Streetsville. I was lying in my usual spot at the top of the stairs listening to them talk in the living-room.

It would be the longest separation my parents would have had since the week my mother had spent in the hospital when I was born. In spite of that, Frank didn't seem as upset about our going as I think Mavis might have liked. He'd have his lunches downtown as he preferred to do anyway, and he knew, as did Mavis, that the neighbourhood wives would outdo themselves having him over for evening meals. He promised to come see us one Sunday, and to phone once during each week. He was so cheerful about what he called "batching it" that I felt less guilty about being glad to leave him too.

When he leaned down to kiss me on the forehead at the bus station the day we were leaving, he didn't say he'd miss me, or that he hoped I'd have a good time with my cousins. "You behave yourself, Elizabeth," is what he said. "Do as your mother tells you and no talking back, you understand?"

I squinted up at him balefully in the way I knew infuriated him. "Yes, Daddy." Wondering if Mavis had put him up to it, if she had said, "You had better have a word with her, Frank, before we go. She'll listen to you better than me. What *will* I do with four to look after?" Or whether that was really all he had to say to me ever, any time. "Behave yourself." As if he were suddenly aware of the harshness of his tone, he reached out and straightened the shoulder strap of my sundress. "There now, away you both go."

We got our seat near the front, and my mother waved her handkerchief so that he could see where we were through the dusty glass, and then we were off, enclosed in the smoky, musty smell of plush seats and other people's perfume, settling into ourselves for the trip ahead. Mavis was wearing one of her smart little hats and a striped cotton dress that made her look taller, more chic than usual. I wanted to tell her how wonderful I thought she looked, but it sounded false when I rehearsed it in my head so instead I sat silently, flipping over pages of my comic book while she opened out a new issue of the *Ladies' Home Journal*.

Reading on the bus made me feel like throwing up; my usual remedy, sucking peppermints, so annoyed Mavis with its accompanying smacking noises that in the end I put down the comic and looked out the window. After Guelph the country got flatter, less lush, more open, as if paving the way for the towns and cities to come. I was happy to be leaving home; life in Streetsville was bound to offer me adventures not possible in Garten. I thought about Ted and Charlene, and wondered if they would play with me or not. We had always seemed as much friends as cousins, yet the last time I'd seen them, during the Easter holidays, they had pretty well ignored me, had played games that were too difficult for their sister to understand and had left me to play with her. Somehow, since Aunt Mabel's death, we were no longer in the same league; cousins still, but they had something from which I was excluded and it seemed to make them much older. "They've been through a lot," my mother soothed when I complained about feeling left out.

"Don't forget that. Death leaves its mark." If *she* were to die, I wondered, would we then be equal again?

Uncle Rennie and my mother stayed up very late that night going over the past, organizing the present. He left the next morning after breakfast, and we all gathered out at the end of the driveway to wave goodbye. It was a very hot, clear July morning, and the edges of everything seemed brighter and sharper than normal. As his car pulled away, my cousins followed it down to the curb where they stood, barefoot on the grass, holding hands. Mavis wiped her eyes and put her arm across my shoulders and I knew I was supposed to be feeling something, love or sadness. But I longed only for time to move more swiftly.

"Come now, children, we'll go inside and talk about all our arrangements," my mother said, and I saw Ted and Charlene raise their eyebrows at each other after she'd turned and opened the screen door. Having an aunt around every minute was going to be a big change in their lives and I recognized that. I wanted to raise my eyebrows back at them in some kind of comradely gesture, to show that I was on their side. But I didn't. I knew, intuitively, the protocol to be observed here was the same as in Garten: one waits to be asked to enter the charmed circle, the secret society; one does not attempt to wink and weasel one's way in.

We sat down around the kitchen table and looked at each other. Ted played with his spoon in the remaining cereal and milk in his bowl, stirring it around and mashing it, a habit I knew drove my mother wild. But she didn't say a word to him, she was busy with a pad of paper and a pencil, checking the notes she and Uncle Rennie had made. Ted was very much like his father in appearance, angular and square-headed, with fair hair that wanted to grow at right angles along the back ridge of his scalp. His hair was greasy, and although he wouldn't turn thirteen until the end of the summer his face was already blotchy and bumpy. I didn't know anything about puberty at that point, I only recall thinking that he had become, as if under some awful enchantment, horribly ugly.

Unlike Charlene, who at ten was long-limbed and slim, whose hair was combed back smoothly into a pony-tail that flicked back and forth as she tossed her head and chewed her gum. She had a way of sauntering that made you think she wasn't scared of anything, and I envied her wholeheartedly; even her clothes lay loosely on her body, did what they were supposed to, didn't stick and bind and wrinkle the way mine did in this hot weather. She began stacking the breakfast dishes by the sink, and looked back over her shoulder.

"I don't mind doing the dishes every morning before I go to day camp, Auntie," she said, "if that would be a help. I'm used to doing chores."

"Oh no, dear, there's no need for that. You could clear the table for me, of course, but that'll be fine. You and Ted just take care of getting yourselves ready. We'll make up your lunches the night before and put them in the fridge, wouldn't that be smart?" Mavis smiled, at her kindly, efficient best.

The two older ones would be gone every day from nine until four, leaving me to play with Gracie. Or, as Mavis put it, "being responsible for your cousin." I didn't mind at all; Gracie was far and away the easiest one to get along with, and I rather liked the status of being her caretaker. Besides, Ted and Charlene had made it clear since my arrival, by ignoring me and lumping me in with their sister, that they wanted nothing to do with me. Trailing around after them would only end in heartbreak, I felt sure of that.

It was decided that I would share Gracie's room instead of staying in my mother's bed—a move I heartily approved. Aunt Mabel had made the room a mauve-and-white bower with floral wallpaper, white furniture decorated with gold scrolls and curlicues, fluffy curtains and ruffled cushions, and shelf after shelf of stuffed dolls and toys. Gracie had such a placid, generous nature I knew she would let me play with all her things—she never argued or wanted to do things "her way" the way other children did—and she might even give me a doll to take home. No wonder everyone loved her, I thought wistfully. What must that be like? Maybe if there was something wrong with me Mavis and Frank would give me whatever I wanted, would give me ruffles and stuffed toys. It must not be so bad having the mind of a three-year-old. I tried to remember what it had been like to be three, but all that came was a fluttering of shreds and scraps, like torn-out pictures from a book or bits of cloth being tossed from a ragbag. Maybe that's what it was like, just not remembering much. Well, I wouldn't mind that, I thought.

"Can Gracie and I play in the woods?" I asked, seeing in that the opportunity for adventure. My mother looked hesitant, and glanced at Ted and Charlene as if for their sanction.

"Oh sure, Auntie, the little kids play at the edge of the bush there by the school all the time. You just have to be sure that Grace doesn't wander off, Elizabeth," Ted said. "You have to keep an eye on her because sometimes she'll go off and then not know the way back."

"Do not," said Gracie, offended. "Do not. Gracie's a good girl."

"Of course you are, dear," my mother said, reaching over and patting her arm. "And you must be good when you are with Elizabeth and stay with her every minute so that *she* doesn't get lost in the woods. Do you see?" Mavis thought she was being so clever, I thought, and it was such a transparent ploy I was sure even Gracie could see through it as well. But we all smiled then and nodded at each other and finished our orange juice and went out. Ted and Charlene went off on their bicycles to their day camp at the Y, riding side by side down the street at exactly the same speed. They swerved their front wheels slowly in sweeping rhythmic movements leaving a trail of invisible *esses* in the air behind them. There was a smooth, effortless quality to their riding, as if they had practised this routine so often they could do it with their eyes closed.

Mavis stood at the door behind Gracie and me, and when I turned to say goodbye I thought how worn down and lonely she looked, how out of place. I wondered what she would do without her Garten friends to talk to on the phone. Would she sit at the kitchen table now and sip coffee by herself and miss her dead sisters? Well, there was nothing I could do. I couldn't make her feel better. I would just get out and away.

I held my cousin's hand crossing the street to the school-yard and then we ran across the open grass to the fence at the far end where the bush began. There was a section of fence pulled up so that it was easy to crawl under into the long uncut grass on the other side. Queen Anne's lace and milk vetch and sweet clover, I could name all the flowers for Gracie. And then out of the tickle of grass against bare legs, into the enveloping shadow of the trees. At the edge of the woods there was very little undergrowth, but as we went farther it became thicker and heavier, the saplings crowding for every last bit of soil and light. The farmer who owned the bush must have stopped clearing it out once he saw the direction the development was taking; he must have known that he'd soon be a richer man than he'd ever have been from lumber or maple syrup.

I wanted to keep going, right into the dense heart of the woods, where I imagined there'd be a clearing, a small tranquil pool. But in some places the thin wiry branches were so interwoven that we could barely get through, and

Gracie whimpered as they whipped against our arms and faces. "Don't cry, Gracie," I said. "We'll turn round in a minute." I felt dizzy with new sensations, the heavy scent of growth, the closeness and overwhelming sameness of all the green around us. What if we *did* get lost? They would find us here, huddled beneath a tree, starved to death, our souls gone to heaven. Like the babes in the wood. The illustration from my nursery storybook flashed into my head then, and I saw two sleepy, chubby children cuddling by the roots of a tree on the edge of a path. A path. That's what we would do. We would make a path and then Gracie wouldn't cry any more and she wouldn't get lost. It would look just like the picture in the book.

"Do you want to make a path, Gracie?" I asked. "Do you want to help make a beautiful path?" She nodded, enthusiastic about anything to put a stop to this trudging forward through the underbrush. We turned back, and sat on the edge of the woods while I thought about what we'd need. Just clearing the leaves away from the forest floor wouldn't be enough, we'd need clippers too and maybe a trowel. I was sure Uncle Rennie would have everything we needed in the garage, and I warned Gracie not to tell anybody what we were going to do. "My Mom would think you might hurt yourself with the clippers or something," I said, "so we'll just borrow things without telling for now. You understand? It's our secret. Our secret path." The idea became more and more appealing, and I began to see a small hut at the end of the path, with walls and a roof made of twigs. The summer started to take on the shape and colour I'd been hoping for.

It was easier than I'd imagined to get the tools out to the wood without anyone noticing. Mavis was often on the backyard patio of a neighbour, drinking iced tea or lemonade and talking about dear Mabel. Ted and Charlene didn't come out to the bush—they treated me as if I were as babyish as their sister—in case they'd get stuck with us, and although occasionally at supper one of them would ask "What do you *do* out there?" an answer such as "Just playing" was always sufficient, barely acknowledged. Even when Mavis missed the little whisk broom we borrowed for sweeping the leaves away, it never occurred to her that we might have it. And to Gracie's credit, she never once volunteered to help find it.

The only trouble with Gracie was her slowness. Unless you kept reminding her, she'd forget what she was doing and sit and daydream in that blank-faced way of hers. Sometimes I wanted to shake her or pinch her, but it was impossible to get really angry with her. It would have been like punching mist; there was no resistance in her at all.

She did try to work very hard, and would help me yank at the larger saplings when the clippers failed to break a woody stem. We tried to clip everything right down close to the roots so that the path, which was nearly two feet across, would be as smooth as possible. After the small seedlings were pulled out we turned to the anonymous greenery left after spring flowers had stopped blooming, the green leaves of wild leeks, dog-toothed violets, bloodroots and hepaticas. The path made two or three abrupt twists around patches of trillium leaves, which we knew we mustn't pull on pain of death, ours or the flowers' we weren't quite sure. And we left a little group of jack-in-the-pulpits and decorated around them with some stones we took from the schoolyard. But all else vanished under our busy hands, until we were down to the bare soil.

The removal of the leaves was the task we both loved. The scooping up of the first light dry layers of soft brown and yellow like bits of fragrant paper, and then under that the leaves nearly turned into humus, dark and moist and smelling rich and heavy. Secret. A smell that made me want to bury myself in the leaves and just lie there and be. Only that, just be. I think Gracie felt the same things, for we would lift handfuls of leaves to our faces at the same time, kneeling on the ground together, and breathe in the smell and then smile at each other. Two small animals, noses buried in the wet, dark pre-earth. I didn't know anyone else in the world with whom I might share such moments.

After that layer had been off for a day and the ground below allowed to dry, we would sweep it all with the whisk broom and straighten the edges with small twigs. Except for the occasional knobby stub where a sapling's life had ended, the path was smooth, looking exactly as I had imagined it would. It was hard work, but so perfectly satisfying we kept at it day after day, doing little else. Obeying, perhaps, some primitive, atavistic urge to clear the land that our ancestors must have had pushing them on to make fields out of forests when they came from Germany and England in the last century. The repetition of an ancient dream, being played out by children in a bush on the edge of a city. But all I knew then, at that age, was that we had to keep going, we had to push farther into the centre of the woods.

On Sunday morning at the end of that first week, Mavis got us all ready for Sunday school and church at some cost to her composure. She wasn't used to four children getting washed and dressed at once, and she became edgy and flustered. As we were standing by the door for a final review, she opened her purse to put in the necessary handkerchief and peppermints, and to check, she said, that she had enough change for the collection plate. At home, she and Frank gave each week in little paper envelopes on which the offering was marked for use at home or abroad. But here she would need a dollar for herself and quarters for us. As she opened her change purse, her face wrinkled in puzzlement and then flared in anger.

"I had several dollar bills in here only yesterday," she said. "Somebody has been in my purse and taken them."

She looked right at me and I hated her with all my heart. How dare she accuse me in front of these cousins? I hadn't ever taken money from her in my life.

"It wasn't me, Mommy, honest," I said, my face flaming and the backs of my eyes feeling on fire.

"No-one said it was, Elizabeth," she said, in that calm voice I knew was meant to sound clever, as if she had caught me out. "But *someone* took this money and I want to know who. Now."

Silence. Ted and Grace and Charlene standing at the door looking back and forth at each other and at me. "Oh Auntie, we'd never do anything like that," said Charlene, her eyes wide open with hurt at the idea of being a suspect. "And you mustn't think, just because, you know, Gracie doesn't understand everything . . . she still knows the difference between right and wrong, she would never steal, would you Gracie?" She knelt before her sister, who was nearly as tall as she was, so that Gracie had to look down at her. "You wouldn't take anything from Auntie's purse, would you?"

Gracie began to cry and Ted said, "Look what you've made her do, Charlene, you've started her bawling." Mavis dabbed at Gracie's eyes with her handkerchief and patted her cheek. "There, there," she said. "I know Gracie's a good girl. She wouldn't take money to play with, would she?"

"Gracie's a good girl," Gracie sobbed, as the cousins turned and glared at me as if it were all my fault. I stared back, squinting and blushing, wondering how I would ever get even with them for this. It had to be one of them and I was sure it was Charlene; sneaking money was the kind of thing I could imagine her doing. I wondered if Ted knew, if he was in on it too. I'll bet he is, I thought. They're always in things together now. They're going to make sure I get blamed.

My mother gave up and said we'd discuss it after church,

and that what each one of us better do was pray to God for forgiveness and for the strength to confess our sins, whichever of us it had been. We marched down the sidewalk in silence, a sad little band, Gracie no longer crying but sniffling and wiping her nose with her hand. "I love you Gracie," I whispered, and took her hand when we got to the curb and then didn't let go. "You are my favourite." That made her smile and we squeezed our fingers together and lagged behind the others—Ted all awkward and skinny, his white cotton shirt sticking to his shoulder-blades in the heat, and Charlene mincing along in her crisp turquoise sundress beside Mavis, whose back was stiff as she walked, as if all her distress had concentrated itself in her spine.

At lunch, oddly, Mavis didn't mention the money and we all waited for the topic to come up—you could tell by the way that none of us looked at each other and kept talking about other things. And again at supper, nothing. I could barely swallow from anxiety and I noticed that no-one else seemed very hungry either. Mavis spent a long time talking to my father on the extension phone in the bedroom and when she came out she said, "Oh, Elizabeth. I meant to let you say hello to Daddy."

"That's okay, Mommy," I said, and tried to look wounded but brave. In truth, I was immensely relieved; the idea of listening to Frank lecture me on the telephone was too awful to contemplate.

The next day came cool and cloudy, a kind of temporary relief. I was eager to get back to the woods after the weekend, to see how the path looked, whether it would be as perfect as it had been when we left it. I lived in constant fear that other neighbourhood children would come into the woods there and find it and mess it up or claim it for their own. But none of them ever came; they were all off at camp or swimming-lessons, or else they felt that since Gracie had someone to play with they didn't have to, and so they left us alone.

One or two days that week it rained, and there was always a lot of work to do after that, for the path would be strewn with new leaves and twigs and in need of careful cleaning. We'd brush and pluck and pull together, munching on snacks of carrot sticks and occasional arrowroot biscuits. Our hands and knees were always dirty when we arrived home and my mother would say, "How *can* you get so dirty?" but in that exasperated way that didn't expect an answer.

At the end of the second week the worst heat wave of the summer settled down to stay in the flat treeless streets of the subdivision; the little bungalows shimmered in the sun and became airless traps. Mabel's house, which had seemed so wonderfully modern and bright, now showed itself for the nasty little box it was. "What I wouldn't give to be back in my own house this minute," my mother said, as she set the electric fan in the hallway to "stir up some circulation." I thought about our old-fashioned house with its wide front verandah and all its wooden trim painted green, the snowball bushes and spirea that I hated for their drabness. The lawn and the house seemed to sit in a pool of shade cast by the big maples that grew along Brubacher Street, leaning over to form an arch above us, hemming us in. But it *was* cool under that canopy. I smiled at Mavis. "Me too, Mom," I said. "I miss it too." We looked at each other with affection and marvelled.

On the Friday afternoon she took to her room for a nap after lunch, with a cool cloth to put on her forehead, and urged both of us to do the same. "I'll leave a note on the kitchen counter for Ted and Charlene to tell them we're resting," she said, "and maybe they'll put their feet up before supper too." Gracie obediently went off with her damp washcloth to lie down and within minutes fell asleep. I roamed about the house, restless and uneasy, until I could

72

bear it no longer. I went out to the bush with a plastic glass full of lemonade and ice but by the time I drank it, it was warm. The heat had seeped in through the trees and lay close to the ground; there was no coolness in the shade, only heaviness. Mosquitoes nipped at the back of my knees and neck, insects hummed everywhere in the air, everything seemed too alive and sticky. I looked at the path, the intricate design it made through the brush, and felt very tired. Without Gracie along it didn't seem fun and I didn't know why. I decided I would go back and sit in the basement the way Nana, my grandmother, did at her house when it was hot. She kept a rocking-chair down there and in summer often took her knee chores, as she called those jobs she did in her lap, down to her cool cellar to get them done. I had sometimes helped her shell peas and snap beans in the grey half-light.

The house was still except for the whirr of the fan in the hallway. I went down the steps carefully, my eyes unaccustomed to the darkness. It *was* cooler; it had been a good idea. I crawled behind the furnace in the farthest corner, behind a pile of suitcases and boxes, and imagined myself hiding on board a ship—a runaway orphan, a stowaway bound for who knew where.

There was a slightly sharp odour to the basement, a clean cement smell that was at odds with the dark dampness I knew in the woods. It was so impersonal and anonymous I felt safe and hunched down happily, grateful to have found a place where I could avoid everyone upstairs. Ted and Charlene kept acting as if they were waiting for me to confess that I had taken the money, and they had all kinds of ways of making me feel guilty. Sometimes Charlene would sidle around the doorway to Gracie's room and would lean there, looking at me without speaking. I put my thumb in my mouth for comfort in the dark then, and thought about how to get her to admit that she had done it.

I must have fallen asleep like that and dozed for some time, for I woke to voices nearly next to me on the other side of the furnace. Ted and Charlene.

"Don't twist my arm, you're hurting!" She was hissing with anger.

"Give me a dollar then," he whispered.

"I don't have any left, I really don't," she said. She seemed now to be nearly crying. I was going to come out at that point and accuse her and say that I was going to "tell," but I was frightened, the way you are when you wake out of a bad dream and then can't make it go away. I was frightened of what they might do to me if they thought I had meant to spy on them. So I huddled down and tried to stop breathing.

"Don't tell, Teddy, please," she was saying. "I'll give you something else, I will, I will. Just don't tell." Then I heard her gasp as if he had twisted her elbow behind her back even harder. It was the kind of torture I most feared, that wrenching, burning pain as your arm nearly gets pulled from its socket. Why did boys always do that?

"Okay, but you have to do everything I say or I tell," he said. "Promise. Swear to God."

"I promise, swear to God, amen."

Then the rustle and slide of cotton against skin, the *zzzzt* of a zipper, the sound of their intake and outtake of air. Ted's breathing fast and shallow, Charlene's a kind of gulping sob.

"You have to, you said you would do anything I said," he was saying, and she was whimpering. I heard a kind of thud of flesh and bone on concrete, as if one of them had knelt down, but I couldn't tell which one.

"I'll just rub it for you, okay, Teddy?"

"No. Suck it. Put it in your mouth." His voice was rushed and urgent, like the beginning of a windstorm.

"I can't, I can't, I'll be sick!" Charlene's voice a whine,

like the mew of a cat. Then a kind of swallowing sound and Ted moaning. The most grotesque images flooded my mind. I was picturing something that had never entered my head before. She had *it* in her mouth. What if he peed? I felt my stomach heave and my throat fill with acrid, burning vomit. "Aaagh. . . ." In my little corner behind the trunk and boxes I threw up between my feet, shuddering with disgust. Behind me I heard noises as they moved boxes to get to me, the gasping of Ted and Charlene's sobbing.

"You little puke!" he said, yanking at my hair. "You little spying puke! We'll get you for this Elizabeth, we'll get you, just you wait. We'll kill you if you ever tell your mother. If you ever tell anything to anybody I'll make you do it too. I will!"

I retched again, this time at his feet, more terrified than I knew how to be. My eyes had become used to the dim basement light and I could see Charlene's pale face behind his, pleading with me not to tell. But . . . if I didn't tell, then Ted would keep on making her do this. She *had* taken the money; maybe this was meant to be her punishment. God always evened things out, I knew that. But what had *I* done wrong? What was going to happen to me?

I made my solemn vow never to tell and promised to clean up the vomit and sat there shivering and crying long after they left. I heard Mavis walking around the kitchen upstairs and finally found some rags and newspapers to clean up the mess and threw the whole works in a cardboard box and put it in the garage. I went outside and lay on the lawn until I was called in to set the table for supper.

That night Mavis served us cold canned salmon and lettuce with yellow Jell-O for dessert, and we sat in the late afternoon heat and tried to eat. None of us could, and finally she said it was okay, and gave us ice cubes to suck instead. We sat out on the porch and watched the sun sink behind the maple bush, a violently red ball promising more heat for the next day and the next after that. There was no wind at all; we were too far from Lake Ontario to get even the faintest breeze. Only the falling of the dark and the oppressive heat bearing down.

Lying in bed in Gracie's room that night I asked her who she loved the best. "My dead Mommy," she said.

"Who next?" I pressed. "Who else?"

"You," she said, and started to cry.

"Don't, Gracie, it's too hot," I said. "I love you too. I love you the best of anybody." And we fell asleep.

The next morning I could barely wait through breakfast to get out to the woods. I made Gracie bring her last piece of toast with her, and in a bag full of dolls and toy dishes, in case Mavis looked to see what I was carrying, I hid a jar of nails and a hammer from Uncle Rennie's workshop. It was time, I suddenly knew, to build a little shelter at the end of the path. A place where Gracie and I could hide and be safe if we had to. I saw myself fashioning something out of branches nailed together and perhaps bound with rope, if I could just get some rope somewhere. I had found four small trees growing in such a way that they made the corners of a rectangle, and I imagined a roof attached, somehow, to each trunk. There would be ferns and moss on the floor for mats, and we would live on beechnuts and berries, and water from a nearby stream. Or we might have to bring food from home . . . but we would think about all that later.

I explained to Gracie that her job today was to clear the path from beginning to end while I organized our new hut. She took the whisk and began, on her knees, to clear away the debris, patting the dry soil with her hands to make it smooth. We were both content, in control.

Late in the day, into the green stillness came the sound of voices. Ted and Charlene. Why were they coming? Would they wreck the path? Were they going to do something to

76

me? They stood, Ted with his arms folded across his chest, several yards away from where Gracie knelt, scraping away at the ground. She looked up, happy to see them, to have the secret over, able now to show them how much she and I had accomplished. "Look, Teddy," she said. "See what I can do." And she dug with furious energy, pulling up plants and scattering dry leaves in the air.

"Does Elizabeth make you do that?" Ted asked.

"Yes, she makes me. I'm a good girl," Gracie said, not understanding the intent of his question as I did. There was a cutting tone to his voice that made me feel very alert, as if something had altered the slant of light through the trees, as if the whole scene was changing before my eyes. I smelled danger.

"I don't *make* her do anything," I said. "She likes doing this. We both do. She's good at it. Leave us alone, we're having a good time and we're not hurting you."

They stood for a moment, as if unsure whether to join us or run, and then they moved off, wordlessly, leaving Gracie sitting on the dirt floor, digging with a spoon, looking sad.

"They didn't like our path?" she asked me. "Not pretty?"

"No, no, they liked it all right. Never mind, Gracie. It's me they don't like any more." I turned back to the hut, and the unsolvable problem of how to make the branches and twigs stick together onto the tree trunks. It was going to be much more difficult than I had thought, and I wished Ted were still my friend so that I could get him to help. We gave up finally and gathered up our bag of dolls and toy dishes and went home.

After supper that night Ted and Charlene offered to help Mavis do the dishes while Gracie and I were sent to a neighbour's garden to pick green beans. When we came back with our full baskets, my mother's manner had changed—she had become tight-lipped, aloof, and her eyes were red. She told Grace to go upstairs and get into the tub she had readied for her, and she told me to come to her room.

"Your cousins have told me what you've been up to," she said, as soon as she closed the door behind her. Her face was taut, and she had the kind of expression on her face that I knew from experience would soon give in to full-blowing rage. Sure enough, as I sat on the edge of the bed looking confused, her voice became louder, harsher, the words came faster and faster. "The *idea* of you taking advantage of that poor child when she can't think for herself makes me sick, Elizabeth. Sick. To think that a child of mine could be so heartless, so unfeeling...."

"But what did they say that I *do*?" I broke in. "I don't even know why you're mad at me. I haven't done anything bad, I really haven't!"

"Calling your cousin Grace your slave and making her grovel in the mud, Elizabeth? You don't call that *bad*?" She stopped and shuddered. "If I had had any idea of what was going on out there.... Oh, it's all my fault, I should have kept an eye on you. I've been too preoccupied with the older two, keeping the house straight and yes, chatting next door. It really is my fault. I've just let you go your own way, I should have known you'd disgrace us. But I never thought... really, Elizabeth, your own cousin!"

They had convinced her. I could see I didn't stand a chance of explaining anything. They had told her that Gracie was too frightened of me to tell her what was going on, that I had threatened her, that I had twisted her arm behind her back to make her do what I wanted. "They feel very responsible for their little sister, you know, Elizabeth, because she can't always tell when she's being taken advantage of. Oh, where have I gone wrong with you?" The sorrowful gaze, her hands to her face, her head shaking back and forth—I knew all these movements intimately, could predict her next words. "I've failed, I've failed."

When I tried to speak, she asked me to keep still. "Your father is coming tomorrow. I'll take him out to the woods and we'll see these roads you've made your poor cousin work at. We'll see what he thinks, but I'm afraid we'll have to send you home, Elizabeth, we'll have to work out some kind of arrangement, I don't know. . . ." Her voice trailed off; the whole awful thing was becoming far too complicated for both of us.

Gracie emerged from her bath, being towelled dry lovingly by Charlene, as my mother opened the bedroom door. "G'night, Auntie Mavis," she said, and came toward us to give my mother a kiss, her rosy naked body still damp and shining.

"Put your nightgown on, dear," Mavis said, "and then we'll say goodnight. Elizabeth, you go and get washed up."

After it was dark, and I heard Gracie's breathing change to the deep rhythms of sleep, I lay very still and waited for the rest of the household to settle. I heard their voices, Ted's and Charlene's, and I tried to remember what it had felt like, back before Aunt Mabel died, when I had liked them, had wanted them to like me. And now it had all changed. I knew these terrible things, and we would never like each other again. We couldn't even look at each other. They were going to get me sent home so I wouldn't know any more about what they did, so I couldn't tell. Did they really think I would tell Mavis about *that*?

It was nearly midnight when the light under my mother's door went out, and then another hour after that passed before it seemed safe to move. It had been so hard keeping my eyes open—but the anger and hate I felt seemed like a kind of energy, strengthening my resolve. I was not a creature of stealth by nature, so that getting down the stairs was difficult and I was thankful for the thick carpet. I chose the back door out of the laundry-room for my exit, moving the lock with careful, careful fingers. Then out through the garage and down the side of the driveway, looking up only once to see whether anyone was watching from a window. No-one. I was safe. Barefoot, worrying about the sharp gravel sticking up through the asphalt on the road and the thistles in the schoolyard, I kept going. It didn't matter if my feet hurt. Nothing mattered but what I had to do.

A three-quarter moon hung in the sky, a white and fleshy thing giving off bright light and pale shadows so that I was able to see where I was going. I was surprised not to be frightened. It occurred to me that I was more frightened of the people in the house behind me than of anything in the woods.

The little path shone out in the moonlight, a silvery ribbon through the leaves and underbrush. I walked on the velvety soil, occasionally feeling the stub of roots under my feet, having to bend sometimes under the overhanging branches. It was beautiful, just right. The very kind of path Hansel would have scattered his crumbs along. I got to the place where the hut was to be, and gathered up the rest of the tools we had hidden there, the spoons and clippers; then with the whisk broom and my hands began sweeping leaves and twigs back over the bare ground, covering it over, making the path disappear. It took a long time and my arms got tired, but finally I reached the edge of the bush where our work had begun and I looked back where I had just been.

There was no path. You could tell there was a clearing of underbrush here and there, but it might have been natural; the path had been so twisting and winding it had never made a straight clear course. It would have looked like this again in the fall—but now, right *now* there was nothing, nothing to show for our days spent here. Only now to go back and put the tools in the garage and get into bed without getting caught. I would have to clean my feet, I thought, and my hands, but I would manage somehow. Suddenly, I was very tired, and my limbs ached from the exertion I had made. I turned slowly and bent down to crawl under the hole in the fence. And saw another pale nightdress in the moonlight, another pair of bare feet, another tear-stained face. I scrambled through and got up as fast as I could.

She stood there, looking at me, weeping quietly, her chin quivering as she tried to speak.

"Oh Gracie, I had to, I had to," I said. "I can't explain why. They were going to spoil it all anyway, they had already spoiled it. Everything is ruined. Can you understand?"

"My path," she said. "You broke my path. I'm a good girl and you broke my path!" And she began to sob in earnest.

"Please Gracie, don't cry. I love you. I had to. It was my path too and I had to. . . . Please. Honest, please." I reached out and turned her shoulder so that she was looking right at me again, and we were face to face, out there in the open on the edge of the bush. The same height, head to head, and I couldn't make her see. Ever. I couldn't do anything about it.

Queen Esther

Her name was Esther Bauman, and she always seemed to me a little different from the other Girls. Although she wore her hair in the same severe way, pulled back into a tightly braided bun, somehow on her the hairstyle looked stylish, like the sleek chignons of the models in my mother's fashion magazines. Esther's colouring was dark (almost Spanish I thought), which meant that in later years her facial hair darkened too so that a moustache along her lip was noticeable but it never grew as coarse and wiry as some of the other Girls' did. In every way she appeared to be more refined than others, not conventionally pretty but what my mother called "striking." She was taller and slimmer than any of our Friday Girls; they in turn were not so wide-hipped as their country sisters whose diet was far richer, but they still had a stout sort of shape because of the way their ankle-length dresses bloused over their round, unbrassièred bosoms.

They were called the Girls not only by my mother and her friends but by themselves as well, so it mustn't have been as derogatory as it sounds today. It had nothing to do with their age (most were well over 40 and anything but girlish), only their unmarried state. There were around a dozen Girls, Mennonites who had moved into Garten when it became clear that life held for them no husbands, no farms or families of their own. Perpetual virgins with no altar to tend, they hired out as cleaning women, babysitters, housekeepers, supporting themselves in a humble way that suited their beliefs. They lived together in small groups, refusing electrical services or telephone connections in their apartments or houses, keeping themselves as firmly removed from worldly intrusion as their relatives in the country. In their sparsely furnished, curtainless rooms they supplemented their income by doing needlework and knitting for women like my mother.

There must have been other women in Garten who went out doing housework, but no families I knew hired anyone but a Girl. There was no minimum wage in those days; if there had been, the Girls' pay would surely have been below it, for they were known to work for very little money. Still, my father believed they were overpaid.

"They just give what's left over to their families back on the farm," he said once, when I was old enough to ask questions about how much the Girls made (wondering how much I might earn for an allowance if I did similar chores). "They want so little themselves there's no sense giving them more than they need," he said. "No sense at all, do you see?"

My mother agreed but I said I didn't see what was wrong with them giving their money away if they wanted to. My father laughed his worldly, banker's laugh. "Well, Elizabeth, those Girls sending money back to the farm is like raindrops falling in the ocean. Those farmers are already so rich they don't know what to do with their money."

It offended my father that the Mennonites who farmed around Garten were so disinterested in the services his bank had to offer. As if they purposely kept a space between their money and their lives, they maintained a non-materialistic stance that still allowed them to buy the best cattle, the finest horses, the highest quality lumber for their barns. That was the paradox to puzzle over: having given up earthly pleasures and vanities, the Mennonites were tied to the earth, through their farming, in an intense way none of us townspeople were. They lived in profitable harmony with the very same earth they renounced in favour of God's heavenly kingdom. I never understood the belief they lived by, but I felt it as a crosscurrent pushing against me, running counter to the flow of life in Garten.

"Only place they squander their cash is the doctor's office," my father said, gladdened by the thought of Dr. Waddell's savings account at the Imperial. It *did* seem that the clinic waiting-room was always packed with Mennonite families on those days when cold or rainy weather prevented outdoor work. "I swear some of those old fellas take their cough syrup by the bottle instead of the spoon!" (Dr. Waddell, at my parents' bridge club in the living-room, everyone laughing. And at the top of the stairs listening, me laughing too.)

There was often joking about the Mennonites, especially concerning that waiting-room where barn smells and body odours would rise, nearly visible, from the damp dark clothes of the men. "Really June, the place reeked. I was there waiting for my annual and by the time I got in I felt quite faint. Do they *ever* wash?" (My mother, on the phone in the morning.) Jokes too about the babies lying on the broad laps of the women, so swaddled and bundled in layers of blankets you could hardly see their faces. "They don't grow arms and legs until they're a year old, that's why they keep them wrapped up like that!" (My friend Dieter, on the way home from school. Laughter. More laughter.)

No babies, limbless or whole, for Girls like Esther, except for the town children they minded. Minded—such a curious phrase, as if there were meant to be some element of brainwashing in the care they gave us. As we grew older, many of my friends resented the stern and unworldly attitudes of the Mennonites: forbidden to listen to the radio, Mayor Shultz's two children tied up their Girl with a clothesline and put her in a closet while they tuned in to the Lone Ranger, a scandal that nearly cost the Mayor his spot on council. I, on the other hand, felt nothing but gratitude for the Girls no matter what rules they imposed; for even at their most strict they were easier to be with than my parents, willing to play games of dominoes and Parcheesi.

I listened contentedly to their stories about growing up on the farm—walking beams in their bare feet, milking cows in the freezing dark, stooking grain in the blazing heat, making apple butter in the fall. Most of the women who minded me were the same ones who did the cleaning on Fridays, and over the years a procession of Rebeccas, Rachels, Blendinas and Marthas waxed our floors and told me about life in the country. But my favourite was Esther, who came on Tuesdays to do the family ironing until the year I was in Grade 9.

I would watch Esther ironing our clothes and wonder what she was thinking as she edged the point of the iron along the lace collar of my mother's good blouse, or flattened with broad strokes some floral housedress. Did she want clothes like these instead of the sombre dark cotton that she always wore? Or did she think that my mother was a fallen woman, given over to vain self-indulgence? There was no way to know, I would never have asked her. But eventually I convinced myself that Esther ironed our clothes as a way of reaching out and touching another world. Like me, she wanted more than the life she had.

She *was* different, she wasn't meant to be a Girl, I'd tell myself. Through some trick of fate she had come into a Mennonite family when by rights she was meant to be a lady of means, a ballet dancer, a movie star, a queen. A queen. In Sunday school our Bible stories were printed in small pamphlets with colour illustrations; in a series of Old Testament tales we were given a wonderful picture of Queen Esther. Seated on a throne, regal and long-necked, she was draped in a deep-red garment that flowed down her body like the marble angel's dress at the Cenotaph. Brave, beautiful, clever, adored by both her people and her king. Why did no-one love *my* Esther enough to make her his wife, his queen?

I invented dramatic and tragic explanations for her spinsterhood and by the time I was ten or so my favourite involved a handsome Mennonite I called Abel, who suffered a fatal accident while repairing a buggy wheel by the side of the highway. Her heart forever broken, Esther became a Girl, forced to observe happy families in Garten while mourning her lost love.

That was as close as I ever let my fantasies come to her actual life. Usually I created a rich existence with variations that took her to castles, ballrooms, theatres, the *worldly* world of music and excitement and romance. I accomplished all this secretly with paper dolls, drawing a likeness of Esther on white cardboard and cutting it out carefully. The face, as I remember, was very like hers, although I had a difficult time drawing the pulled-back hair—the doll simply looked mannish with no hair around the face—so I drew two enormous curls of the sort flamenco dancers wear on each cheek. (I would look at her, bent over the ironing-board, and imagine those spit curls pasted on her sallow cheeks and feel amazed at what change a few strands of hair might make. Were our lives really so precarious?)

I drew for Esther a wardrobe unusual for its emphasis on off-the-shoulder ballgowns in shades of red: crimson, scar-let, magenta. I paired her with store-bought cut-out dolls and gave her a continual parade of boyfriends with whom to dance. My friends Trudy and Sharon pointed out early that my doll Esther didn't look at *all* like Esther Williams; I said it wasn't supposed to anyway, and showed them the back where I'd written "Queen Esther." They snickered that the doll looked more like our Girl than a queen. "Imag-ine a Girl a Queen!" they said, and collapsed with laughter. The idea was just too ridiculous.

I was Esther's favourite town child, she said. She often told me stories about how badly behaved other children were, "but you're such a good girl, Elizabeth," she would say. I'd glow with pride at such rare and coveted praise, since my mother usually held exactly the opposite view. Of course I knew Mavis loved me—and she tried to be affec-tionate in a careful, specific sort of way—but there was al-ways a darkness under us, as if we were floating on a deep river of distrust and suspicion, pretending to each other that our little raft was safe and sure. We knew, both of us, that her motherhood had not turned out. But for Esther I was just a sunny, talkative child who kept her company while she ironed.

Everything was ironed at our house, even the sheets and towels. The wind often twisted the washing around the line so that there were knots and creases around the wooden pegs, but even when things came off the line unwrinkled the procedure was always the same. As soon as I was tall enough, my household chore on Mondays was to bring the wash in after school. It was a job I never objected to, even when in the winter my fingers ached as I pulled at the pegs on the frozen shirts and sheets. The clothes, stiff and un-wieldy, would be stacked like boards in the basket, and be put in the basement where overnight they'd go limp and damp, perfect for ironing on Tuesday. The grey-blue shad-ows on the snow, the sky like clear rosy tea steeping darker, the creak of the line—the only part missing in winter was the smell. In all other seasons I buried my face in the laun-dry and breathed it in, the delicate aroma of virtue.

Mavis showed me how to sprinkle and roll my father's shirts into tight cylinders, how to pile the basket in such a way that there was a logical progression from item to item, ready for Esther the next day. The cleanliness and order and peacefulness of Mondays made me want to be good for-ever, to be there forever on the wooden porch bringing in the line, folding clothes into a basket.

Even underwear was ironed, including my father's white undershirts and underpants. I remember one flushed mo-ment when I was sitting on a stool across the ironing-board from Esther, suddenly aware that her hands were smooth-ing the crotch of Frank's white cotton briefs. I had seldom given a thought to the anatomy my father possessed, but now it seemed so bulging, so evident in its absence there under deft fingers, that I felt engulfed by shame. At that moment Esther looked up, and for one brilliant flashing instant our eyes met. Then she lowered her eyes and went on working, applying the hot iron in small, precise strokes.

◆

One spring afternoon—I am eleven at the time—Esther asks my mother if I can go out to her brother's farm to stay overnight on the weekend. "She always has so many questions about the country, Mrs. Kessler," Esther says, "I was thinking maybe she'd like to see it all for herself once." My mother frowns in that way that means she'll have to clear it with my father, and she does, and he agrees. On Friday after an early supper, he and I pick up Esther at her apartment. Although it is a warm evening she has her long navy blue coat buttoned to the neck and her black bonnet tied under her chin. She has a small black valise that Frank puts in the trunk beside my mother's maroon overnight case. We sit side by side in the back seat of the Plymouth sedan, unable to think of anything to say, and I watch the back of my father's neck as he drives. You can tell so much about a person from behind, I think. Everything I know about my father is there in his thick, rounded neck, like a beige marble column, a pillar. I've seen pillars in Toronto in the museum and at the head office of his bank; I've heard Frank called "a pillar of the community, a pillar of the church." My father is a pillar. What does that make me?

I stare out the window at the scenery I know so well I can hardly look at it. The Bauman farm is only ten miles along the road that goes into the city, so I know the route, every house and barn by heart. If you count to fifteen after you've passed Ezra Martin's mailbox then you're at the curve where an enormous billboard proclaims that the kingdom of God is not here on earth. After that there are two barns with scripture painted on the side; although the billboard message changes every few months, the barns are always the same. And the fields falling away into the half-light of evening are the same, everything is the same. The things that I see out this car window weigh on me with their ordinariness. The land hums with new wheat and corn coming up green, even the woodlots look prosperous and tidy now that leaves are filling out the maples. The country rolls so gently it is nearly flat, but now and again—three times, I've counted them—there are dips where small creeks run and cedars rub against each other. These are the only places wild flowers and grasses grow; everything else is planted, cultivated, useful. I think I hate this country as much as I hate Garten but then consider that no, not quite as much, there is a little more chance in the open country for escape, even this country. But I long to go to places I have seen in movies, read about, imagined; dangerous mountains, furious seacoasts, even the treeless expanse of prairie would seem open and generous after this.

Sometimes we've driven up to Owen Sound to see Mavis's cousins and we've passed through little towns that my father calls "poor and nasty," through countryside that makes him shake his head in mock despair. "Don't know why they came here," he says of the Scottish settlers who moved into this area a hundred years ago. "I suppose it looked like home, as bleak as they could get after the Hebrides." The land up there *is* pretty barren, full of thistles and rocks even though it's all been cleared and there are stone walls separating the fields. Now there are plenty of deserted houses and broken-down barns and overgrown cellars, and the fields are patchy with stubbly grass or corn in spindly rows. Still, I like it much better up there than down here, and I think about how it would be if I ran away by myself to one of those grey-weathered windowless houses. I would live like a wild thing and have adventures. Here, I am trapped. Trapped in the back seat of my father's car, I think, and I feel a tremor of excitement. The night and day ahead of me have not yet been lived out—I don't know what to expect. None of my friends has ever been to a Mennonite farm overnight; I'll be the first, for whatever that's worth. I glance over at Esther and wonder how she feels about bringing an outsider home with her. Mavis said I must remember every single thing to tell her when I get home. My father said I must be careful not to give offence.

We turn off on a concession road toward the setting sun

and Esther says, "Second lane on your right, Mr. Kessler." We turn again and I see ahead a large brick house with two small brick additions on one side and a wooden addition on the other. There are several outbuildings and an orchard and bits of green showing where the garden is, before you come to the front yard, and farther back an unpainted barn, looming up in the violet light.

My father parks the car and gets our cases and Esther and I walk over to where a man and woman are coming out the screen door. They shake my hand and introductions are made all round—Israel and Ruth Bauman, my father, me —and then my father kisses my forehead and tells me to be helpful. "Ach, there's lots for her to help with," says Mr. Bauman, winking. "We'll have her up milking at five." He and the two women laugh in a kindly way, and we stand together and wave as the car goes down the lane although I am sure Frank is not looking back.

There is a wonderful smell in the air, wet earth and sweet manure, smells that seem to spring out of the darkening air itself. Inside, the smell is of sour milk and apples, and something else like bread or wood, I cannot name it. There are oil lamps that flicker when we come in and their fumes rise in smoky drifts up out of the glass chimneys. Like incense, I think. There are four children sitting at a table in the middle of the room and two teenage boys on a day-bed at the other end. They are all perfectly silent, watching me with smooth, barely curious faces. They have round unfathomable eyes like all the Mennonite children I have ever known—there have always been Mennonites in my classes at school—but I am aware that these are *real* Mennonites who go to a country school and come into town only now and again. There are three girls, all smaller than me, and a boy who looks to be nearly the same size. He is wearing the same clothes as his older brothers, a collarless white shirt and black trousers held up by braces. The girls' long dresses are pale blue flecked with darker blue flowers, and their hair is pulled back from their foreheads into thick braids.

In Garten I am used to seeing them as the odd ones who just won't fit into our ways; but now, here, I feel strange and out of place with my short hair and a skirt that only just covers my knees. Their parents have made them stand up to be introduced and as they are named in turn I am blushing so violently that my ears seem to be full of rushing blood and I cannot hear properly so I don't ever find out what they are called.

When we all sit down at the table, the mother asks me if I am hungry and I don't know what the correct response should be. I look to Esther for help, who says, "A piece of pie would go down, Ruth," at which everyone laughs in agreement. Two pies are brought out of a pantry and a brown jug of milk, and I am given a piece of what they call shoofly, sticky and sugary and satisfying. Everyone else eats busily too and no-one talks until we are finished. Then the father asks me about school, trying to make conversation in a friendly way. He asks me what I would like to do tomorrow, what I would like to see. "Everything," I say. That seems so enormously funny to the big boys they nearly fall on the floor until their mother hushes them.

I have finished my pie so Esther says she will show me my bed. I'm to have my own small room on the third floor. I carry my bag and she the lamp, and I remember to stop at the bottom of the stairs to say thank you for the pie and goodnight. They all reply in English but as we are climbing the stairs I hear them starting to talk and the sound is the rich ebb and flow of Pennsylvania Dutch, the guttural German we make fun of in the school playground. I know they are talking about me and so does Esther, who begins to speak to distract me. She says she will bring me warm water in the morning to wash, and that there is a pot under the bed. We reach the door and she opens it to show me a small room with a sloping ceiling, plain white walls stained blue by the failing light, and as the lamp moves farther into the room I see a bed covered by a patchwork quilt, a small wooden table on which there is a pitcher and basin and a wooden chair at the edge of a rag mat. That is all there is and I am surprised at how much I like it.

Esther tells me she will wake me early so I can start the day with the family, sets the lamp on the table, takes the pitcher, reminds me to say my prayers and goes out, leaving the door slightly ajar. I undress quickly and pee in the cold porcelain pot, wondering if anyone is listening to the noise I make. I can hear all kinds of things, the night sounds of the house that become louder once I have blown out the lamp and pulled the covers up over myself. There are groaning floorboards and random faint murmurings, a laugh and then another, and I try to imagine myself living here, part of this house. Belonging. Finally I sleep.

It is still dark when Esther comes with the warm water, telling me to get dressed and come down when I am ready. In the kitchen she is waiting for me and we go outside together. The sun is at the edge of the far fields and there is enough light to see by when we enter the whitewashed cellar of the barn. I see ahead a long double row of cows— twenty Holsteins and four Guernseys, Esther says. Mr. Bauman and the three boys are already milking, their arms moving like pistons as the milk squirts into the pails. There are two striped cats sidling around Mr. Bauman who aims a teat and sprays the smaller one in the face. Dripping milk, the cat retreats happily, licking itself; I am shocked but I cannot say why. Esther asks me if I would like to learn how to milk, and although I am afraid of these animals flicking their tails and shifting their feet restlessly, I say yes.

First she sits down on a stool and with a rag from a pail of sudsy water she washes the udder and each teat and wipes it all dry. Then she takes an empty metal pail and puts it beneath the cow and in front of her own legs; in each hand she takes a long pink teat and begins to pull them in succession. I can see that the ball of her thumb is pressing hard and the sinews and veins in her wrists stand out like cords. Within a few seconds there is a hissing stream of milk hitting the bottom of the pail; soon the spurts become heavier and the hollowness of the sound decreases as the pail begins to fill. After a few moments Esther turns and looks up at me with a smile, as if she had nearly forgotten me. She belongs here, I decide, not at my mother's ironing-board, not even in my imaginary ballrooms. Against the black and white stomach of the cow her elegant face makes everything here more beautiful, more real.

She finishes the two teats and gets up. "Now you try, Elizabeth," she says, and shows me how to hold the teats. They are surprisingly firm and yet there is a squishiness, a rubbery quality that embarrasses me. I think of penises and wonder if anyone else has such wicked thoughts. I try to hold and press and pull at the same time as I saw her doing, but nothing happens. The cow, sensing a novice hand, is annoyed, tries to move away. "Keep trying," Esther encourages, and I see that the two elder boys have come up behind her, smirking. Their father calls them to get on with their work and again I yank and squeeze, but no milk comes. Esther is soothing the cow with words I don't understand, words that sound like the barn itself, musical like the *whssst* of milk in a pail. I stop and rub my aching hands together and feel tears welling in my eyes. I cannot cry or they will think I am not having a good time. But I am not having a good time.

After the barn there is breakfast and the table is laden with food—I have never seen a breakfast like this. There is cold roast beef and ham and summer sausage, a bowl of scrambled eggs and a big crockery plate of fried potatoes,

along with several smaller dishes of stewed prunes, straw-
berry jam and apple butter and maple syrup and pickles and
pale fresh butter. There are two loaves of bread and left-
over pie and a platter stacked with doughnuts and coffee
cake, and at both ends of the table, jugs of milk. There are
prayers said in German before we eat and I keep my eyes
open so I will know when it is over. I see the family's bowed
heads, and am sure that the boy my age is watching me
from between his fluttering lashes. During the meal Mr.
Bauman tries again to talk to me, this time about the chores
that are done on Saturday. I will help the other girls in the
garden, and will learn to make fetschpatze for dinner, and
then in the afternoon will play in the barn before my parents come for me.

When the barn time comes I am tired. I have worked
harder and eaten more than I have ever done and I wish I
could find a dark corner and sleep. But the little girls are
eager to show me their playing-places, the ropes hung for
swinging from the rafters, the secret hiding-spots up in the
loft. Because it is spring the bales of hay are nearly gone
and I am disappointed that it is not as Esther described it to
me, full nearly to the ceiling with fragrant golden hay.
There are ladders leaning against the rafters and the boy
my age clambers up quickly, shouting at the swallows who
are swooping in great arcs from one side of the barn to the
other. Two or three dive very close to his head as if to warn
him away and he hoots at them and waves his straw hat,
then flings it at one bird and laughs when the hat falls to
the bare plank floor below. I stand with his sisters, looking
up and giggling. Nearly a whole day has passed and we
have managed to avoid speaking directly to each other—
there is no way now to break our shyness. The boy shouts
down at us to watch and he eases himself off the ladder and
onto the wide crossbeam, and stands up.

He is far, far above us, his arms held out like a tightrope

walker's and his head high, proud and cocky. Shafts of speckled light fall across his path and he steps through them, a creature both magical and real, with swallows wheeling around his head. He gets to the far side, kneels and lets himself down onto the ladder leaning there. After a few rungs he is able to reach out and grab the rope that is tied to the beam above. Swinging out into the open air he yells, a sound I want to be able to make myself. It sounds like being free.

He slides down the rope and lands with a thud, looking at us, me, all the while. Triumphant, challenging. "Who next?" he asks, and pokes the biggest of the three girls, who laughs and runs to the ladder. She has taken off her shoes and in her bare feet she makes the procedure look graceful, ballet-like. I am becoming more envious than I have ever been, watching her walk slowly along the beam. Imagine, I think. Imagine being up there and not being scared. She completes the same circuit as her brother but climbs down the ladder instead of using the rope. She comes over to me as if she had read my mind and says, "Do you want to go?" They are all standing around me, looking at me with those round, impassive faces, grey-blue eyes wide open to see what I will do now. The competitive thrust here seems edged with curiosity rather than the jealousy and malice I know at home on Brubacher Street. No urging or taunting, only the smallest girl saying "Just try it once." *She* can probably do it backwards, I think, and bend over to take off my shoes. The world around me spins and swims, I am dizzy before my feet even leave the floor.

As I climb the ladder I feel very determined and very brave. I have never done anything like this before—once my friend Dieter jumped out of his bedroom window and dared the rest of us to follow but no-one did. And here I am now, nearly at the beam. I have done it, climbed right up without any help. I look down to see whether they are ad-

96

miring me, and the fit of dizziness sweeps over me again. I
hang on tightly and wonder how to get my body from the
ladder up onto the rafter as swallows dart at my face and
the walls of the barn tilt and dance. My body seems to be
pulling away from my head, willing itself to fall backwards
in space. It looked so easy from down there but I can't see
how it is done now that I'm here. I know I can't do it. I
know I am too scared to try, and with that thought I begin
to cry. At first just a few tears that blur the striped light
around me but then I hear myself sobbing. The next thing
is Mr. Bauman's scolding voice; he is speaking German so
I know he is scolding the children, not me. And then he
says in English that I should stay right here and not look
down and he'll come up and get me.

I feel the ladder shake as he starts up the rungs and that
makes me cry even harder even though I know now everything will be all right. "Step back and down now," he says,
and I move my leg obediently, and begin letting go of the
beam, feeling safe with his body behind mine. Soon we are
at the bottom and I turn to see the solemn faces regarding
me with mild surprise. I am humiliated by their charity, and
feel certain they will laugh about this once I am gone. And
now Esther comes, running up the ramp to the open barn
door. her hand at her heart, out of breath.

"She could have killed herself," Mr. Bauman says sternly,
and the boy flushes red as if that thought had already
crossed his mind. I feel very important. I could have killed
myself. I haven't ever been so near to real danger before.
There is a thrill here I didn't know about until now, a sweet
plummeting drop and then a spreading out of burning
wind through my body. Esther comforts me, puts her hand
on my shoulder. "Ach, Elizabeth, we learn when we're
small and when the loft is high with hay so if we tumble
there's no hurt. But *now's* no time to try."

"Oh Esther," I say, "I was so scared up there. We won't

97

tell my folks about it, okay?" I can see that she is relieved this idea has come from me, and we agree. She tells me to go and get my things ready since my parents will soon be here. I walk back to the house without looking again at the children, thinking what a mistake this has all been. It doesn't work, this overlapping of people. I should never have come.

Frank and Mavis arrive within the hour and although the Baumans press them to stay for supper we depart after all the handshaking and thanking is accomplished. One of the big boys tickles the palm of my hand with his finger and I can see he is laughing at me. I wonder if I will ever see him again. It doesn't seem likely.

We are turning from the lane back onto the highway when Mavis begins her steady drill of questions, a habit that always distresses me and makes me resolve to tell her nothing. I am getting better at fending her off, keeping little sections of my life private from her prying; and today it is not difficult to resist her need to know, for I truly have nothing to say. I feel as if I have been coated with something clear, like mineral oil, for the entire time at the Baumans'. I have absorbed nothing. I know nothing about what it is to be a Mennonite except that I do not belong there. And I know that Esther should not be ironing my father's shirts—and that I am no more able to change things than I am able to walk the beam.

The only good thing has been being free of my parents for these hours, and it turns out they have had the same revelation. "Really, I think this little change has been good for all of us," my mother says, and lays her hand on my father's on the steering-wheel.

✽

In one of those inexplicable reversals, Esther became more fond of me after that disappointing visit, and I felt my interest in her waning. Perhaps it was something as simple as outgrowing my paper dolls; or perhaps my curiosity, satisfied, no longer embraced Esther either as person or object. Although I still took great care in preparing the Monday laundry basket, I seldom joined her on Tuesdays, never sat around and talked—I always seemed to have something else to do. Sometimes she tried to start up a conversation with "My brother's children say hello," but I never sent any messages back. Worried that maybe they were supposed to be invited now to *my* house, I avoided the topic of the Bauman farm whenever I could.

That visit, however, caused major repercussions in my life. My absence had so revitalized the Kessler marriage that my parents began to look forward to another respite and my mother asked me if I would like to go to camp that summer. Only for a week, and only to a church camp down on Lake Erie (not like the expensive private camps up in Muskoka where the Waddells and Lutzes sent their children) but still, a chance to get out of Garten.

With Sharon and Amy from my Sunday school class, I went off in July to Camp Zion, a well-weathered collection of white cabins set on the edge of a wood facing the lake. Each of the cabins contained eight girls—we were in Intermediate Camp, ages ten to twelve—and a counsellor; ours, a freckled redhead named Betty, had come out the other side of Senior Camp and now wanted "to contribute to Camp Zion." She said our week would be a "rich experience," which is what we were also told by Zion's leader, Mrs. Davidson, whose camp name was Dee-dee. We were told we would learn about God's glory as it manifests itself on earth and then we sang both verses of "This is my Father's world," a hymn that always brought Frank's face to mind, which spoiled it.

Both Betty and Dee-dee told the truth; I learned more about God's glory at Camp Zion than I had ever known, and during Bible study I memorized the Beatitudes and several long scripture passages by heart. I learned to make a fruit basket of Popsicle sticks, and a wooden plaque on which I glued alphabet macaroni to read GOD IS LOVE. I learned innumerable songs featuring choruses heavy with hosannas and hallelujahs, and I learned to shout "pee-yuke" at the sight of tapioca pudding being passed down the long tables in the dining-hall. I learned, when Dee-dee's shrill whistle called us to rise and salute the dawn, to blot out the sound of her nasal voice reciting poetry and hear instead the sweet clatter of morning birds. I learned several dirty jokes I didn't understand, and I learned that Emily who slept in the bunk beside mine came from Simcoe and had never heard of Garten.

"It must be pretty small," she said scornfully, and I felt a peculiar twinge, a terrible need to defend the very place I hated.

"It's not *that* small," I said. "You must be pretty dumb." And so ended whatever budding friendship there had been between us. But there were other friendships that grew and thrived from that first summer through to the next year, when we converged on Camp Zion with the energy and enthusiasm of true initiates. "How did we ever sur*vive?*" we asked each other, wondering how the months apart had not destroyed us entirely. Here we were again, ready for all God's glory and morning dip and evening tuck and camp-fire reverie. By the third summer, even though Sharon and Amy chose a co-ed camp closer to home, I would have let nothing come between me and Camp Zion. I didn't need friends from home; I was just as happy to leave them be-hind, to concentrate on these brief, intense friendships with girls from Brantford, Hamilton, London, St. Catharines. These were girls who could teach me about life outside Garten, who knew about things I had never encountered— Chinese egg rolls, pizza, perverts in movie theatres, how to steal stuff from stores, how to wad your brassière with Kleenex (I didn't need to and for that had some status), how to slick your hair back into a ducktail and wear your blouse collar turned up at the neck. Endless, the things there were to discover at Camp Zion.

I learned, now that I was at Senior Camp and regarded as an Old Camper, that everyone, including the counsellors, thought Dee-dee was a real jerkball, a confirmation of my instinctive reaction so profound that it gave me lasting confidence in my own judgments. I learned that Betty, now nineteen, came back year after year only because of Lefty, the camp cook's nephew. I learned that no matter what sin you had committed, Jesus would love you and forgive you if you told him. And I learned how to kiss.

The kissing began on the second evening of camp. So titillated were we by Betty's revelations about herself and Lefty, our cabin sent Joan and Wendy on a spying expedition to find out "how far they went." It proved an easy task, since the urgency of their passion had taken the lovers into the bushes only a few feet from the back of the dining-hall. Guided to the spot by Betty's audible sighs of "Lefty, Lefty!" the girls crept undetected to within good viewing range. Lefty had long been the focus for many of our amorous fantasies, a thickset boy with dark greasy hair falling in curls on his forehead, and a sensual, pouting mouth. The city girls said he was a true hardrock. If he caught any of us looking at him as he did his chores around the camp, he wiggled his middle finger at us in the most lewd way. "Lewd," in fact, became a catchword that last summer at Zion. Everything our eyes lit upon became lewd.

"It was so-o-o-o lewd!" Joan and Wendy breathed their astonishment at what they had seen. "He had his hand inside her sweatshirt and she was moaning and saying 'No, no!' and he kept on kissing her like he couldn't stop."

"Like how?" we asked, curiosity rising to fever pitch.

"Like this," they said, and lay down on the cabin floor, and put their arms around each other, and writhed about, moaning, their faces fastened mouth to mouth.

"Oh God," we said. The girl holding the flashlight switched it off and we sat there in the dark, shivering with nameless agonies we didn't recognize. Wendy and Joan sat up, coming apart with a start once the light was off them, and it was a long time before anyone said anything. I was sitting on my top bunk, legs dangling over the side, feeling nearly as if I were floating, as if Lefty's hands were on my breasts, his lips on mine.

"What does it feel like?" I said, half to myself, half to the cabin, where only dark shapes showed, only eyes and teeth glinted in the shadows.

"Here," said Wendy, and she got up from the floor, and stood on the edge of the lower bunk. "Bend down. Like this." She put her arms around my neck and pulled my face down toward hers, and kissed me. Her lips pressed hard against mine and I was aware of having to breathe with a nose that was squashed against her cheek. I pulled away. "It feels like rubber worms," I said.

Someone in the dark began to laugh then, and then another until the cabin was filled with hiccupping, gasping laughter, girls thumping their pillows and crying "Rubber worms!" and sobbing with laughter. Finally there was an exhausted silence. And in that silence we began kissing each other.

This time Wendy and I moved our faces so that we could breathe, and we found that if we moved our mouths a little as we were kissing there was a variation in pressure that became quite pleasant. Made us want to stop only for a moment and then start up again. I let myself down from the bunk and stood with Wendy, who was nearly my height, our bodies tight against each other, kissing and kissing. I opened my eyes once and in the darkness could make out other pairs standing and kissing, stroking each other's backs with hesitant hands.

"All change!" someone called out, and we all laughed again, and again there were cries of "Lewd!" and "Rubber worms!" but not so vigorously, not so hysterically as before. Now we were settling into a delicious dreamy pattern of changing partners, everyone kissing everyone else, laughing in a quiet way that became less and less embarrassed. It began to seem very ordinary, like something we had done before, maybe in our dreams. We were teetering on the edge of craziness but because we were together it held no danger. Sometimes one of us began giggling during a kiss and our mouths came unglued and we peered at each other in the darkness, a little amazed we had not discovered this business until now. Eventually we heard Betty outside the cabin and we scrambled into our beds and lay there quietly, listening to Betty undress, thinking about her body moving under Lefty's hands.

The next morning no-one referred to the night before, no-one winked or pursed her lips or muttered "rubber worms" at breakfast. But at night, as soon as Betty had slipped out to her rendezvous in the bushes, we began again, this time without preliminary joking, to kiss and kiss and kiss.

We were on fire. For the remaining days of camp everything we did or sang or ate or said was only waiting until the darkness and the kissing. The true glory of God had been revealed to us, we had been touched by the tongues of Pentecost. We stared boldly at Lefty, we lowered our swim-suit straps invitingly whenever we could arrange to stroll past the back of the dining-hall where he sat much of the day peeling potatoes and carrots. But he never took the bait —he had his Betty, after all—and we were left with each other, confused and passionate.

I returned to Garten at the end of camp dreading the

awful loneliness I knew I would now feel. I had no-one with whom to share this knowledge—although some of us exchanged letters at intervals through the year, no-one had the nerve to make any reference to what we had done. It was as if it had never happened.

At the end of the summer came the start of high school, and I was back with all the friends I'd known since kindergarten plus a whole new group bused in from the country. And from being at the summit at Camp Zion, I plunged to the murky depths of despair. I was a misfit. There was no-one in my class, from town or country, boy or girl, as tall as I was. My body seemed purposely to lurch itself at people and objects so that I was constantly bumping things, breaking things, causing a disturbance. Teachers, when they heard a pencil case drop or a book fall to the floor, snapped, "Pick it up, Elizabeth," without even looking. I felt picked on, awkward, unloved and ugly. Except for math class where I found solace in algebra, I hated school.

Mavis and Frank were not oblivious to my unhappy state and in their own ineffectual way they tried to make me feel better, but nothing could, of course, nothing but some mythical Lefty who would kiss and stroke me far into the night. What intensified my anguish was that I saw the girls around me beginning to discover first hand what it was that I was only dreaming of. By the end of October Trudy reported that she and Wilbur had kissed for half an hour after the Hallowe'en Teen Town Dance . . . and Sharon announced soon after that she was going steady with a boy in Grade 11 and no longer had time to spend doing homework with me.

At dances in the gymnasium I would stand against the wall hunching my shoulders, with my knees slightly bent so that from across the floor I might look not much taller than the girls beside me, even though I knew all the boys *knew*. I would take off my glasses and squint into the crowd, hoping that my lounging attitude against the wall might be taken as seductive by one of the older, taller boys from the upper grades. But my plain, open face and solid, ungainly body attracted only the truly lonely or charitable, and the occasional classmate who wanted to discuss algebra problems. ("You *must* go," my mother urged, wanting me to do well, to be popular. "Don't think of your*self*, think of how to make the boys feel comfortable and you won't be self-conscious a bit. It doesn't matter if you're taller if you can make *him* feel important.") With each dance I attended, my sense of self-esteem decreased.

By the mid-winter, I was as sad and lonely as I would ever be. The days dragged on, one after another, and mine was the only body that seemed to flourish and grow in that frigid climate. It was all my father's fault, I decided. My mother was a decent height, a little under 5′ 4″, but Frank was a big, heavy-boned man with long fleshy arms and legs and a graceless, thick body. And it was my father's family that I "took after." I transferred some of my self-loathing onto Frank's shoulders, which eased the burden only a little, for even if I knew who to blame for my misfortune, it was still Elizabeth in whose shape I dwelled.

One afternoon after a basketball tournament there was a tea-dance in the gym, which still smelled of boys' armpits and rubber running-shoes, a sharp, precise smell that quickened the nostrils and brought to mind images of combat. I stayed for nearly an hour but eventually, humiliated to have stood for so long without being asked to dance, I got my coat and books from my locker and went home. I scuffed my feet along the snowy streets, aware only of how much I hated Garten, how much I wished I were somebody else. I let myself in the side door and entered the back part of the kitchen where we left our snowy boots in winter. Where Esther had the ironing-board set up. She was there that day, working at my father's shirts, and she seemed pensive and withdrawn. Maybe the peaceful rhythm of the ironing made her introspective, or maybe she had learned to anticipate my moody silences. "Your mother said to tell you she'll be at the church until five," she said. "She's at a missions meeting and she wants you to get the potatoes on before she gets home. I've turned on the oven so you can put the meatloaf in any time."

"Sure, right," I said, feeling myself listless in her sight. Mavis was at the damn church more afternoons than not. It was a relief in some ways but God, I hated all that messing around I had to do in the kitchen. Why couldn't goddamn Esther peel the damn potatoes? Wasn't she our Girl? Wasn't she supposed to do things like that? I slumped with exaggerated despair and told Esther I was going to lie down. "I've had a bad day," I said, thinking how much I sounded like my father but how like Mavis it was to go and lie down. I could never escape them.

I didn't lie down. I went into my closet and sat in the back corner, the way I had when I was younger, when I used to play cards by myself by the hour, poker hands and clock solitaire. Still taped on the closet walls were magazine photos of movie stars—Debbie and Eddie, Jeff, Tab, Jimmy, Doris and Audrey and yes, there was Esther, not anything like our Esther, posing under palms with Fernando. She had rather wide shoulders, I judged, looking closely at the photograph, and her hips and legs weren't all that small either. She was probably pretty tall and strong too, not that different from me, really. I didn't have to be a recluse forever; someday someone would see me as beautiful and rescue me. But when? I studied the photograph closely for more clues, and finding none, began to cry.

All the sorry thoughts of the desolate winter crowded round my brain just as the hems of my dresses brushed my forehead where I sat. "I am the saddest person in the world," I thought, "but someday I will be the most beautiful and everybody will love me." The very childishness of that idea made me cry harder.

*

Then there is the sound of footsteps in my room, the closet door opening, the light being switched on and Esther there, an armload of freshly ironed blouses ready to hang. She seems to fill the whole doorway, a giant like me, and she says "Oh, Elizabeth?" in a way that isn't really surprised, as if she knew all along this is where I'd be. She hangs the blouses and then crouches down, bends toward me. She smells of sweat and scorched cotton.

"Ach, you are having a bad time?" she asks, and her voice is so warm, so genuine, that I see her face as I haven't for years. She is beautiful. If only I could be that beautiful, the world would just come right.

"Esther," I say. "Esther." I lean forward, and put my arms around her and kiss her. I have my hands on the back of her shoulder-blades so she can't move, and I press my mouth against hers firmly, pressing hard, opening her mouth with mine, feeling all the pleasure there is to gain from lip on lip, tongue curling on tongue. It is exquisite. It is all the burning, rushing, sinful excitement I have ever known or dreamed of.

But this is Esther the Mennonite, the Girl Esther, whose moustache bristles slightly against my skin, who irons my father's underwear.

She is pulling away as I am saying "Oh Esther, I'm sorry, I'm sorry, I didn't mean to. . . ." She is gathering her dark purple dress around her as she stands up, looking at me with eyes that say I am a monster, but that she still loves me. She turns and runs from the room. I sit there a long time and listen to her leaving, hear the noises of her putting away the ironing-board, getting her coat and bonnet and boots from the front closet, shutting the door behind her. It must be five, my mother will soon be home, I better peel the goddamn potatoes. I think I will probably never hear Esther leaving this house again.

✱

Mavis read out to me and Frank the letter she received Monday with the kind of Pennsylvania Dutch accent that townspeople affected when they tried to imitate Mennonites. "I chust feel I kennot work for yous eny more, Missus Kessler, eefen though I haf enchoyed my yearss in your howss. I pray to God for all of yous."

She raised her eyes from the letter. "Now what do you make of this?" she asked my father. "What is going through that woman's mind?"

"Lord only knows," Frank replied. "You know how those Girls take notions. Which was it, Rebecca? Rachel? Who thought I was in love with her?" They both laughed. Mavis looked at me.

"What do you know about this, Elizabeth?" she asked sharply, suddenly intuitive, on target.

"Well, don't ask me," I said. "All *I* ever did was get the laundry basket ready for her. Maybe she didn't like the way I've been rolling Daddy's shirts lately." And I flounced from the table, insolent, uncaring.

"Dear Jesus," I said, as I climbed the stairs to my room, "I am telling you about this, so you have to forgive me."

Sorrows of the Flesh

Because my father was a banker, I was never allowed to have any pets while I was growing up. It wasn't, as you might think, because of the expense that he objected, although he usually brought that up as an additional factor. No, it was because he couldn't tolerate animal hair on his clothes. He wasn't allergic, just neat. He wore navy three-piece suits winter and summer, and the notion of meeting the public with dog hair or cat fluff clinging to his trousers was unthinkable, as unlikely to happen as his neglecting to visit his barber once a week to have his own hair trimmed close to his head.

"Now see here, Elizabeth," he would begin on those occasions when I was wheedling for whatever newborn kitten or hand-licking stray had taken my fancy. His voice would be patient, but sternly turned to the problem at hand, as if we were doing arithmetic questions together and I needed extra explanation. "We've been over this before. I cannot afford to turn up at the bank looking as if I had slept in a nest of monkeys. People need to have absolute trust in their bank manager, they have to look up to him as someone who knows what he's doing. Now what impression would I give with hair sticking to my suit?"

"But Daddy . . ." I would be allowed to break in, but only as a matter of form, to give the appearance of rational dialogue between father and daughter.

"And I've never known a man yet who came from a house where there were pets who didn't look like it!"

"We could keep it outside all the time, Daddy," I'd say, getting specific on the idea of a big dog on a rope by the back door.

"Fine in the summer, too cold in the winter," he'd reply. "Not fair to the animal, anyway. Now think about *that*, Elizabeth. Think about that!"

I would offer to brush his suits every morning, to vacuum the house every night, to never let so much as a hair go ungroomed on the body of the longed-for pet, but always the answer was the same. "It simply isn't worth the fuss, Elizabeth. No."

Once, reading about cats, I came across a variety called "Russian Blue." The Prussian blue in my paintbox was a lovely dark greeny blue, and hope sprang up as an idea took me—maybe this kind of cat had dark blue fur and then, oh maybe, if the hair didn't show on his navy suit. . . . I went to the Carnegie Library the following Saturday and looked up cats until I found a colour photograph and two descriptive references: a distinctive grey coat with a bluish cast, nothing like navy at all. I gave up on cats.

When I was in Grade 4, I became friends with a boy named Billy who lived on the edge of town. He and his sister Beatrice were known as "the poor kids" because their house looked more like a shack than anything else, and because the clothes they wore seemed always to be faded, patched and the wrong size. They were as mysterious as foreigners and I would not likely have made any attempt to know them except that one day during composition, Billy read aloud his paragraph about raising rabbits. After school that day I asked if I could come and see them, and he said yes, I could even help him feed the rabbits and clean their cages.

There was a whole wall of rabbits along the back of his father's chicken coop and Billy pointed to it with pride, beaming. Cage after cage of breathing fur, silent and un-blinking. Not until he opened a cage door and gave me a big black female to hold did I understand what there was to like about rabbits: the heavy warmth against my body was so comforting I knew I had to have one or die. I began then to save from my weekly allowance and by early June had the dollar to pay him for a black-and-white baby rabbit. Billy said I could borrow a cage until I could buy or make another, and I set off for home with the rabbit in its cage balanced on the handlebars of my bicycle, full of plans, a little worried, but confident. I set the cage behind the gar-age in the shade of a lilac bush and went inside to ask my mother for some lettuce and old newspaper.

Although I had tried to sound offhand it was such a peculiar request, and I was so flushed with excitement, that she followed me outside. "Your father will never allow it," was the first thing she said. I argued with her a little, and knew when I said, "I just want something of my own to take care of and love," that I had scored a telling point. It worried her, I knew, that I was an only child and she felt guilty that she might have deprived me of a normal childhood. Sure enough, it had been exactly the right thing to say, for I heard her through the kitchen door when my father came home.

"Listen to me, Frank, this is important. That child has gone out and bought a rabbit because she wants a pet so badly. She can keep it out in the garage, it'll never be in the house. Really, by the end of the summer she'll be bored with it and the whole thing will be over."

Such insight and compassion on my mother's part was nearly unheard of, but for her own reasons she had decided to take on my father and he gave in, grudgingly. He came out once to look at the animal and grunted something about "stew," warned me to keep it outside, and that was all.

I sold the rabbit back to Billy before school was finished for 50¢, which I spent on butterscotch wafers. My mother smiled knowingly at my father, but she was wrong, I had *not* become bored. I had begun to hate the rabbit with such passion I was frightened to death I was going to kill it. The damp newspaper and pellets of poo gave off a sickening smell, and the pulpy bits of nibbled lettuce on the bottom of the cage were disgusting—but it was the animal itself that I loathed. The very thing that made it lovable to begin with, its idiotic passivity and furry heartbeat, grew to offend me so much I wanted to wring its neck. It was stupid, stupid, stupid, and my hands would clench around its little neck tighter and tighter. "Stupid goddamn rabbit," I would whisper. "You are too stupid to live."

The foolish creature would twitch its ears and whiskers and nose, and look blankly at me with its glassy eyes, and my heart turned to stone. I discovered that no matter how much love I lavished on it, or how much hate, it stayed exactly the same. I wanted something, *anything* to happen. I would have been charmed at that point if it had bitten me.

But it didn't, and I had nightmare after nightmare about squeezing the soft fur around its neck until the head lolled to one side, finished with rabbity thoughts forever. Full of guilt and fear, I made the deal with Billy, and told my mother I couldn't bear to see the poor thing caged. She was touched, and we had a little talk about freedom, and how awful it must be to be my grandmother's canary. And that was the end of it.

By the time my father was no longer a banker, I was well over the need for a pet, had even completed the brief but obligatory fling with horseflesh that all my friends went through. By that time I was in love, and whether my father wore navy suits or hairy suits or none at all didn't matter to me. All I cared about was Mr. Wheeling, and staying in Garten the rest of my life.

I was fourteen, three inches under six feet and going into Grade 10 when Jerry Wheeling, teacher of junior biology and senior chemistry, came to Garten District High School. He was 24, at least 6' 5", with long bony wrists that hung from his shirt-cuffs so poignantly it made me want to cry until I watched him on the basketball court, coaching the boys' team, and I saw those same wrists fluid and flexible as rubber. It was like visible music. "It is wonderful to be in love," I wrote in the diary I began that year, "because it means you notice all the little things about a person."

There were far more obvious things than his wrists to notice about Jerry Wheeling. He was good-looking in a Hollywood way, with a thatch of cornsilk hair and a square but not jutting jaw. He was the first honest-to-goodness American many of us had ever met, and he had come up out of Ohio like a live advertisement for the great United States. He talked with a slight twang that soon all the basketball players were copying, used American slang like "cool" and "neat," and wore "sneakers" instead of running-shoes.

The reason he had come to Garten was that his bride of a year had become homesick for her family who lived about 40 miles away. He had applied for teaching jobs in a 100-mile radius of her home, he said, and Garten was the first town to reply. Her name was Mayruth, and when he spoke of her it was not with the professional detachment that other teachers used if it was necessary to speak of their spouses in the classroom. He called her his sweet Mayruth, and long before we met her, when he brought her with him to chaperone a dance that autumn, we knew all about her. We knew, for example, that they had met while she was down at Oberlin studying music, that she could play the piano with her eyes closed, that she was just a little bit of a thing, and that she was going to have a baby soon after Christmas.

He was, besides being our science teacher that year, homeroom adviser for 10A, and he changed my life. I rose an hour earlier so that I could practise my piano scales before breakfast (a discipline I had resisted for years), and then I would rush to school to get to the room, to be the first one there. He'd be sitting at his desk, marking assignments or reading, yet he always seemed accessible, open to conversation, even eager. I had never known an adult to be so casual, so ready to talk. Sometimes we would talk about sports, a favourite subject of his, and the boys would cluster around his desk too, showing off and butting in. One of these mornings he singled me out and said, "Now you, Elizabeth, have a natural advantage with your height. You'll be on the junior team, right?"

Said as an assumption, as if no-one had told him how awkward I was, as if he couldn't see it with his own two eyes. The boys all hooted, derisive as always, and said, "Oh, Mr. Wheeling, she's no good!" And he smiled right at me, so that it felt as if my chest was opening and my heart fluttering and flaming up into the air the way it does in Roman

Catholic holy pictures, and he said, "Well, she *will* be good. Won't you, Elizabeth?"

So of course I tried out and got on the team for exactly the reason he had mentioned—I was big enough to be of some use. Sometimes he would drop into our practice sessions and chat with Mrs. Ridley, who'd been leading girls' teams to early defeats for years and years. Eventually he had her warmed up enough so that she didn't object when he came on the courts with us, showing us all kinds of neat plays we could do even within the rigid confines of Girls' Rules that prevented us from taking more than three steps with the ball and kept us on certain sections of the floor according to our positions, forwards and guards. Oh, how I longed to dribble down the floor, ball bouncing tenderly beneath my palm, the way Mr. Wheeling did. And then up, in a smooth, effortless muscular curve, the arm arching up and up and in, the ball would flip itself over the red rim and plop through the net and he would catch it, casual as fate, in his outstretched cupping hand.

I wanted to *be* him, and to be the ball at the same time. It was as near as I ever came to understanding the Holy Trinity.

In some ways Jerry Wheeling did become a kind of religion for me, supplanting all the old ways of seeing the world, bringing my life into a new focus. I had always been naturally inclined toward maths and sciences, high marks in these subjects balancing my lower grades in languages. I had an aptitude for the logic of the scientific method, loved the slow, peeling process of discovery in the labs, learning the names and functions of parts. Grasshopper, petunia, amoeba, everything had its place. Somehow, learning the names, you got power over the universe. It was Mr. Wheeling who first put that idea into my head. And then more. "The more you find out about the world," he said, "the more you find out there is to know. In science, every answer brings another question. You must never stop asking. Never." Then he would hand out the day's assignment, something so utterly removed from our normal school routine we would be baffled. Something like: *On the front desk you will find a (dead) frog. What are ten questions you might ask about it? Arrange these questions in a logical sequence of investigation.* And after our initial nervous laughter we would begin, and I would think of twenty questions, 30, more than enough to share with the girls around me. In Mr. Wheeling's class, I was popular.

Almost overnight I also became a good basketball player. My body suddenly slimming found within itself a core of energy, an intuitive knowledge of where the ball would arrive in the air, of when to jump and where to turn, when to block and where to run. I had never even dreamed of such success for myself and so quite naturally attributed everything to Mr. Wheeling. "If it weren't for him . . ." I would think, and then shudder. He, in his turn, must have found me equally necessary for his own view of himself. I was scientific proof of his growing skill as a teacher; and my devoted enthusiasm encouraged him in the face of a groundswell of opposition in the school and in the town.

At first, it was only a vague and predictable resentment of anyone new, especially one with that abrasive American openness so foreign in Garten. But worse than his manner was his confidence in new "educational methodology" and his disdain for old ways. We heard what the teachers said about him in the staff-room from Wendy, whose mother taught us Home Economics. She said they didn't much like him because he really thought he was somebody, didn't he? *And* because he refused to use the prescribed biology text that had been in service in Garten District High School for seventeen years and done us all very well, thank you. But that was just normal griping and would have eventually faded away, had he not made mistakes that kept him in the foreground of public attention.

The initial error was his usurping of Mrs. Ridley's authority with the junior girls' team. He didn't mean to, but if he was there, as he was more and more often, we turned to him for advice or praise and left her watching us from the side of the floor, swinging her whistle on its yellow rope in smaller and smaller circles. Possibly it came from her, the spinning threads of ugly speculation about why a young man would want to be hanging around girls' basketball practice. It had never been done before in Garten—women coached girls and men coached boys and any variation of that was "unnatural." Or maybe it came from one of the mothers—but it soon reached Mavis and she would ask peculiar, obvious questions like, "He doesn't touch you at all, does he dear?" I would lie and say no, of course not, all the while my body still thrilling to the memory of his hand on my shoulder-blade, his twangy voice urging me, "Up, up, Elizabeth!"

However, Mrs. Ridley and the mothers were soon silenced by the fact that our team, like the boys' teams, was suddenly winning every game they played with neighbouring towns and villages, and had a good chance to bring back to Garten trophies and cups at the end of the season. The male teachers, who had now begun to think of Wheeling as "a real asset to the school," and the principal, who saw the possibility of a little glory rubbing off on his shoulders, helped to quash the unsavoury rumours. In no time, tongues were stilled.

Then, in December, he made his second, more serious error. In our science class the conversation turned from the earthworm's procreation to more conventional methods, and Mr. Wheeling was asking us questions, I guess to see how much we knew. Half the class was bused in from the country and knew the facts of life from the barnyard on up, certainly knew what they had and what it was for. But Mr.

Wheeling asked Amy, who was bright-looking but not very smart. She had taken, that year, to sitting hunched over with her arms folded against her chest, hoping to hide the truth we all knew; her breasts had not arrived. Nor had her period, according to Trudy who was the class informant on such matters. "What is the female organ of procreation in the mammal?" he asked her, as he leaned against the board, a yardstick held between his two flat open palms. Hesitant, hunching down with embarrassment, Amy asked back, "The belly-button?"

One of the boys at the back guffawed, but before it could roll and gather more laughter across the room Mr. Wheeling silenced us all with the tapping yardstick. "No, Amy," he said gently. "Not at all. That's where the umbilical cord connects while the baby still lives in the womb."

The room went as still as church as the image of sweet Mayruth rose up before our eyes, the way we had seen her two weeks ago at the dance—short, dark-haired, with a flat, freckled face, sitting pale and unsmiling with the chaperone teachers. She had clearly been uncomfortable, her enormous belly jutting up and out so that she seemed nearly deformed, a less than human thing. She had stayed sitting most of the night, her hands folded over the giant puffball of her body, watching wistfully as her husband roamed the floor among the dancers, now and again giving his basketball players approving pats on their shoulders. He introduced some of us—"my homeroom girls," he said—but of course none of us knew what to say. She seemed hurt by our open, curious stares and lowered her eyes after a few moments as if giving us a signal to leave. We did. In the girls' washroom there was a sudden flurry of supposition about what it must feel like, how heavy and awful it must be, and how Mr. Wheeling had stuck his thing in her to get her that way and he was so tall and she was so little, how did they ever...?

Now, in the classroom, we waited for his next words. "Let me show you, Amy," he said. He turned to the board and drew the stylized bull's head of uterus and fallopian tubes, the double squiggle of ovaries, and the long narrow channel of the vagina, like a stem. "These are the female organs, Amy," he said. "With some minor variations, they are present in the abdomens of all female mammals." Throughout the room girls put hands on their stomachs involuntarily, aware of themselves as mammals whose hidden organs procreate the race. Faces flaming, hearts pounding, praying inside ourselves, don't stop, don't stop.

He didn't. He went on to trace the egg from the ovary down the tube where it met a quick, chalky sperm he drew to look like a tadpole. Then the cell division, and the embryo, his blackboard brush working in jerky sweeps as the drawings grew and changed, the uterus enlarging to accommodate the next curling foetus, and then, as he was finishing the final stage, where the bulging baby lay connected to its placental home but ready to emerge, the end-of-class buzzer rang. The room jolted, as if out of a dream. We had all, Mr. Wheeling and each of us, been growing and growing inside the white outlines of sweet Mayruth's womb. It had been magic and peaceful, hardly a word spoken, the secret of life unfolding before our eyes, flesh conquered in his diagrams. Beautiful, sad and frightening: because the narrow stem below the baby hadn't changed at all. How could the baby get through that? How? We left the room quietly but as soon as we were in the hall the talk began. Maybe tomorrow he would draw *that*.

Of course, there was no tomorrow. Phones were ringing around Garten that very night and by nine o'clock a white-faced Mavis was standing at the door of my bedroom. Inquisitor, guardian of virtue.

"No, Mommy, no, he didn't," I said. "It was just the place where the baby is."

"But didn't he show you how it got there?" she asked, her mouth nervous around such details.

"Only the little sperm thing that meets the egg, just like in that book you showed me *years* ago," I said.

"Mrs. Tabor says that she heard he drew (here, a grimace of disgust) the male organ inserting itself." Horror and shame manifest in my mother's wrinkled nose.

"Oh honestly, no, that's a lie! That's just kids making up a big story, honestly, believe me. Really, no," I said.

(In fact, Josh, one of the big farm kids who sat at the back, spread the even better lie that Mr. Wheeling had taken out his own penis, laid it out on the desk and said, "That there's the male organ what done it!" Probably nobody believed it, but the story was titillating enough to make the rounds for some weeks after.)

I barely slept, so frightened of what might happen. I knew what could happen if men like my father decided someone was a bad influence in Garten—he'd be fired, banished tomorrow. But luck played fair with truth for this one time, and Mr. Wheeling was able to convince the principal that what he had done was not conducive to impropriety. In return for his promise never to take sex education into his own hands again, the principal backed him against the irate parents—after all, there were the basketball trophies in February still to be won. All that Mr. Wheeling had to do was to apologize to our class the next day, and ask any of us who had made notes from his blackboard sketches to turn them in. And we returned, relieved and chastened, to the lowly divisions of the earthworm.

Then it was Christmas and we all forgot about the excitement of scandal in the swollen anticipations of the season. What would we get this year? What my father got at Christmas was a letter he had long been expecting from the Toronto office, telling where his next appointment would be. To have stayed ten years in one town was either a rare privilege the bank gave to those managers considered a credit and an influence, or else a punishment for those who were better left in the backwaters. Until he learned where they would be sending him next, my father wouldn't really know how he was regarded, whether he was on his way up or down.

"North Bay!" my mother said. "Oh Frank, we can't, we can't!" She'd waited so long, praying for so many years that we would be sent back to Toronto, that he would be given a nice bank in Weston or even Willowdale. She had dreamed and dreamed of getting out of Garten, of getting back into what she called "the mainstream of life." The blow was severe; she said she felt shattered. She and I united immediately in an odd sort of partnership against my father, neither of us willing to move to a place we'd never been. I would not leave Mr. Wheeling, I promised myself in the dark, listening to the urgent whispers from their bedroom across the hall. Somehow, somehow life had to stay as it was, there had to be some way of halting the awful flux threatening to sweep me and Mavis along.

"The north is opening up," my father said, trying to calm my mother. "This is a great promotion, Mavis, I'll be manager of a bank doing very big business. Mining, forestry, it's all happening up there. North Bay is the heart of the province, the heart, Mavis."

My mother would not be comforted. I think she would have preferred Sudbury, ugly as it was, where she had an uncle and there would be the wealthy Inco wives to play bridge with, to have to tea. Some kind of establishment, some kind of connection with Bay Street in Toronto, the real world of finance and culture. But North Bay? Who in the world had ever heard of North Bay? A town for tourists, she sniffed, but not a place of consequence, not suitable for giving the child a proper education. The bush, it was really just glorified bush!

Frank Kessler looked at his life, his wife and his daughter united against him, and for what was (as far as I know) the only time in his life, he gambled. "If you had a choice, Mavis, would you really rather stay here forever?"

"At least I know Garten," she said. "At least I have a *place* in the community."

It wasn't an unequivocal yes, but it was enough for him to pursue an offer that had been made to him months before. Three men had come to his office in the summer, saying they wanted a loan to begin a wholesale hardware business in the town. "Say, Frank," one of them had said, "if you ever get tired of the bank here, we'd take you on as an accountant, make you a partner, even. What do you say?"

At that point, still waiting for the Imperial to steer his life onto some more rewarding course, he had demurred, given them a good loan, and ushered them out of his office. Good men, all of them, with good sound business sense. Two were Mennonite, a blacksmith and a buggymaker, and the other of German stock, like himself. Men who saw a need and a way to fill it, opportunists in the classical mould. Able to take a chance, which he, by his very nature, was not. But here, now, the odds had changed—if he followed the bank's orders, he would have a living hell with his wife and child. And if he defied the bank, asked for an extension or showed any hesitancy, they'd see him as deadwood, a man of 50 not able to handle new fields. And he'd be passed on down to far worse, far smaller places than Garten. No, he thought, there was no point in refusing the post unless he had somewhere else to go. I heard him telling my mother all this late one night in the living-room as I lay at the top of the stairs, my heart thudding dangerously loud in my ears.

So he phoned Elisha Martin the blacksmith, and they talked, and in a matter of days a deal was made and he agreed to take out his pension as a lump sum on leaving the bank and invest it in the new company. They would supply hardware stores in the area and let owners of stores buy shares in their company so that all profits would be shared and it would be in their interest to invest. It would be called Honesty Distributing and they would run the company along the most Christian of guidelines. And they would have all those Mennonite farmers, all the small hardware store owners in all those small towns in the county falling over themselves investing. It *would* work, he told my mother. Everything he knew about business from all those years in the bank told him it would work. And now, here was a chance for him to be part of the action, not just the man behind a desk doling out loans. "Oh Mavis," he said, "trust me. I love you."

Lying on the carpet, my body froze as if his words were needles of ice injected in all my limbs. Frank loved her. I'd never heard him say it before—oh, it had been written on birthday cards and on anniversary and Christmas presents and was of course assumed. But this had been the voice of someone other than my father, doing his husbandly duty. It had been the voice of a young man, pleading; for everything was out there to gain if only his true love would trust him.

She did. She really had no choice, and she was not particularly giving or gracious about it; in fact, she went through six or seven months of the worst tension headaches she had ever had. Coinciding as they did with the hot flushes and depressions that were the bane of her existence those days, life was not easy for any of us. But the Imperial Bank accepted my father's resignation with regrets—27 years he had given them, and for that he got a plaque on his marble desk set. His pension, as he had requested, was immediately transferred to his savings account from where it went as part of his investment in Honesty Distributing. All I cared about during these events was that the outcome meant we could stay in Garten, and I could see Jerry Wheeling five days a week, and he could smile at me and say, in his twangy American way, "You are one neat kid, Elizabeth."

The trials of my father's life were overlaid in my mind by a tapestry of a far more tragic, vivid design. During the Christmas holidays, we learned when we got back to school, the Wheelings' baby had been born while they were visiting Mayruth's parents. A girl, named Nancy. Born three weeks early, with spina bifida. None of us had ever heard of spina bifida before, and relying on Wendy as we were for all our news, we were in a froth of horror and excitement by the time Mr. Wheeling returned, a week late, his face white and drawn.

"I'm sure you have all heard, from one source or another, that I am now a father," he said to our homeroom that morning. The winter sun shone mercilessly through the windows as if this was an occasion when we should all be smiling. "Her name is Nancy, and she is a beautiful baby with reddish-blond hair. But she has an impairment of the spine that I will describe to you in science class later today."

And he did, with clinical detachment and great care not to frighten us, tell us then how the vertebrae had not connected at the base of the baby's spine, and how there was no likelihood that she would ever walk. "She's still in the hospital now so they can keep observing the spinal fluid for a few more weeks," he said. "But when she comes home, you may all come visit and see what a pretty little girl she is."

This is what I choose to remember about Jerry Wheeling: his courage, his compassion, his concern for our ignorant fears of what might lie ahead for us when we grew up, had babies. Explaining and explaining, as if scientific language could dispel our misgivings and his disappointment.

The tragedy softened the mothers' hearts in Garten and took the starch out of their opposition to his brash, foreign ways. "Poor thing," they all said. And he was invited to homes for supper all the time Mayruth was away, given encouragement and support and sympathy. Not by the Kesslers, though. Mavis was having so many nervous headaches that our house was perpetually draped in twilight as she lay in various rooms with curtains pulled, blinds down. My father and I walked softly, whispering whenever we spoke, which was not often. We barely communicated, each of us in our own egg of pain. I know now that he was going through a very difficult time then, wondering if indeed he had done the right thing, wondering if these fool Mennonites knew what they were doing with his money. But there was no-one for him to talk to, no-one to give him comfort. Mavis lay in the dark with a cool cloth on her forehead, seeing before her a nightmare, the wrong choice made, the rest of her life as the wife of a merchant, a hardware wholesaler. And I? How could *I* suddenly give Frank Kessler *comfort*? I knew only to avoid him and study my own grief.

My sadness took on the gaudy colours of guilt as it became apparent to me that there was something wrong with the baby because of my feelings for my teacher. God worked in strange ways; that had been drummed into us all since earliest Sunday school. Maybe this punishment had been sent down on Jerry Wheeling for invoking my love. "Oh punish me, Lord," I would weep into my pillow. "Punish me, but heal poor Nancy's spine."

Poor Nancy and sweet Mayruth came back to Garten in March, after our team had won the junior girls' basketball trophy for the southwest end of the province. Mr. Wheeling had been able to devote hours and hours to our improvement on the courts, and we repaid his efforts with absolute determination. The junior and senior boys' teams won as well, and only the senior girls, still coached solely by Mrs. Ridley, failed to place. The school honoured us all with a Celebration Dance at which Mr. Wheeling was the star. He was wearing a pale-blue shirt and his fair hair was longer than usual so that it curled a little around his ears and fell forward on his forehead. He seemed feverish from the adulation being heaped upon him, he was flushed and his eyes were skimmed over, unfocused. He must have had a flask of vodka in his jacket; it is a boozy kind of looseness I recall in his jaw. But of course, I didn't think that then, only that he seemed so relaxed.

"Will one of the stars dance with her coach?" he said as I passed him, coming back from the girls' washroom where I spent most of my time at dances.

"Sure, sir," I said, and let myself be taken by the hand and led out into the protective dark of the gymnasium floor. It was crowded and noisy and Jo Stafford's voice flowed like warm honeybutter from the loudspeakers. It was the first of many times we danced together and for that the most memorable. My height suddenly became the same advantage it was on the basketball court, for with my high-heeled shoes on my face came nearly even with his, and as we danced sometimes his cheek would brush against my hair. I was a good dancer—so light on my feet for a girl my size, Mrs. Ridley had often said when we were learning polkas and horas and foxtrots in Grade 9—and now I was like a shadow, following his lean body around the room.

At the end of the first dance we stood for a moment, self-conscious, until he said, "May I have the next, Miss Kessler?" and I said, "Of course, Mr. Wheeling," and then before the third we didn't say anything, we just looked at each other. My legs felt as if they might splay away from my body at any moment and then *Stars Fell on Alabama* came on and he took me in his arms and we moved like fish in a darkened aquarium through the seaweed of music and bodies. Like fish in the deep, like stars in the dark, we clung and glided. He was making me happier than I'd ever been —in every cell of myself I felt expanded, filled with an entirely new sense of purpose.

At the end of that song one of the other chaperones cut in and said, "Hey now, Jer, just because you're the coach doesn't mean you get to dance with the pretty girls all the time, eh?" and before I knew it I was in the arms of Nels Ferguson, the math teacher, who was, by common consent, a real turd, and smelled under the arms.

It didn't matter. Nothing mattered except this: I knew now I wasn't just fantasizing the way I used to do with movie stars. He liked me too; I knew it. It was all true.

Then, when Mayruth came home, he suddenly became a distant, remote figure on the edge of our lives. Once basketball was over there was no reason for him to stay around the school after classes, he went right home at four. And in the mornings, even if we were in the room early he had so many papers to mark he never had time for talking. "Sorry," he'd say, if one of us tried to open a conversation with him. "I'm up to my neck."

No-one ever saw either of the Wheelings out and about, and he never invited us to see Nancy as he had promised. Mayruth seemed more reclusive than ever, and we speculated endlessly on why they were never seen on the streets like everyone else in Garten—shame, or grief, or shyness? Finally, in May, I could stand it no longer. "Look, Mr. Wheeling, if you ever need a babysitter so you and Mrs. Wheeling can go out, I take care of kids in the neighbourhood all the time, I'm sure I could sit Nancy for you. Just ask if you ever need me." He looked at me with the most startled expression and I blushed because I knew my motives were not pure. I simply wanted greater access to his life. But he said, "Why, Elizabeth, what a good idea. Terrific."

Mayruth called me the next week and I went over after supper on a Friday night and they went out shopping and then to a restaurant. She was so nervous and grateful I felt as if I were doing something truly good, letting her out of a cage. They lived in one of the wartime houses, right across town from Brubacher Street, and I was struck by the temporariness of the place in contrast to the solid brick walls I knew. Everything there was clapboard and peeling paint, small wooden porches and bare lightbulbs over the front doors. Inside, the Wheelings' house had the same unsettled quality, as if they had never meant to be there. On the turquoise plaster walls they had hung several family photographs in an attempt to personalize the rooms; but for some reason that only heightened the sense of transience.

The baby's room was painted a violent pink colour, and all the furniture was white. Nancy slept in a large wooden crib, covered by pink and white blankets. She was asleep when I arrived, and as soon as they left I went into her room to look at her. Her little face was puckered and her fist clenched by her cheek, as if she were worrying. Gingerly, I lifted the covers from her small body and turned her over so that I could look at her back. But all there was, under the loosened diaper, was a raised dome of flesh, about the size of a small half-orange. Only that, and her legs would never work. I stood in a kind of sickened fascination for a long time, watching her sleep, wondering what it was that I felt. And then I returned to the living-room and read through all their back issues of *Time*.

I took care of Nancy several times before they left in July to spend the summer with Mayruth's parents in Muskoka, and came to know the house and their lives in a peculiar, vicarious way. Girls like Trudy were openly jealous when I flaunted my knowledge ("They have a book called *The Sexual Side of Marriage* on the bedside table") and called me a teacher's pet. But I felt my prestige as spy was above such pettiness, and I made the Wheelings my primary topic of conversation. I kept secret, however, the feelings I had about being walked home by Jerry Wheeling through the tree-lined streets of Garten—they had no car, and he was compelled by custom to see the sitter home once it was dark. The pale night sky of late spring and early summer, the heavy fragrance of lilacs and false orange, the sounds of the last late tag-players on Faber Street calling out "Home free!" . . . and the slow, earnest conversation we would have about stars, or birds, or God. It was, even at the time, very nearly like dancing.

By the time school began again in the fall, I was an inch taller than I'd been in June, but mercifully that was the end of it. The extra height seemed to finish me off, so that I appeared as graceful as I ever would, and I used to stand alone in my bedroom, underpants and brassière simulating cheesecake bathing-suit, posing in front of my mirror so that I could admire my shape. But after I was dressed, in layers of crinolines and full cotton skirt clinched in by a wide elastic belt, I looked badly put together, drawn too large for the page. And once I got to school, I felt myself looming over the smaller, more appropriately sized girls.

We didn't have Mr. Wheeling for homeroom teacher that year, nor did we have him for any classes. This was the year we had to take physics, and his courses, chemistry and biology, would come in our final two years. Happily for me there was still basketball, and there I was able to see him, be touched by him. My mother's health had improved over the summer, as had the chances of Honesty Distributing getting off the ground, so that the attention at home could again be focused on me, on what I was doing at school, what I was thinking, how I was acting, where I was going. Inevitably my mother's scrutiny turned to the amount of time I spent in the company of "that American."

"Why I've heard from June that you even walk him home after school," she said, her face taut with distaste. "I've never heard the like. What *can* you be thinking of?"

"Oh, Mother, that's not even true," I said. "Sometimes after basketball practice my legs are sore and he said a brisk walk is good for the muscles, loosens them up. So I walk to the post office corner and then back home. Sometimes he's on his way home but usually I'm alone. Honestly, that's just Trudy telling her Mom stories because she's jealous, she wishes she were on the team and she's not. Honestly."

He had come back all tanned and crisp in his pale blue shirts and his hair seemed even more fair. But he was different, even more aloof than he had been in the spring. He never wanted to talk the way he had. "Just walk along like a good quiet friend," he would say, and we would take long strides together.

In early October Mayruth called me to sit with Nancy while they took the bus into the city for a Saturday matinee, and I could see immediately that the baby had not thrived during the summer. She seemed awfully puny and weak, and it was apparent now that she couldn't move properly, that she was going to be a cripple. When they came home Mayruth invited me to stay for supper but I said I had better go, my mother would be expecting me. "Come and see Nancy any time you like," she said at the door. "You can come and visit, you know, you don't have to wait to be called to babysit."

I looked down at her pale freckled face with much confusion. Was she saying this because she thought I was devoted to the baby? I wasn't; I didn't much like her, she made me feel far too much pity and guilt. Or was she asking me to be *her* friend? After all, there were barely six years between us, and she was desperately lonely and shy. But I couldn't. I couldn't be her friend because I loved her husband; it just wouldn't be right.

But I couldn't stop myself thinking about Mayruth's small sad face, her breathy, hesitant voice asking me something under the words. I could feel her plucking at me and eventually I knew I would give in. One afternoon, when there was no girls' basketball practice, I left school and walked directly to the wartime houses. It was unseasonably warm; I would offer to take Nancy out for a carriage stroll and that way make peace with myself.

It took a very long time for Mayruth to answer the door, but I rang the bell several times and waited, knowing that she must be there because she never went anywhere without her husband. Eventually the door opened, only a little. She had her hand over one side of her face.

"Oh, Elizabeth, it's you, come in. I wasn't sure who it might be, I look such a fright. . . ." Her voice trailed off and in an apologetic way she lowered her hand and I saw that the whole side of her face was a massive, yellowish bruise. "I didn't turn on the upstairs light and I tripped on a pile of laundry I'd left on the top step," she said. "What an idiot, eh? Well, I've learned my lesson, that's for sure. I'm just glad I didn't break my arm." And she showed me her elbow and upper arm, black and mauve like a summer-storm sky. I felt my stomach heave and twist in revulsion; confronted by such clumsiness, such vulnerability, I only wanted to run away.

But I stayed, and shook little rattles at Nancy to make her laugh, and pretended that I thought she was a lovely baby. And I listened to Mayruth tell about how she'd been on a music scholarship to Oberlin and in her first year had met Mr. Wheeling. "Well, I guess I can call him Jerry in front of you, Elizabeth," she said. And she showed me some old photographs of what they'd looked like just four years before when they'd been going out to proms and football games together. He was lanky, awkward-looking in whatever clothes he wore, with hair cut so short he seemed nearly bald in black-and-white snapshots. She seemed always to be dressed in something full-skirted and tight-waisted, aiming a dimpled, adoring smile at his shoulder. In some pictures she held a plaid wool blanket over one arm and had a tassled toque pulled down over one eye.

Flirtatious, raffish, coy. Only later do I think to comment how much her demeanour changed once married. Then, I only thought how much better I would have looked by his side, tall, straightforward and unafraid. And I thought how unfair it was, the way life worked itself out so badly.

That night at supper I told Mavis and Frank about what a nice time I'd had with Mrs. Wheeling that afternoon and how lonely she seemed. "We should have them over for dinner sometime, Mommy," I said. "She's awfully shy and they really don't ever go out with the baby. There's still that old crib in the basement we could bring up for Nancy, so they could bring her too."

I knew better than to pester, so that the next two or three weeks passed without any plans to have the Wheelings over. My father was usually out every evening with his hardware partners, working on their plans for a warehouse, and my mother said we would just have to wait until he wasn't so busy before we could invite company. And then it was too late. In November, I heard in the corridor at school that Mr. Wheeling wasn't in that day because his baby had died in the night.

"Crib death," said all the mothers of Garten, a chorus on the edge of the tragedy, eager to explain events in the light of their own experience. And sure enough, that's what Dr. Waddell's verdict was too. "We don't know *why* these poor little tykes die," he said to Mavis that same week during a bridge party she and Frank attended at the doctor's house. "But for some reason there are infants who simply stop breathing and pass away in their sleep. One of God's mysteries we still haven't solved."

It was the same explanation that Mr. Wheeling gave when he returned to school a week later, looking as if he had not slept himself during all that time for fear of his own life ending. I went to his room after classes, feeling as if I should make some gesture. I had, after all, been the

132

babysitter for that frail little soul, and I should be mourning her death—even though I felt nothing except relief that she was gone.

"Elizabeth," he said when I came into his room, and I was horribly afraid he was going to cry. His face crumpled and reformed around my name and he finally said, "Mayruth said to thank you when I saw you for the card and the flowers. She's going to stay with her folks for a few weeks. She's taking the whole thing pretty hard."

"How are *you*?" I asked, emphasizing the last word with the implication that it was insensitive of sweet Mayruth to leave him alone during such a sad time. He looked startled, surprised no doubt by the personal tone of my question.

"Oh well, I'll make out," he said, and he suddenly smiled. "It was all for the best. You know that, don't you? It's just that Mayruth can't see it that way."

"I love you," I said suddenly, unaware I was going to say it until it had been said.

"I know that, Elizabeth," he said, his face becoming long and sombre again. "I know that. But we won't speak of it, not now."

I ran from the room, humiliated by his gentle tone. Later that afternoon I felt such embarrassment at the thought of facing him I told Mrs. Ridley that I had period cramps and couldn't stay for basketball practice. When I got home I told my mother I thought I was getting the flu, and went to my room where I sat on the bed, laying out cards for clock solitaire, until suppertime.

We didn't exchange words again until early December at the Christmas Couples' Dance, to which I had bribed Tommy Bauman to take me by promising him all that term's physics experiments. Mr. Wheeling had come to the dance alone and stood against the back wall with three other male teachers, neither talking nor dancing as he usually did. Tommy was the tallest boy in our class, which is why I had asked him, but he couldn't dance very well and he didn't much like me and so we shunted around the floor in an aimless, loosely held way, both miserable. All night long my body felt empty and concave as an open clam shell, wanting to be gathered up by Jerry Wheeling's long sad arms and crushed against his chest. Half an hour before the dance was over he came to where Tommy and I were standing in resentful silence and said, "Coach's choice, Tom." Tommy was one of his senior boys and would have died for him; giving up a dance with Elizabeth Kessler was pure pleasure. "Keep her as long as you want, Sir," he said, and ducked out the sidedoor of the gym.

We danced only one dance and I can't remember the song. My body was pulled up against his so tightly that my breasts felt flattened and bruised and the side of my face, where it touched his jaw, burned. He hummed in my ear, a low tuneless moan, and his fingers pressed into my back, each fingertip a separate, exquisite pressure. And I felt within myself a gathering sadness, a sorrow in the flesh, as if my body knew too much for the mind to bear, as if the blood humming up and down my limbs held more awful knowledge than it could tell.

He went to Ohio for the holidays, and we heard when he got back to school in January that he had come back to town with Mayruth. I kept meaning to go and see her but after school there was always basketball and I didn't want to go on the weekend in case he might be there. She, for her part, became even more reclusive than she'd been when Nancy was alive, and the neighbours said they never saw her out.

The basketball finals were in February that year and we expected to win. Mr. Wheeling had devoted himself to our team and we in return had mastered every intricate play and trick he had taught us. We had become experts at the fast pivot, feinting a pass one direction and then turning and throwing the ball another. The forwards had picked up his easy style of rising up off the floor just at the basket and flicking the wrist up and out so that the ball would flip sweetly up, out and down through the net. The guards became confidently aggressive and sly, always ahead of the game. I had turned into the kind of player I most admired —fast, light and totally unpredictable, always in control of the ball.

We won the game easily, and on the bus back home to the Celebration Dance at the school, Mrs. Ridley suggested to us girls that we go over and ask Mrs. Wheeling to join us, since she had given up her husband to the team for so many weeks. We all laughed and said what a good idea that was, and Karen and Diane volunteered to go. "Don't tell Mr. Wheeling," Mrs. Ridley said. "It'll be a nice surprise for him when she gets here."

When the bus arrived back at the school, the two girls went off on the run. They were back in half an hour, without her. "She came to the door like a scared little rabbit," Diane said. "And when she turned on the porch light we could see she had bandages on her face. She said she had been putting her suitcases away at the top of a closet and they all fell down on her, and she wouldn't think of coming out when she looks such a mess." Inwardly, we were all relieved, I think. We *all* wanted to keep Mr. Wheeling to ourselves that night, he had shown us the way to glory. But when he heard what had happened, that the girls had gone to see Mayruth, he decided to leave the dance and go home. I felt betrayed, and without him the celebration soured and died. Who cared, really, about winning, if he weren't there to say how terrific we were, how terrific, how neat.

Two weeks later it was all over.

Sweet Mayruth fled to the neighbours in the middle of the night, bleeding from the mouth and bruised all about her head and shoulders. Phone my parents, she is reported to have said. Have them come and take me home. Get me out of here before I die.

The neighbours, an elderly couple who were the care-takers for our church (and so Mavis got many of the details from the minister's wife), phoned not only her parents but the police, and Jerry Wheeling was arrested and booked for assault.

None of us ever saw him again. I wanted to testify at the trial but I was under sixteen and the lawyer, when I called him, said he would convey my best wishes to his client and hung up. I wanted to say, "Tell him I love him" but I knew he knew that already and it might have been the wrong thing to say to a lawyer.

My mother said she could sleep nights now that that man was locked up. "I never did trust him," she said, "and it used to make me quite ill, all the time you spent with him, Elizabeth. I shudder to think what might have happened." My father said that what could you expect, violence had always been part of the American character, and we should all just consider ourselves lucky he took it out on his wife.

There was some stirring of renewed interest in exactly how poor Nancy had died but Dr. Waddell stood by his original statement of natural causes and the matter was let alone. Mr. Wheeling's trial in the city wasn't until several months later, and although there were rumoured to be all manner of complications, he was eventually found guilty. The week he was sentenced to four years in jail, the Garten *Enterprise* had a big story on the front page, with a photo of him taken from the school yearbook. At the end of the story it mentioned that Mrs. Wheeling was suing for divorce.

My mother said there was no justice, that man should have been put away for life. My father just grunted and said he would read about it in the paper when he got back from the warehouse. My mother said, "At least when you were with the bank you were home some evenings." My father turned and looked at her with as pure a hate as I have ever seen.

He became a rich man, Frank Kessler. There are Honesty Distributing outlets across the province now, with plans for the Maritimes in the near future. He retired at 60, so that he and Mavis could enjoy his money in good health, spending half the winter in Florida, and the rest travelling across North America in their mobile home.

Secrets

My mother and her friends had secret lives. Growing up in Garten I learned that duplicity was as necessary, as natural to their existence as breathing. Their lives were made up of layers, like the parfait desserts they took to church suppers, and at some level or another they all shared different secrets with each other. I sometimes wondered how my mother kept it all straight, who knew what about whom. I always seemed to be making mistakes, divulging Linda's secrets to Amy or Sharon's to Joyce, not with any malicious intent but from forgetfulness. Mavis had no such difficulty. Entrusted with her friends' secrets, she gave back in kind.

Here is a secret. My mother and her friends Beverly Mutch and Nelly Tabor all slipped into the city regularly to have electrolysis treatments on their chins and upper lips. That was *their* secret; if you didn't keep it hush-hush, then it was money wasted, wasn't it? I wasn't officially admitted to that secret until I was seventeen, when one day Mavis made me stand by the bathroom window while she examined my face.

"Oh dear, I'm afraid you've inherited my skin in more ways than one," she said, and her voice was regretful yet filled with something like enthusiasm. Here was a fault we both shared and it could be plucked out. We could be made perfect together. "Rena Louise said I should check your facial hair for darkening. You come along in with me this week and we'll let her have a look."

In this way I was initiated into the secret rites of little jabbing needles and quick searing pain and women with perfumy hands and peppermint breath leaning over me, grotesque through the underside of the magnifying glass with which they would study my face. Rena Louise had smooth, waxy skin that made me think of pale pink tulips, and she wore a deep pink smock with a large floppy bow at the neck. She said she could fix me up in no time and I wouldn't have "so much as a shadow on that pretty face." In fact, the treatments often left little red welts that made me as self-conscious as hair would have, but she had told the truth and my secret was safe. Only my mother and Rena Louise and Mrs. Mutch and Mrs. Tabor knew that God had meant me to have a moustache. I suppose my father must have known, since it was his money that paid for the treatments, but like all matters of a female nature it was never mentioned between us.

❋

My mother is teaching me how to dance. I am already taller than she is but she is playing the role of the man, leading. We are dancing first in the living-room but the rug interferes with my mother's sliding turns so we move to the smooth hardwood floor of the dining-room where we circle around the table. We do the foxtrot and the waltz, we spin past the china-cabinet and the sideboard, we dance until my arms ache from this strange, formal position, one hand on my mother's shoulder and the other clenching hers in mid-air. She is flushed and her eyes are bright. "Oh Elizabeth," she says when we stop. "I do love to dance."

＊

Men were generally excluded from secrets, as if there were a conspiracy among the women to keep things from the husbands. In fact, those men were often involved in the secrets themselves—they simply weren't part of the intricate network of telling and not telling. For example: Beverly Mutch wasn't really a widow; her husband had gone to Montreal a long time ago and sent her a postcard from the LaSalle Hotel that said "Goodbye, Bev." Only Mrs. Mutch's most intimate friends (Mavis being one) knew that. Just as none of Peggy Bonnet's friends would have dreamed of telling her *their* secret, that her husband fondled their breasts whenever he got the chance.

Here's another. Vera, who played the organ at church, kept a bottle of sherry right out on her kitchen counter where she could get at it during the day, which is why she sometimes played so badly at choir rehearsals on Thursday nights. Sometimes the entire soprano section, which sat near the organ, could smell it on her breath but they never let on because our minister, Reverend Hartwell, was absolute death on drinking and everybody liked Vera. Since she was always sober on Sunday mornings, the sopranos agreed among themselves, they'd do their part too. It was a secret for years. As was the information that when Mrs. Hartwell went off to visit her relatives in Halifax she was really over in the sanitorium having one of her bad spells.

A lot of women in Garten had bad spells of one kind or another. I didn't really think of it at the time, it seemed to be part of being a woman—they kept secrets and had bad spells. With my mother it took the form of tension headaches, certainly more acceptable than Mrs. Hartwell's nervous breakdowns but still not to be mentioned. That was because to ease her pain she visited a chiropractor in the city for manipulation treatments, a fact that had to be kept quiet so that Dr. Waddell didn't find out. "If I ever hear of you or *any* of my patients going to one of those quacks I won't have you in my office again!" he had said when she asked him what he thought about chiropractors.

"It just burns me up," she'd say to her best friend June on the phone, "the way Bob Waddell thinks those pills he prescribes are the reason my headaches are better when I know full well it's the treatments." But she could never bring herself to tell him, to risk losing the pills or incurring his wrath. In case someday she really needed him if I were sick or Frank keeled over. In case it made things awkward in the bridge club they belonged to. It was easier to keep it all secret—and if that made her tense, well, there was June to talk to, and there were always the pills.

*

My mother is teaching me how to dance. There's going to be a dance after the Grade 8 graduation on the weekend and she is preparing me. I don't expect anyone to ask me except in the Paul Jones and the Snowball, but I go along with her cheerful delusion that I will be dancing my feet off. "It isn't the steps you need worry about, Elizabeth," she says. "*A good dancer just follows gracefully. There now, don't pull like that. You can't go your own direction, you must flow with your partner. Flow. That's it. Don't look at your feet, look at me. There now, see?*" Embarrassed, I look directly at my mother, into her blue eyes. I feel she is forcing me to love her. I cannot resist the insistent rhythm of the waltz. I let myself relax and think that she will take care of me if I love her, that I will float above the ground and never trip or fall. "*There now,*" she says again with satisfaction. "*You're getting it. You're dancing like a dream.*"

❋

The cause of my mother's headaches, and a host of other tension-related illnesses she suffered, was no secret. Over the years I heard her on the phone talking about what a difficult, unmanageable child I was and I knew it was all my fault, all her disappointment and frustration. The phone-calls themselves were part of a secret life she led with June and Nelly and Gladys and Wilma as soon as my father was out the door in the mornings. I was often home from school with ear infections in the winter months, and lay on my stomach at the top of the stairs listening to my mother's voice down in the kitchen. She and her friends reviewed their lives in such elaborate detail that although I only heard my mother's end of these conversations, I learned to piece together, from her comments, what the other women were saying. Sometimes there was laughter, but what I seem to remember best are the endless exchanges of daily events delivered in a weary, resigned sort of way. They knew each other's menus ("I think I'll heat up that roast beef with the gravy and add a few potatoes, maybe a chopped onion for supper tonight") and financial matters ("Frank says $2.95 a yard is madness but I just told him you have to pay if you want quality that will *last*"), they told each other about their ailments ("Well, Wilma says she's found that taking a little lemon juice in warm water right when she gets up makes a world of difference, it's worth a try, I think") and their heartaches.

"I simply don't know which way to turn, June," Mavis would say, her voice rising with anxiety, and I'd be wondering if she *meant* me to hear, if she knew I was there at the top of the stairs. "That child gets more headstrong by the day and nothing I do does any good. I don't know, I simply don't know." Silence then, while June would offer advice or solace, possibly in the form of some complaint about her daughter Trudy, my classmate. I would get up quietly and tiptoe back to bed, huddle under the covers and hate her for talking about me. There was no privacy, no protection; all my mother's friends knew how impossibly bad I was. My life was not my own when it was being told about that way, and I thought my mother was wicked and disloyal.

Now, of course, I can see how useful those telephone conversations were, and how much more I would have suffered without them. Women like Mavis, married to men like Frank, with children like me . . . women like that needed each other. Without that receiver into which to pour their troubles, there would have been little comfort or release. Their secret phone life provided them with an escape from the realities of Garten they'd not have had otherwise. Although some of the younger and more adventurous women she knew took jobs in the city selling cosmetics or working as receptionists, Mavis mainly had friends whose husbands preferred them to stay at home. After a certain time, a married woman had a responsibility to stop work and raise her family—none of the tellers in my father's bank, for example, was over 25. There were rare exceptions—Mrs. Mutch who ran her own lingerie store but of course she didn't have a family—but it would still be fair to say that in Garten women were expected to be housewives. "Keeping the home fires burning," my father called it.

Mavis and June decided one year—as a lark, they said—to apply for the seasonal staff Moodies took on during the Christmas rush, to make themselves some extra money for presents. Moodies was a genteel department store in the city, with extremely refined salesladies waiting on customers from behind glass cases filled with kid gloves, cashmere scarves, hosiery, lingerie, handbags. It was so genteel that these women didn't have to handle cash—they sent their customers' money up pneumatic tubes in small brass cylinders to a department that dealt with the harsher aspects of commerce such as making change. Mavis and June, being exactly the kind of women that Moodies catered to, found themselves hired on the day they applied. But the next day, right after breakfast, my mother got on the phone.

"He says absolutely no, June," she said. Her voice quavered with a peculiar whiney note, the way I knew I sounded when my parents prevented me from doing something. "I talked myself blue in the face but he wouldn't listen. He just kept on at the same old thing, no wife of mine, no matter what . . ." Silence, and here June must have come in with her own sad tale. Her husband Arthur was thought to be more easygoing than Frank but he must have put his foot down too, since in the end neither woman ever worked at Moodies. "I'm not telling a soul about this, are you?" Mavis said near the close of their conversation. "It's too upsetting. Well, it'll be our little secret now, won't it June?" As far as I know, that was the last time they tried to earn money.

What Mavis and June and the others did with their time and energy was to throw themselves into church work. If the church hadn't already been there, they would have invented it, or some similar structure that would have collapsed without their support. They made it seem, with their fervour, that the word of God was dependent for survival on their tubs of potato salad, their bales of cast-off clothing, their rummage sales and socials, their countless projects. The division of labour within the church was reflective of the way that marriages worked in Garten: the elders of the church, the husbands and fathers, were its brain, figuring out the finances, hiring the right kind of preachers for what we wanted to hear; and the body of the church, including its heart, were the wives and daughters, who arranged the flowers on the altar and took turns cutting Weston's white bread into little Communion cubes. The first time I was allowed to help Mavis with this job down in the church kitchen I stuffed myself with cut-off crusts and said I wished there was some jam to go with them. She turned on me with an angry, stricken face.

"This is a sacred task," she said. "You must take it seriously."

"It's just dumb old bread," I said, knowing that was heresy and not caring. I hated it when Mavis took that tone about churchy things, making them far more important than I knew they really were. She was so angry at me that if we'd been alone she might have slapped me, but there were other women in the kitchen and so she held herself in check. She told me to get my coat and wait for her outside after I'd apologized to her and the others. I stood in the doorway in what I meant to be a defiant pose and looked at the bunch of them, flushed and busy in their flowered aprons, looking back at me with charitable faces. I wanted to say the most awful, mean things I could, to somehow make Mavis stop cutting up bread like it mattered, to free us all from the rules for believing in all this dumb stuff. But instead, of course, I mumbled that I was sorry and ran upstairs.

We belonged to Bethel United Church, whose congregation had changed from Methodist to United in 1925, and in which Mavis always said she felt right at home. Her family had been Methodist until union, and she liked the plain interior of the church that reminded her of her childhood. The white walls, varnished oak pews and pulpit, the panes of pebbled glass in the windows—there was nothing in Bethel to distract from the word of God. She liked it too, I think, because it represented a minor victory in her life with Frank. He had been raised a Lutheran, and in the first years of their marriage in Toronto they had gone back and forth to one another's churches, neither one giving way. But the transfer to Garten meant starting afresh; and here Frank found that the United was a real up-and-coming church, attracting the new people in town, the young couples with growing families, the very people he wanted to put money in his bank. As for the Lutherans, he had all the connections he needed there because of his German name and heritage; he could make himself at home in this predominantly German community with a well-chosen German phrase or two. By going to the United Church he was covering more bases for the Imperial, he said. We still, when we visited my Nana or she visited us, went to the Lutheran church—but I grew up believing that after centuries of dithering mankind had found the true way in the amalgam of the Uniteds.

Religious affiliation was an important part of Garten life, not only for the women who ran the bazaars and sang in the choirs, but as social definition. It told as much about you as where you lived or what your father did or whether you went into commercial or academic in high school. You always had to know what people "were"; it was like knowing their name or phone number, and when you met someone, it was one of the first questions you asked.

My parents always made a point of finding out early whether newcomers to Garten would be joining our congregation or not. I remember one couple, who had become quite friendly with my father while discussing loans and mortgages, who came to dinner their first week in town. The conversation turned to which church they'd be attending—there were plenty to choose from, my father said, but for his money you couldn't find better than Bethel.

"Actually, we're going to drive over to St. John's in Guelph," the wife said.

"Oh, you're Anglican, then," my mother said. (I heard her the next morning telling June she'd known all along they were just from the snooty way the woman acted.) "Why don't you go to St. Margaret's here in town?"

"Well, what we *really* go for is the music, you see," said the husband, little suspecting he was sealing his fate with the Kesslers and would not be thought well of again. "They have a marvellous choir at St. John's, simply marvellous. And an excellent organist, as good as any I've heard. His postludes alone are worth the price of admission."

Polite laughter and the topic was swiftly changed; only after they'd gone did my parents dissect their impiety. Going to a particular church for business reasons, now that was practical, even necessary. But "Imagine!" my mother kept saying, as if to elicit from my father even stronger declarations of shock. "Imagine going for the *music!* If that doesn't beat the band!" Anglicans were prone to this kind of excess, it seemed, so likely to stray off onto wayward paths that had nothing to do with God, she ought not to have been surprised, she said.

*

My mother is teaching me how to dance. It is a rainy Saturday afternoon and I am listening to the radio in the kitchen as I stand by the sink polishing silver. I am helping Mavis get ready for a dessert bridge that night, for which all the pie forks must be shining. I turn up Connie Francis singing

*"Who's Sorry Now?" just as Mavis comes into the room.
"Heavens, is that back?" she says. "That was popular when
I used to go dancing with Tim, goodness, 25 years ago."
She comes over and slips her arm around my waist, humming. I am startled and pull away, not used to this kind of
impromptu embrace, but she is determined, and begins to
turn me around the floor. "Come on now, Elizabeth, this
is a good song. No wonder it's come back." "Who's Tim?"
I ask. "Was he your boyfriend before Daddy?" "Oh, I
suppose you could say so," she says. "He was a brother of a
girl in our office and he used to take me dancing out on the
Pier. Oh my, he could dance!" Her voice is reflective and I
can tell she is seeing things I am not. The song ends and I
want to ask her more but I can't think how to start. As if
she reads my mind, she volunteers some information. "We
saw each other for a few years, Elizabeth, but all we had in
common, really, was the dancing. And when you decide to
settle down with someone, you have to have more in common than that!" She smiles and leaves me here at the sink.
I am thinking about how she and Frank never dance, how
he says it's a waste of time to walk around to music. I wonder what it is that they found in common.*

◆

There were more than enough churches in Garten to keep
the women busy, but no synagogue—the nearest Jews
were twenty miles away in the city, evident chiefly in the
clothing-stores of the business section. They were said, by
my father, to own the entire street, one way or another. My
mother and her friends used to entertain each other on car
rides back and forth by imitating the Jewish saleswomen
in the dress and hat shops they went to when Moodies didn't
have what they wanted. "Liss-en, maaa-dam, it's you. Trust
me!" they said to each other in heavily accented voices,

affecting gestures and mannerisms I never observed in the Jewish women themselves but that brought them to mind. They *were* different, those ladies, and I liked them. They had dark hair and eyes and gypsy-like jewellery and they smelled like spice. They'd try to make you buy things by telling you lovely lies. They told me I looked wonderful in bright reds and pinks when Mavis said any fool could see my colour was navy blue.

I liked the Jewish stores for the same reason I liked going to the city—it was all proof that another world was waiting for me after Garten, a world in which the rare and exotic would be commonplace. I saw it as a beginning, a step in the right direction; for my mother I think it was like coming up against a stone wall, facing the fact that her life was limited by my father's, that she'd never get back to the real city, to Toronto, again. She did not pine for youth the way some women do, she longed only for Toronto itself where she had been a secretary on Bay Street during her twenties. Whenever she reminisced, she always interwove street names throughout the memories, like a sweet essence penetrating her present life.

"I took the Danforth car," she'd say, or "Of course, Eileen was up at Pape and Eglinton, no wonder!" or "Right at St. Clair and Yonge, I nearly died of embarrassment!" Everything, everything was anchored in *place*; everything happened at Eaton's College Street, over on Spadina, somewhere off the Kingsway, down at the foot of Bay. . . . She always said she could find her way blindfolded in Toronto, she knew its grid of streets by heart; oddly enough, anywhere else she had no sense of direction, and the small towns and cities around Garten confused her utterly. "Here, you follow the map," she'd say. "I don't know where we are."

After I turned sixteen and got my driving licence, I was allowed to share the driving with Mavis, an arrangement that suited us both. While she kept her various appointments in the city, I went to the library and looked up books unavailable in Garten's Carnegie, or else wandered through the art supply store across from Moodies. Sometimes I nicked down a sidestreet to a small Chinese restaurant where I ordered egg rolls and green tea and smoked secret Du Mauriers.

In those years after my father had left the bank and was setting up the hardware business, my mother's visits to her chiropractor became more frequent. Occasionally we'd be accompanied by June and Trudy—June was the only friend who knew about the treatments—but most often we went alone, which I much preferred, since I loved to drive and Mavis would never allow me behind the wheel ("I'd never forgive myself if anything happened") when there were other people in the car. All Trudy ever wanted to do was to shop for clothes and talk about her boyfriend Glen, and I sat in the back seat with her on those journeys in an agony of bad temper and boredom. I'd find myself listening to Mavis and June instead of us as a way of tuning out Trudy, but I had to be careful about how I listened, for my mother's eyes would flicker to the rearview mirror every few moments to check whether or not they were being overheard and if she saw my face attentive she'd let her voice drift away to a whisper, or raise her eyebrows at June to caution her. I never grasped what their conversations were about, she need not have worried; the two women had set up a code in which little was said but much understood. "Well you know *Arthur*," June would say, and I'd be no wiser; yes, we all knew Arthur, but what, but *what*? What was the information they were passing back and forth? Their voices would have a humorous edge, but there was something else under that, a brittle, discontent, unhappy sound. "You know *Arthur*. . . ." What did that mean? What did they know about Arthur? What did they know about Arthur and Frank and each other that could not be spoken? June's voice sounded, it seemed to me, as if she had given up on Arthur. Was that it—had Mavis and June given up on something?

Our usual routine was to leave for the city as soon as I got home from school and be back in time to get Frank's dinner on the table. One winter afternoon when we'd gone in alone, we parted as we always did in the parking-lot behind Moodies, and agreed to meet at 5.30 in the lingerie department where there was a sale. I stood for a moment by the car and watched my mother going down the street and thought how right she looked in the city, in her fur jacket and matching hat, how much more in place she appeared here than on Front Street at home. From the back, I thought, she didn't look as if she had blinding headaches; you could imagine she was happy when you couldn't see her face.

I finished making notes at the library with nearly half an hour to spare, and decided to sneak down to the tea-room in the basement of Moodies for a quick Coke and cigarette. I hurried down the marble steps to the glass doors of the tea-room and was pushing them open when I recognized the back of my mother's head. She still had on her fur hat but her jacket was draped over the back of her chair. She was leaning forward across the table and I could tell from the movements of her head that she was talking to the person facing her. I had never seen him before in my life.

He wore the black shirt and white collar of a minister or priest, and had the kind of humble, wishy-washy face I'd often seen on such men. His rimless glasses caught the light and shone at my mother in a benevolent way; what little hair he had was sandy-grey and I could see he was quite thin. I let the glass door swing shut and stood there on the other side, trying to think who he might be. I didn't want to get involved in a discussion about religion with some fanatic—it occurred to me that my mother might have heard about the fuss my essay "Science, the New Religion" had caused in Mr. Hawthorne's class, and it'd be just like her to worry that I was losing my faith and go and get help from some city church. She knew I couldn't stand Reverend Hartwell.

But it wasn't about me. It was about her. I knew that when I watched the way his hands reached over and took hers, those agitated creatures with a life of their own; the way he placed them on the table and patted them, the way he left his hands there over them. I knew when I saw how her body caved in toward him, and their heads bent forward and what they were saying was making them sad. More sad than my losing faith. More sad than I wanted to know about. I turned and ran up the steps and stood at the top, panting. Watching them through the glass I had had to consider an alarming possibility: what if my mother had *real* secrets?

Whoever that man was, he had seen me through the door without any expectation or recognition; he and I were truly strangers. But where did he fit in *her* life? Where? I went directly to the lingerie department. My heart pounded as I stood fingering rows of lacy slips and crinolines, wondering what it all meant. I thought of running back down to the tea-room, surprising them, but some other part of my brain held me back, suggested that now I still had power; I knew something and my mother didn't know that I did. Once I confronted her she would somehow turn the tables. If I wanted to know more, if I wanted to know it all, I had to hold this secret in.

Mavis appeared right on time, looking as if she'd just come in from outside. "Let's have a look at these nighties," she said. "You could do with another, Elizabeth."

"I already looked and I don't like any of them," I said, in what I hoped was a peevish tone indicating that I'd been

152

there for some time. "Let's just go home. I'm beat." I paused, wanting my next question to be a little dangerous, but only a little. "Do you feel better?"

She looked surprised at my solicitous concern but answered easily. "Oh my yes, dear, it's a miracle what that man can do. If I could see him more often I'd never have an ache or pain."

All the way home in the car we were silent, watching the windshield wipers make their hypnotic sweeps against the oncoming snow. From time to time I would look over at her with amazement—whatever she was up to, she was a liar. A vague kind of excitement flushed through me and I sensed that my life was changing with this knowledge.

Sure enough, at the dinner table that night I couldn't look at my father without thinking of how my mother was pulling the wool over his eyes too. I saw before me the minister's hands holding hers, and wondered if he were in love with her. Oh, how awful, my mother cheating on poor Frank! A new and tender concern for my father surfaced, and with a clarity sprung from pity, I saw him for what he was. . . . So diligent, so faithful, working so hard to give Mavis the things she loved, like her fur jacket and our new dining-room suite. Okay, he hadn't moved back to Toronto the way she'd always planned they would—was that his fault? Oh, it wasn't fair, it wasn't fair!

•

My mother is teaching me how to dance. We have been doing this for years now but there are always new things to learn, increasingly intricate steps. There are quick little reversals, neat crossovers and slides, and an exquisite balancing on the ball of the foot that is like something we do in basketball when we pretend to pivot one way but then throw the ball the other. All these steps, my mother says, she perfected in Toronto back in the days when she was a working girl. "We could dance all night until the band went home," she says, laughing. "Why, we were so good we used to win dance contests time after time out there on the Pier. It got so the other dancers hated to see us arrive."

❋

The winter pressed down on us and pushed us together for warmth. I felt as if I couldn't breathe much of the time, questions for my mother were clogging my throat. Yet the longer I went without asking her who the man was, the stronger I felt within myself.

I decided to follow her about three weeks later, a bitterly cold and windy afternoon. In the parking-lot I turned in the other direction as if I were going to the library, but as soon as she'd got around the first corner I turned and ran back. Sure enough, she wasn't going up that street to the chiropractor's office but down the other way, across the busy main street. I edged my way through jostling afternoon crowds, keeping close to shop windows in case she turned, but she never looked back. What I was doing was very wrong, I thought to myself with a feeling of pleasure. It was almost satisfying to be doing something so unequivocally wrong, like reading someone's mail, with a real excuse. I was only doing it for Frank.

Two blocks off the main street I saw her turn and enter a small grey stone church. I recognized it as St. Barnabas, an Anglican church, which at least meant he wasn't a priest. But I remembered what Joyce had told us in CGIT group about being in St. Barnabas with her aunt last year, who said it was so high it might as well be mick. She said there were statues and candles and incense just like in the RC church in Garten—we all knew about that because we'd been taken there by our CGIT leader one afternoon and Father Fultz had shown us around, tried to explain to us the stations of the cross and the intercession of the Virgin Mary and all the beauty of the Mass. All we saw was the glisten of gold and fluttering rows of cranberry glass, and our hearts turned to stone against these pagans.

I crouched behind a car and waited for a while to see if she meant to stay or whether she was just calling for that man. After a few minutes I was so cold that I turned back toward Moodies, mulling over new possibilities. Mavis hated what she called "fancy Anglicans," so she couldn't be going to St. Barnabas for anything but to see the thin little man. He wasn't nearly as attractive as my father— now that I thought of it, Frank was quite handsome for a man in his fifties. I was having to re-evaluate my parents' marriage in the light of what I knew about love and marital fidelity, all of it gleaned from movies and women's magazines. Romance, that's what Mavis was missing in her life. Romance. My father should take her out, buy her flowers, stuff like that. Hold her hand across a restaurant table, that's what he had to do.

Frank was reading the paper when I approached him in the living-room. "Daddy, I was just thinking. I don't mind staying alone if you wanted to take Mommy out on her birthday next week . . . like, you could go in and see a movie." He bent the paper down and looked at me oddly. "Or something," I finished lamely.

"What are you up to? Stay alone, eh? Invite your friends over and get up to Lord knows what. No sir, Elizabeth, it's not that easy!" He laughed then, and called for my mother. "You hear that, Mavis? She wants us to go out so she can have the house to herself. Wants me to take you to a movie."

My mother came in from the kitchen, untying her apron. "You know watching anything on a big screen like that gives me a headache, Elizabeth. Why are you so thoughtless?"

The next time I followed her, nearly two weeks later, it was raining, one of those wicked March days that promises spring but never delivers. Mavis held her umbrella at an angle as she walked, her head tilted forward as if in a great hurry. This time I waited until she'd been in the church a few minutes before going forward, inching behind parked cars, to have a look at the sign on the corner of the lawn. It was shaped like a church window, and under glass, white letters on a black board provided all the information St. Barnabas wished to impart.

Rector: Canon Timothy Box
Second Sunday in Lent
8.30 AM Holy Eucharist
10.30 AM Solemn High Mass
Church School and Nursery
7 PM Choral Evensong
Lenten Weekday Services
12.05 PM Holy Eucharist
4.30 PM Evensong

Of course. Timothy Box. Standing there with icy rain streaking my glasses so that the world around me blurred and ran into itself I suddenly saw, I suddenly knew. Heard music, heard Connie Francis singing, saw my mother dancing in the arms of her old love Tim. They had found each other again after all these years, destined to be together but kept apart by . . . here I stopped, unsure of my ground. Had he fled to the church when she chose a banker as a more suitable husband? Or was his Anglican faith what she meant when she said they had nothing in common—had she rejected the life of a canon's wife and taken up with Frank on the rebound? Infinite speculation.

I saw them as they'd been, young and whirling happily to the music out on the dance floor above Lake Ontario. I imagined them now, as they were, down in one of the Sunday-school rooms of St. Barnabas, her fur jacket hung on a chair, her hat off, yes, definitely her hat off, and he, Timothy Box, placing a record on the record-player, turning up the volume just a little so that only they could hear. "Who's sorry now, who's sorry now, whose heart is aching for breaking each vow?" Or maybe something more upbeat, there were so many old songs that Mavis liked to dance to—"Making Whoopee," that was one of her real favourites. Down there in the basement of the church, my mother and a nearly bald minister, dancing in secret. My mother, capable of deception, unfaithful and getting away with it.

The image began to fade and was replaced with a sombre realization: now that I knew, I had a responsibility. It was up to me to put a stop to this, to bring her to her senses and back home to Frank's waiting arms. Around the edges of this thought suddenly blossomed new, frightening ideas. Maybe I was too late. Maybe she could never love Frank again. Maybe, after all, I didn't blame her. Maybe I no longer knew whose side I was on. All the way back to Moodies in the rain, I wondered what I would do.

Studying for Easter exams prevented me from going into the city with my mother the next few weeks, which was fine with me; I knew I wasn't ready yet to make my move, whatever that move was. Mavis herself was easier to get along with than she'd been in some time, and although we didn't have much to do with each other except at meals, I hated to jeopardize the feeling of peace there now was in the house. She seldom lay down in her room any more, and never took Dr. Waddell's pills after meals the way she had the last couple of years. What I found hard to understand was how my father didn't seem to be noticing any of this— he seemed as distant and preoccupied with his hardware as ever.

Still, I decided that I would go into the church the next time, and find them together, and tell my mother she had to stop, no matter what. The scene played in my head along with remnants of movies and excerpts from "Playhouse 90." I rehearsed my lines, the declaration of shock and grief with which I would punish that dancing pair.

A warm April afternoon, the snowdrops and crocuses on Brubacher already fading and the tulips well up; spring was here. The moment of disclosure was at hand.

As if scripted, we left the parking-lot behind Moodies agreeing to meet in an hour. Smiling at her, saying "See you, Mom," and wondering why she didn't suspect me. How could she not know that I knew? She had always said she could read me like a book.

Waiting until she turned the corner, waiting at the intersection, waiting until she went in the side door—all so familiar now, these steps of the plot. I wondered if the front doors were locked, or if the side door led right down to the basement where they met. Did he put his arms around her? Did he say "Bless you, Mavis, you've come!" Did he *kiss* her?

I noticed, as I stood hesitating on the corner, that some other women had gone in the side entrance, followed by an old man with a cane and another woman on her own. They must be going in to pray, I thought; how shocking to think of those two dancing in the basement below them. Dancing or . . . no, I couldn't let myself think anything else but dancing. That was enough, that was bad enough. I waited until another two women started up the walk to the church and then slid in the side door behind them.

I stepped into the gloom of the vestry, where I could make out display cases of pamphlets and booklets, and a table covered with a purple cloth with a brass plate on it, and a wooden money box on a stand with a black and white photograph of an Eskimo child above it. The women went ahead and pushed through wooden doors into the body of the church. As they did so, and the doors swung open and shut again, I heard my mother's voice. High and clear, echoing, a half-singing sound.

And our mouths shall show forth Thy praise.

Then, a solemn male voice I was sure must be Timothy Box, for it sounded as thin and sandy as he looked.

O God, make speed to save us.

Then my mother again, and underneath her voice I could hear whispery, faint voices, like crumpling paper, the voices of the other women, the old man.

O Lord, make haste to help us.

It was like a love duet the way their voices went back and forth like that, like Kathryn Grayson and Howard Keel, or Jane Powell and . . . who? I couldn't think. I wasn't sure I'd ever felt exactly this way in a movie, although what was happening here seemed more like a movie than real life. Carefully, I pushed the doors and looked in.

Directly ahead of me stretched a red carpeted aisle and to the left of that, halfway up the row of pews, sure enough, my mother. Her head was raised so that she was looking up to where *he* stood at the front of the church, now reading verses from a Bible held in the wings of a brass eagle. When he finished, everyone began to recite something together, and I saw that Mavis was holding in her right hand a maroon book, open but barely glanced at; her head never inclined toward the book, she kept her face tilted up looking at Timothy Box. But she was speaking, I could hear her voice. She knew all the words, I realized with a jolt. She must have memorized all this stuff.

He hath put down the mighty from their seat,
and hath exalted the humble and meek.
He hath filled the hungry with good things;
And the rich he hath sent empty away.

Pale April light leached in through the stained-glass windows, came to rest on burnished brass and wood, was absorbed by velvet and stone. There was a musky smell I guessed must be incense, and in niches along the walls there were indeed small statues, some with little bouquets below them. The place had a festive, dressed-up air, not like a church at all; there'd be a lot of things to look at and enjoy here whether or not you were listening to the words or thinking about God. I could imagine liking a place like this myself, but I couldn't understand what Mavis saw in it —St. Barnabas was everything she said she despised. This Box person must somehow have her in his power, that was it. I knew that women would do anything for love.

With that he was chanting again and the scattering of women were saying something back in the same way, and then there was a scraping noise, a rasping shuffle and every-one was kneeling. My mother was kneeling too.

Christ have mercy upon us.

Like a Catholic, her, the one who loved the plain white walls of Bethel.

O God, make clean our hearts within us.
And take not thy Holy Spirit from us.

God, I thought, was it Timothy Box she came for or *this*? Was this the dancing? What I was planning to do . . . now I was not so sure. Maybe I would be taking the holy spirit from her.

I let the door close silently and went back into the vestry, aware for a moment only of my own terrible loneliness. There was simply not a soul to turn to, no-one who would make haste to help me. If that was how Mavis felt. . . . But it was still wrong, all her lies, all her deceiving ways. I picked up a couple of pamphlets that welcomed strangers to St. Barnabas, thinking that I might use them some day as a weapon if I needed to. I could leave one lying on my desk where she'd see it if she were snooping around my room, the way I knew she did. It would serve her right. Or I could send it in an envelope to my father and watch her face when he opened it and said, "Now what the devil is this, Mavis?"

But I knew I wouldn't, even as I was imagining it. I kept seeing her head bent forward, her forehead resting on her clasped hands on the pew ahead, kneeling and praying. This whole thing made me want to cry, to run in there and blame her for even more than I'd made up in my head these past weeks. It wasn't fair.

I let myself out the side door into the sunlight and began walking back to Moodies. I didn't want this secret, I didn't want it at all. But I knew, as I stood over a grate by the curb and ripped up the pamphlets into little pieces and let them fall through into the sewer below, that I had it now, and that I'd be keeping it.

Getting Out of Garten

Dieter and I always sat in the same booth at the Cozy, the one directly behind the jukebox where we couldn't be seen from the street. Since Mr. Pfaff had put in a plate-glass window across the front of the restaurant it was the only place we had privacy. We weren't concerned about being seen together—from the beginning of Grade 13 we'd been regarded as a couple—but neither of us could afford to be caught smoking. Dieter's mother had said that only if he gave up cigarettes could he join his elder brother in Timmins for the summer, and he had promised. Although nothing specific hinged on my getting caught, I knew it would involve some loss of privilege so that my father could make a point about obedience, if nothing else. He had forbidden me to smoke simply on the grounds that it was a filthy habit: this was an explicit criticism of my mother, Mavis, who really enjoyed a cigarette with her tea, especially when old friends like Aunt Eadie came to visit. Smoking was *unfeminine*, my father always added, implying that was worse than filthy.

As if they'd heeded my father's warnings and were determined to remain feminine, none of my girlfriends in Garten smoked. It was with Dieter, who lived down the street, that I smoked in secret. Oddly, tobacco didn't stunt his growth the way he'd been told it would; within a few months of our first cigarettes he had shot up two inches so that we were nearly the same height. We discovered that smoking provided us with a relationship we had needed without really knowing it. "Isn't it weird," he said once, "to think how lonely we used to be?"

Dieter had an old Forties coupe during that last year in high school, which meant that if the Cozy were crowded we could drive out in the country for a smoke, unobserved except by grave-eyed cows who always congregated by the fence when we parked. Although I liked the little car, I loved the noise and the music in the restaurant more. There was an underlying tension there—we had to be ready to butt out and fan away the smoke if anybody who might tell on us came in—and that very nervousness became an enjoyable part of the smoking. Garten was *full* of people who might tell on you, Dieter observed, as if it were an inescapable fact of life. You were never really safe anywhere. He only hoped that if he did get caught he could convince his mother there'd been some mistake, it must have been somebody else who looked just like him.

I had to depend on aids such as chlorophyll gum, Chantilly cologne and a toothbrush kept in my pencil case, but Dieter relied on his voice. It was a rich, resonant baritone that gave the ring of truth to any lie he might tell; he was the person to have on your side in an argument or debate, for he spoke with such measured certainty he seemed to make sense no matter what he said. Every year he got the public speaking award at our school, and then fell out of the race at the regional level—not quite enough wit or originality to win outside of Garten. People said he'd make a fine teacher; he didn't seem to have the fire or drive for either the pulpit or politics, which was a shame when you thought how that voice might stir a crowd.

Dieter did extremely well in languages at school and got a reputation for being a "brain," no matter how he tried to rid himself of that image. He had a thin, unathletic body that gave all its strength to its lungs, leaving his limbs long and reedy. He was fair, with skin susceptible to acne and hair falling over his forehead in spite of how often he brushed it back. I never thought he was as bright as everyone else seemed to; perhaps that was why I found him attractive. He received my affection with the same gratitude I offered him for liking me, and we became allies in enemy territory.

Dependent and close as we were, our relationship was entirely lacking in passion—the first time we kissed, both of us kept our eyes open, swept with curiosity instead of desire.

"Did you feel anything?" he asked, as soon as his mouth was free.

"Well, not exactly," I said, compelled to be honest by his straightforward voice. "But your mouth tastes nice," I added, wanting to say something positive so that he'd respond in like fashion.

"It probably tastes like cigarettes and gum, just like yours," he said, and we laughed and kissed again. Still nothing, only the pleasant warmth of our faces pressed together, arms around each other. It was comfortable anyway, we decided, and felt relieved. The last thing either of us wanted, really, was to fall in love and ruin our plans for getting out of Garten, separately, at the end of that year. He wanted to go over to Western in London to take English and philosophy, and I was set to study science in Toronto. This way we could go around together, smoke and dance and kiss together, and keep our lives unentangled.

We were pretty safe in the Cozy because the regular waitress, Faye, was on our side, and when anybody came in who might tell our folks she'd signal by calling out "double lemon Coke." She knew who to look for—she was only a couple of years older than we were but had quit school after Grade 11 and had been working at the Cozy ever since—and it amused her to be part of our intrigue. Faye was no stranger to intrigue herself, and rumours had wafted around her since her early leaving from Garten District High, for which there were several scandalous explanations—she'd been found with the janitor in the furnace-room without her brassière on, or she'd gotten pregnant and went to the Grace in Toronto to give the baby up, or she'd been caught typing "fuckfuckfuckfuckfuck" by the commercial teacher and refused to say she was sorry. I held her in awe.

There was an open voluptuousness to Faye that was generally so disallowed in Garten that I'd watch her in bewilderment: how did she get away with it? Didn't she know that when she wore those nylon blouses you could nearly see her nipples through? Didn't her mother *mind* that her skirt was so tight? She was a short, stocky girl whose large breasts made her appear curvaceous, whose generous mouth was always slick with bright colour. She was the kind my mother called "coarse," but I found something very appealing in the way she looked. Maybe it was the way her hair puffed out, as if little fans were blowing it from underneath, as if the hair itself was barely attached to her head and only floated there. She seemed so wonderfully tangible under that frothy cloud of hair. Or maybe it was the way she stood —I liked that about her too. I would try sometimes to imitate that stance alone in my bedroom, hand on hip, pelvis thrust out and head thrown back, but it never looked the same. The difference, I judged, was that she "did it" and I didn't. Everyone said that Faye had been doing it with boys for years and now even did it for some of the men at the ironworks factory where her father worked. She knew what her body was capable of and she liked it. I could imagine that. If I had a body like hers I would probably like it and use it too, I thought.

One afternoon in late November, when Dieter and I came into the Cozy, she was behind the counter but instead of her usual salute, a pantomime of drawing in smoke from an imaginary cigarette between her fingers, she just waved us on back to the booth. "It's free," she said, and went back to polishing glasses. I looked at the way she was slouching against the sink, the way her hair looked stringy and slept-on instead of fluffy.

"I wonder what's wrong with Faye," I said to Dieter, as we settled into our familiar space, piling our books, getting out our cigarettes. "Did you notice how awful she looks?"

Dieter coloured. He held up two fingers when Faye called over to see what we wanted, which meant two Cokes, and said to me in a terse, low voice, "She has ears, you know. Keep your voice down."

"Well, really," I said, annoyed. "Excuse me."

"Oh, just shut up and never mind," he said, and at that moment she appeared with our glasses and set them down slowly, looking at Dieter all the while as if to elicit a reaction from him. But he avoided her eyes and said nothing. She went back to the counter slowly, and stood there chewing gum and drying glasses, looking sad.

"You know something," I said. "What?"

"Look, Elizabeth," he said. "What I know you really don't want to know. Trust me."

"Geez you piss me off, Dieter," I said. "I hate it when you use your 'trust me' voice. I'm not your mother. *Tell* me."

From the front of the restaurant then there came laughter and Faye's name and she walked past us back to the kitchen with her face set and angry. "Come on, finish your smoke and I'll take you out in the car and tell you," he said, getting out change to leave on the table for Faye. "You'd probably hear about it anyway."

We got in the coupe and drove out the gravel road past the egg-grading station to where we usually parked. He turned off the ignition, lit cigarettes for us both and passed me one without looking at me. He took a deep drag of smoke as he began. "Okay, here's what I know. I heard in the can today that last night Sonny and a bunch of guys took Faye out in their car and shaved her." He exhaled, his face paler than the smoke.

"What?" I said stupidly, trying to make some visual sense out of what he had just said. I had seen her minutes before; her hair was dirty and flat but she had it. I laughed. "Shaved her? Where?"

"Oh Christ, Elizabeth. For Christ's sake," he said, his face gone from ash to flame. He rolled down the window and looked out, embarrassed.

"Her crotch?" Sudden understanding flashed through me. I had been thinking only of photos I knew from *Life* magazine, French women paraded in village squares, their bald skulls oddly shaped and their faces dead. Shamed by their countrymen for betrayal, shamed for doing it with the Germans. But this, this was some other thing. "Really, Dieter?" He nodded, still not looking at me, still scarlet. "But why?"

"Sonny," he said, and moved his shoulders in that way that means there is nothing else to say. I saw in my mind Sonny, his dark brushcut bristling with energy and rage, heard his harsh voice shouting, ordering people around, cursing and laughing. With two younger brothers who formed the inner core, he had collected around himself a gang of six or seven boys who had slipped behind in school and now lingered in the C and D levels, waiting to see what life might eventually offer. In the winter they hung around the ice-rink and the pool-hall, in the summer and fall they drove their hot-rods up and down Front Street, leaning out the windows and yelling at girls.

We had been in the same class once, Sonny and Dieter and me. I had a crush on Sonny for a little while—he seemed so lively and funny and bold—but our lives had gone in different directions, and for a girl like me from Brubacher Street, driving around with Sonny and his gang from the wartime houses was as unlikely as being allowed to smoke in the living-room. They were foreign, fearsome creatures, those boys, without the sense to know they were inferior beings. I loathed them for their oafishness, for the way they left their snowboots flapping open, for the way they walked with their thumbs hooked in their belts, swaggering. In the Cozy they gulped their drinks and belched loudly, and poured ketchup over everything they ate and made a great mess and lots of noise. Always noise, daring Faye to throw them out for their rowdy behaviour. But she usually only laughed and called them "You pigs!" and only when Mr. Pfaff was in the kitchen did they get tossed out. Faye always seemed to be amused by them in a way I didn't understand, laughing at their dirty jokes and rude remarks and cleaning up after them. And now this. Why?

"Doesn't Sonny like Faye anymore, Dieter?" I asked, feeling that he must have the answer somewhere.

"It isn't that simple I don't think," he said.

"Oh God, did they do anything else to her?" I asked, the image of Faye's bare and hairless body suddenly swimming up before my eyes. Lying there on the back seat of Sonny's car, helpless—did she have to then endure their bodies pushing into hers? Sonny was always making remarks in the Cozy about "pumping it to some broad"; had he pumped it to her as she lay stripped and shaven? Had they all done it?

Dieter looked over at me and then out the window again, swallowing. This was making him feel sick too, I realized. "No, I think that was the point, see, that they didn't. Sonny and those guys had been out at Leonard's getting tanked up and then they came into the Cozy just as she was closing it for the night. They asked her to go for a ride, and she thought that's what they meant, you know, and then when she got in the back seat they tied her hands and showed her the razor. And when she tried to scream they put her underwear in her mouth. And after they shaved her they pushed her out."

"But I really don't see," I said, horrified by what it must have been like, the razor, the dark, the stupid drunken boys. The male laughter, and fear in the air. A nightmare.

"See, I think it's *because* she likes doing it that they didn't do it to her, that they shaved her instead," Dieter said.

"Do you understand that?" I asked, angry at him for so calmly finding an answer, angry at his reasonable tone. "Do you know why guys would *do* that?" I reached over and pulled at him so he had to look at me and I saw there were tears in his eyes. Outside the car, behind him, a few remaining brown leaves were being blown off a maple, one, two, slowly drifting down. I wanted only to watch the leaves and not think about this other thing. But I had to. I looked at Dieter and watched instead the tears leave his eyes and trail down his skin. I didn't know exactly why he was crying and that made me feel even more uncomfortable. *I* was the one who should be upset, I was a girl like Faye whose crotch could be shaved—he wasn't a victim like us, he was one of them. He had no right to cry. But there he was anyway, putting his arms around me, crying into the side of my neck. As if it had all happened to him.

It was beyond me, this thing. If you were like Faye, if you let them have you, then they hated you and abused you. Could the mothers like Mavis be right? They won't respect you if you let yourself go, she said. You mustn't let them touch you, she said. Never. It only has beauty and meaning after marriage. Well, at least with Dieter I didn't even want to, so we were okay, I was safe. I could put my arms around him now and let him cry, and cry too. Yet somewhere dark inside me where there were no words for it, I felt a cold, repellent wind blowing against him, and I cried for that awful feeling as much as I did for Faye.

I wanted to go and talk to her, maybe help her plan some way of getting back at Sonny. But I didn't, I simply thought about it. And one night that week she took everything there was in Mr. Pfaff's till and disappeared. People thought she must have hitch-hiked to Toronto—that's where everybody went who ran away—but I always hoped she kept going all the way to Montreal.

Mr. Pfaff didn't call the police after her or press charges against her. Maybe he'd heard about her disgrace and it was an act of kindness to let her go; or maybe he was really glad she had gone—her reputation had kind of dragged down the Cozy the last little while, he said—and decided to let her have the small chunk of cash as a farewell present. She was nearly twenty so her parents didn't much care that she had gone; they said it was about time she left the nest anyway. Her sister Marge took over the waitressing job but she never cared about watching out for Dieter and me the way Faye had. Things were never the same there again.

*

From the time we decided to go together both Dieter and I enjoyed a level of social success neither of us had known before. It was almost as if by pairing up we proved our coming of age to the tribe and became acceptable. Dieter came up with that; he read stuff by Margaret Mead and tried to see things in a sociological context, he said. Privately, I thought it had a lot more to do with his having a car—once you entered the fray with a vacant back seat, even a very small, uncomfortable back seat, you had absolute bargaining power. We were asked to go places because we could bring others along; that's why we seemed to be popular.

For whatever reason, we were part of a group of six couples who decided to go into the city during the Easter holidays to dance at the Paradise Pavilion. It was the pinnacle of a girl's social life to get asked out to the Double Pee, and I wanted to feel more excitement than I did. But the truth was that going with Dieter removed the romance, left me feeling empty at the centre. Still, I took the preparations seriously, as did my mother, who became engaged in every aspect of what I should wear, how I might do my hair, which of her two evening bags I could borrow. She had always approved of Dieter—she said he had a good heart—and she wanted me to look my very best for him, probably sensing in some primitive, subliminal way that he posed no threat. My father, Frank, said that both sides of Dieter's family were of sturdy German stock, not a lot of imagination but good staying power. Couldn't go wrong with a Henkel, he said. Mavis said you could tell a lot about a man by the way he treated his mother, and she knew for a fact that Dieter helped Mrs. Henkel, who was a widow, with all the household chores. Without complaining, she added. I thought about him smoking, which made my mother easier to take.

The Paradise Pavilion, with its live band and midnight buffet of salads and cold cuts was the only place of its kind in the area and attracted quite a mixed crowd. Even people my parents' age sometimes went there—Frank and Mavis had never been but they knew all about it. "It's still dry, Mavis," my father said, the night they gave me permission to go. "I phoned George over at the Imperial and he said he and Helen were there only a few weeks ago, still the same policy. Not a thing to worry about, not a thing. You be in at a good hour, Elizabeth, you understand?"

The way the arrangements were made among the boys, we ended up with Trudy and Glen in our car. "Look, it could be worse," reasoned Dieter, when I grimaced at the news. "At least with those two they'll neck themselves numb in the back and we can still talk."

Trudy and Glen had been going steady for three years and unless Glen's mouth was preventing her, Trudy did nothing but talk about the future they had planned. How they were both going over to Stratford Teachers' College next year, and how one day Glen would be a public school principal and how she'd teach until they decided to have a family and then she'd quit because of course she felt a woman's place was with her children and so did Glen. On and on. Sometimes I thought the best thing about finishing Grade 13 would be never having to listen to Trudy talk about Glen again. Life had thrown us together for all these years because of our mothers and I was hard pressed to see what either of us had gained except a strong dislike for each other. She was the most boring, self-centred person I knew.

She was also one of the prettiest. That night I could not look at her without envy and had to keep reminding myself how empty-headed she really was. Her curls were pulled back into a chignon and tied with a ribbon that matched her pale lemon chiffon dress, and she wore a wrist corsage of small yellow roses. With her mother's fur jacket over her shoulders, I thought she looked like a movie star. "You look just like Sandra Dee," I said, as she and Glen climbed in the back of the coupe.

"Oh Elizabeth," she giggled. "I bet you look nice too. Do you have earrings on?"

I did—my mother's rhinestone stars—and they pinched my earlobes and put me on edge. I was wearing a new dress of striped taffeta that felt slippery and ungiving against my body, and I knew that the corsage that Dieter had pinned on me, so that Frank could take our photo before we left the house, was being flattened underneath my coat. I didn't really care. It was a little cluster of white carnations, a choice of flower I considered so inferior they deserved to be mushed. I decided Dieter's mother had probably suggested them; they were serviceable and probably had terrific staying power.

Inside, the Paradise was exactly as I had imagined it—a large, cavernous room with rows of long tables at both ends and an open space for dancing in the middle. There was a raised platform where a dance band was playing, ten men in white jackets and a leader with a French-looking moustache who wore pale blue. One of the men, the trumpet player, had black skin. I couldn't stop looking at him and paid no attention to Dieter who was trying to help me off with my coat. There had been so few times in my life when I had seen Negroes that I still remembered the first, a few years before when we were travelling through Niagara Falls. On a street corner I saw a black girl exactly my size wearing the same sundress I had on. Identical. I was so excited I wanted my father to stop the car but of course he wouldn't. I could still recall the way the sun had gleamed like oil on her skin; under the stage lights this man's face shone in the same way and I thought he was beautiful. His cheeks puffed out when he played and his eyes closed in ecstasy when he hit the high notes in songs like "Wonderland by Night." All evening I found myself trying to catch his eye, wanting to smile directly at him, wanting him to single me out of the crowd and point his trumpet right at me when he played.

As the other carloads from Garten arrived we sat down at one of the long tables against the back wall. I wanted to be closer to the dance floor and said so but nobody paid any attention. The boys were as tight-lipped as if they were in church, stiff and caged in their suits and ties. They didn't seem to be themselves, whereas the girls had blossomed, were more confident and at ease in their perfumed bodies. As often happened, I felt somewhere in between, in neither camp and both.

Waiters crossed and recrossed the room carrying soft drinks and bowls of potato chips. One of them came to our table with a tray of bottles and a stack of white plastic cups, which he handed around the table. "Watch your step now, fellas," he said, winking.

"What does he mean, Dieter?" I said. "Why did he wink like that?"

"Well, look under the table at what Bruce is doing. But be subtle, okay?"

I pretended to drop my purse and moved my chair back so I could bend down to retrieve it. In the shadows beneath the table I saw a paper bag between Bruce's knees and as I watched, his hands appeared. With one hand he grasped the neck of the bag so that it took on the shape of a bottle and with the other he held a white cup, tipping the bag and pouring out amber liquid.

"Dieter?" I whispered, still under the table. "Is that booze from Leonard?"

"Yeah, but it's not his homemade stuff," Dieter said. "He said you girls would like something sweeter so he got us some sherry. It's Four Aces, it's really good."

"Dieter Henkel!" I said, coming up too suddenly and hitting the side of the table with my head, feeling a sharp ridge of pain that increased my anger. "You promised you guys wouldn't . . . you said, you did. It's breaking the law, you know. If we get caught, they'll call the police and our folks and then what? *Then* what?"

"Oh cripes, Elizabeth, keep your voice down," said Bruce, looking at me with disgust. "Everybody does this here, what do you think we came here for? Don't pretend you're so lily pure or I'll tell your daddy that you smoke!"

He was laughing as he spoke but I knew he meant it. I straightened in my chair and looked at the other girls who seemed to be waiting to see what my next move would be. "I'm going to the washroom," I announced, glaring at Dieter who hadn't sprung to my defence. Where was his marvellous voice when I needed it? When it came to the crunch, he was one of them. "Is anybody else coming?"

Slowly the other girls got up, sensing that some kind of battle line was being drawn here that had little to do with booze and everything to do with who was really in charge. We made our way along the tables and out to the Ladies', a large drafty room painted pink and maroon, smelling of disinfectant and hair spray and stale smoke. We stood in front of the mirrors, looking at each other's faces in reflection, looking for an answer to Joyce's question: "Well, what are we going to do now?"

"If we make a big fuss about it they'll get mad and we'll all have a rotten time," said Sharon, looking pointedly at me so that I'd know I should have kept my mouth shut.

"Well, they should have told us," Joyce said. "I don't like the way they snuck it in, hiding it from *us* as well. As if what we think doesn't matter."

"Yeah, and if we let them drink they'll go all stupid and get, you know, lecherous," said Amy. Her date was Eugene whose reputation for wandering hands was legendary.

"What *I'm* worried about is them driving home," I said, hoping to sound so responsible that my tone would put Sharon in her place, and make them all acknowledge how wise I was. "I mean, honestly, what if even one car has a little accident—don't you think we'll all still get blamed for drinking? We'll all..."

Nancy broke in, the way she always did. "What gets me is they pretend to be such nice guys and when it gets down to it they're really no better than Sonny and them, you know, wanting to drink and everything. Really."

Everybody began talking at once then, some defending Bruce who only wanted everybody to have a good time, and others attacking all boys as monsters, maniacs. "Well, you heard what they did to that waitress, eh?" Nancy's voice, suddenly high above the others, splintering in the air. We looked at ourselves in the mirrors. That couldn't happen to us. Could it? We weren't like Faye, *we* were good, we were virgins, we were girls of impeccable reputation. And these were our boyfriends, our sweethearts who respected us, who would never plunder our powdered crotches without permission. Silence.

"I'll tell you what I think," said Trudy, speaking up for the first time. "If we stop making a fuss and *let* them give us some sherry they'll have a lot less themselves, you see? And they'll even think we've given in which always makes a guy feel great, right? Later on, like on our own, we could say we won't kiss them any more, and all that, unless they promise not to bring booze along the next time. But not now. Not when they're all together like this."

We stood and stared at her, nodding dumbly, struck by the depth of her understanding. Who would have thought Trudy knew so much about life? Agreeing that hers was the course to take we all applied more lipstick and returned to outsmart the boys by drinking their sherry. As we sat down Sharon said that she had had some wine at her cousin's wedding and it had been really bubbly, and maybe the ginger ale would make this as nice and bubbly too. The boys looked relieved as Trudy announced that we had decided, all of us, to try a little. "We don't want to spoil a good time," she said sweetly, looking significantly at me.

The cups were handed around and we took our first tentative sips. Alcohol was still the mystery, the untasted magic yet to come, the promise of adulthood still years away. I wanted to drink the things I read about—champagne and martinis and manhattans—not bootleg sherry mixed with pop in a plastic cup. I drank it right down and thought how little I liked the taste. Kind of a rotten, sick sweetness that didn't make me feel happy or giddy at all the way it was supposed to. But at least now it was over. There was no going back now.

Later, dancing with Dieter, I nestled against his chest and told him about Trudy's plans in the washroom. I couldn't bear to have him think I had no mind of my own, that I was so easily swayed. He laughed and said, "But you didn't really think that I'd get drunk, did you Elizabeth?" And his voice was so deep and reassuring, I felt foolish and didn't answer. I looked over his shoulder at the trumpet player, and imagined being in his arms instead, thought that it would be more exciting than being pressed against Dieter's thin body. At that moment he took the trumpet from his mouth and saw me looking at him and flashed a bright smile as if he could see into my head. My spine suddenly felt molten, liquid with longing, and I leaned heavily against Dieter, nearly unbalanced with the intensity of the sensation.

That's what I want to feel, I thought, and let my head rest against Dieter's cheek, closing my eyes and thinking that anyone looking at us would guess we were as much in love as Trudy and Glen. I imagined what it would be like to love Dieter, I pretended that I did, and I thought about whispering that in his ear. But I didn't. When I opened my eyes again the trumpet player was smiling at someone else and the music was over.

*

Much later in the spring, when the whole business about the sherry had slipped into the past, Dieter and Glen and Trudy and I drove, not into the city to see a movie as we'd told our mothers, but to a spot about twenty miles away known as the Gorge. It was famous in the area, not so much for its sheer limestone cliffs falling down to a tumbling river as for the number of secluded parking-places among the trees on the cliff edge. I had been to the Gorge countless times in daylight for family picnics and school outings but never at night to park. It seemed silly, I thought, to drive way over to a scenic view you weren't going to look at anyway—but Glen had convinced Dieter that the Gorge was the place to go.

Between Dieter and myself that spring there was the growing conviction that in our own way we were far more in love than that pair who spent hour after hour intertwined in the back seats of their friends' cars. "I don't think they actually know each other at all," Dieter said. "Not like we do. How can you *know* somebody if you spend all your time kissing instead of talking? And you can't love somebody without knowing them, right?"

I agreed, yet it seemed that there might be another level of knowledge that we didn't know about. "You know, the Biblical kind," I said. "Maybe their bodies know each other better than ours do, Dieter. Do you think they go all the way?"

He said he didn't know but he guessed they went pretty far. "That's why Glen wants to go out parking with us, see, because Trudy's mom is keeping a real eye on her. So if they

178

haven't done it, I bet they're on the verge."

We had so nearly given up on the physical aspect of our friendship that the idea of spending a whole evening kissing made us both a little uneasy. "We can still just talk," Dieter reassured me in his most convincing tone when I was hesitating.

All we ever talked about in those last weeks of school was the work we had to do before the final provincial exams, on which our futures hinged. All the way through the countryside to the Gorge we talked, until he finally stopped in a cedar grove by the river and we both knew we had nothing left to say. Suddenly our usual topics—our mothers, our classmates, our fears and hates—seemed too personal to exchange when there were listeners in the back seat.

Not that Trudy and Glen were listening. They made such a variety of noises, little moans and sighs and mewing, grunty sounds, they couldn't possibly have heard anything else but themselves. As Dieter was shifting closer to me on the car seat I turned slightly as I moved toward him so that I could glance over my shoulder. The unwritten rule in these situations, I knew, was "no peeking," but I didn't care —I wanted to see. What I saw was a flash of pale skin, and Trudy's head squeezed against the corner of the window, her pullover and brassière pushed up and bunched around her neck, and Glen's head burrowing down between her bare breasts. I had never seen anything like it.

Trudy's face was the face of someone dreaming, mouth open in a soundless sigh, the eyes closed to lock the world. Dieter's eyes met mine then and I saw t had turned as well, was just as fascinated by what g With the intuition of someone who feels his ba n't watched, Glen stirred, raised his head a little. "Yer or you go for a walk, Diet, okay? Go look at t something."

I was indignant—it was, after all, Dieter's car and there were a lot of mosquitoes out there this time of year—but with his usual good humour Dieter just opened his door and pulled me across the seat behind the steering-wheel. "Sure thing, Glen. See you in a while."

The smells and noises of the night covered us like gossamer. The sharp tang of the cedars, a dark, wet smell that held in it the promise of surprises, lying on our skin so tenderly. And the song of crickets and frogs, and the sound of the river running, and then, as we walked on, an almost imperceptible other noise, one that didn't belong.

We looked back and saw the car's rear end moving up and down ever so slightly—and we had our answer as clearly as if we were still watching the lovers. They were doing it. They were going all the way. The rhythm was already in our heads, our hands and bodies knew that rhythm, that feeling of having to, having to, having to, until everything in us was sprung loose, released. Dieter and I stood close together in the dark and I wondered if he still remembered how when we were small, playing on Brubacher Street with the others, we had all taken off our clothes and rubbed at ourselves until sparks flew in our brains. We had never talked about it, but I was sure he must remember. He must know that feeling too, feel as I did now, wanting what they had in the car.

Stricken with knowledge, we turned and moved farther into the cedars. Bold, needful, aching with something unnameable that erased all other thoughts in my head, I stopped when we came to an open place among the trees, and put my hands on Dieter's shoulders. Pressed myself only and urgently against him. I had had this feeling before I knew it: molten, liquid, running like the river. We kissed and Dieter drew away, looking at me inquisto si took his hand and pulled him toward the clearing, me on the moist ground, to give me those feelings. There was something heavy now in the air, no longer gossamer, pressing us down against each other. Something making me loosen my clothes so I could feel him against my bare skin, something like masks coming down over our faces so that we were no longer Dieter and Elizabeth, we couldn't see each other or ourselves, we were only bodies seeking out that feeling of having to, having to, having to. Once, he tried to speak, and I could tell it was going to be his cautionary voice, so I silenced his mouth with my hand. "C'mon, Dieter," I said. "C'mon."

We did try. I know that and it doesn't help—maybe the memory is more painful because of that. We tried and tried, but Dieter's body would not obey the night, attended instead the reason and sense of his head. When we finally gave up, we pulled our clothes back on our mosquito-bitten bodies and whispered to each other only little wisps of what it was we wanted to say about the sadness we felt. "I'm sorry. . . . It's not your fault. . . . It's nobody's fault." Brushing ourselves off we got up and walked again through the trees, stopping once to light cigarettes and look at each other's faces in the quick blaze of a match. We were prisoners in our bodies, we had neither given nor gotten what we needed. I inhaled and felt the rush of smoke in my lungs like a calming hand.

Back in the car, fully dressed now and giving off a sleepy, smug contentment, Trudy and Glen sat talking in voices that were hazy and dreamlike. We got in the front and Dieter started the engine, turned on the car radio and backed out into the field, anxious to get going. Wordless. We did not look at each other; we stared out the windshield, hoping that out of the night there might come some comfort. Before he turned the headlights on there were fireflies, small flickers of light in the darkness. And then the harsh beams ahead of us, and from the back Trudy's piercing giggle. Her hand tugging at my hair.

"Hey, hey, hey, what have you two been up to, eh?" said Glen. "Little bit of grass there, Elizabeth, or is it cedar? Lay down for a rest, did you?" They went off in peals of laughter and I looked over at Dieter's sad face. He didn't look at me but I knew we were agreeing to let them think we knew as much as they did, because we couldn't bear to tell the truth. Oh, who cares, I thought. Who cares. It's almost over.

*

Labour Day weekend. In other years, the Saturday afternoon has found us at the Garten Fall Fair midway, eating candy floss, trying the ring toss again, taking the rides that make us sick and dizzy. This year, far from the fair grounds, we are here, feeling as if time has shoved us over the edge of the ferris wheel, as if the ground has come up to meet us too fast.

We have come to this place too fast, standing in rows as Trudy comes up the aisle, her head held high and her eyes searching out Glen who waits for her at the altar, his face averted. He seems to be looking over at the side of the church where all his friends stand, the dozen or so boys who have come to see him married. Tying the knot, they call it. Getting caught, they mean.

The last few days there have been flurries of rumours, with some people saying well, they only did it once but once is enough, and others saying they'd been at it for ages, ages. Somebody says Glen was always careful but that Sonny had stuck pins in a batch of safes he sold around town last spring, just for a joke, see, but look what happened. That Sonny, he should go to jail or something, or be made to buy the crib. *He's* the one responsible. On and on.

Trudy is not too far along and had to let out the waist of her yellow dress only the merest bit, she says. Her mother has made a matching lace jacket to make the dress look more modest and you'd hardly recognize it except for the colour. She's wearing her hair the same way she did to the Paradise except this time she has flowers around the chignon and she is carrying a white leather Bible. There are no bridesmaids, and there will be no reception or party after the wedding. There is a functional, getting-it-over-with tone to the minister's voice that he seems to intend; there is a message for all of us in this service. We don't need his funereal proddings—we have only to look at the face of Trudy's father as he walks beside her, holding her hand. Blame and shame and fear vibrate in the air. There are a few adults here, friends and family on both sides; my mother is here to support her friend June, Trudy's mother, whose face is swollen and ugly with grief, and there are others, a scattering of the nosy and mean-minded who always attend such weddings, filling in the pews at the back.

I am with all the other girls from our class on the bride's side of the church. We have come to witness Trudy's downfall, but in a peculiar way we cannot figure out, she does not look as sad as we think she should. "How can she look so proud of herself?" asks Amy, and the question passes down the row as we wonder at the contented smile that lurks under the outward embarrassment. She has what she wants now, we decide. She never really wanted to be a teacher anyway. Glen can stay in town and work with his Dad at the garage and they'll be just as happy as they would have been in Stratford. We are envious, confused, skeptical.

From where I stand I can see Dieter across the aisle and eventually he feels me looking at him and glances over. He has arrived back from his summer in Timmins looking tanned and older, as if he has gained weight, or knowledge, or both. We tried to write, exchanging news about our final marks, our scholarships, our plans for courses, but there was a dead feeling to the letters as if we were writing out of duty. It is finished between us now. The Gorge divided us forever and there is no going back. We failed each other in an unforgivable way that we cannot bear to talk about and heal.

But we are safe. We are free, and unlike Trudy and Glen we are getting out of Garten. I smile at Dieter as I think that, and he smiles, involuntarily, back at me. I think how lonely I will be without him as a friend this year, off in another life with strangers who don't know me the way he does. The minister is reading now from the Scriptures, that stuff he always reads at weddings from Corinthians 13, and Dieter and I mouth the words at each other in a mocking way, these verses we have memorized so faithfully in Sunday school that we have them imprinted on our brains forever. Like all that has happened to us here, we must bear these verses in our memory and still, somehow, get on with it. Wounded though we may be, we are still intact.

To: John Jaquet

My brother + friend.

May God continue to richly
bless and use you.

Evangelist Leroy Freeman

FREEDOM
FROM
FEAR AND WORRY
SURVIVING THE STORM

EVANGELIST
LEROY FREEMAN

Rejoice Printing
West Palm Beach, FL 33409

FREEDOM FROM FEAR AND WORRY
Surviving The Storm

"Freedom From Fear And Worry"
Published by Rejoice Printing
Copyright © 2008 by Evangelist Leroy Freeman

ISBN 978-0-9822739-0-6

Cover design by Rejoice Printing
Leroy and Patricia A. Freeman
P.O. Box 221076 * West Palm Beach, FL 33422
Printed in United States of America

This book is dedicated to my mom,
Eula McClinton Freeman-Williams
who has taught me, prayed for me,
and supported me both in life and in ministry.

Thanks Mom. I love you!

Acknowledgements

Many thanks to my godly, precious, lovely wife, Patricia A. Freeman for her encouragement and much persuasion for me to write this book. When I wouldn't listen to her, God stepped in and confirmed that it should be done.

Also, many thanks to my awesome cousin Adrianne McCauley who has helped me over the years with her many God given gifts and talents.

Many thanks to the educators, family, and friends who have come along beside me and have taken their precious time to help with the proofing of this book.

Just to mention a few: Min. Craig A. Young, Sr., Rosliand Halstead, Mary J. Ford, and Angel Freeman Wilson.

Many blessings to all of you (named and unnamed). Again, I say thanks very much and God bless you.

Evangelist Leroy Freeman

CONTENTS

FOREWORD
by Min. Craig A. Young, Sr.

The Bible states in I John 4:18, *"There is no fear in love, but perfect love casts out fear. For fear has to do with punishment, and whoever fears has not been perfected in love." ESV*

Many believers are in search of that perfect love which the Scripture speaks of and they have found it to be quite elusive. Dashed hopes and unfulfilled dreams have haunted them over the years as they have been **victimized** and **debilitated** by the **crippling effects of fear.**

Yet, there is a solution for the problem of fear and worry. Evangelist Leroy Freeman addresses these concerns in the chapter titled 'What Is Fear?' By sharing his testimony of how he overcame a personal battle with his phobia, Evangelist Freeman gives **Biblical** and **practical advice** on how every believer can walk victoriously in God's perfect love which comes through Christ.

This book is especially helpful because it addresses common problems in a contemporary setting. It calls attention to the kinds of headline news stories that frighten us every other day, it seems. Yet, **Evangelist Freeman shows us through the principles of Scripture how we can eradicate our fears by trusting God more.** As you read, I pray that you are as encouraged and inspired as I have been and I pray that you enjoy the Word.

Grace and Peace,

Min. Craig A. Young, Sr. - *Dallas Theological Seminary final semester of studies for Master of Theology and also Director of Couples Ministry @ Oak Cliff Bible Fellowship where Dr. Tony Evans is Senior Pastor.*

INTRODUCTION

I believe with all of my heart that we are living in the 'last days.' Jesus said that in the 'last days' many fearful and frightening things will come upon the earth. Paul said in the 'last days' there will be some very hard times.

"This know also, that in the last days perilous times shall come."
II Timothy 3:1

According to Scripture, I believe that we are in the beginning of those times. Today, the dominant mood of the hour is fear. Many live in fear and worry due to an uncertain economy, inflation, higher taxes, and high unemployment. This has resulted in much fraud, thefts, assaults, injuries, and even deaths.

For each of us there will always be times of **fear** and **worry** that will attack our lives. God knew this before the foundation of the world.

Therefore, He sent us a Savior and Deliverer, the Lord Jesus Christ who has come and overcame the world, the flesh, the devil, death, hell, and the grave. Jesus died, but after three days and three nights, He arose with all power in His hands. He now sits at God's right hand making intercession for us.

Because Jesus lives and watches over every believer, we need not fear or be afraid of any threat or danger. There is a Savior among us that loves us and cares for us.

It's great to know that God has given us His Word to help us deal with the issues of fear and worry. God's Word is quick, powerful, and eternal. Faith in God's Word is our shield that is designed to help us quench all the fiery darts of fear and worry.

"Above all, taking the shield of faith, wherewith ye shall be able to quench all the fiery darts of the wicked." Ephesians 6:16

If God's Word is a daily part of our lives, reliance upon His Word can help us meet and beat any challenge that the enemy of our soul throws at us.

In these troubling times, our faith must be at optimum levels of trust in God, if we are to live victorious lives of joy and peace.

We believers are in intense spiritual warfare with the forces of Satan. Casual Christianity of just going to church only on Sunday and reading the Bible every now and then will not work in these 'last days.' We must strive to walk close to God and in the power of His Holy Spirit if we are to stand victorious in our profession of faith in the Lord Jesus Christ.

We must also:
- *Practice holiness at all times*
- *Forsake not the assembling of ourselves together with other believers*

Practicing holiness gives us confidence to believe God for great things, and where there is the unity of believers, there is strength.

We face dangerous and frightening situations every day. We are often troubled and worried about many things that threaten us or our loved ones with danger. We must remember that we have a Savior and Deliverer.

If we concentrate on the Savior and remind ourselves who He

is, what He came to do, and what He can do, it should bring joy and peace to our hearts. Our Savior that is within us can handle any problem and help us overcome any situation.

"Yea, though I walk through the valley of the shadow of death, I will fear no evil: for Thou art with me..." Psalm 23:4

The Lord did not promise to always take away the problem, but He did promise that He will take us through it. He is able to strengthen us and give us courage, peace, and joy in midst of whatever we are facing.

We can rest assured that no event or circumstance can come into our lives that will be more than our Savior can handle or can take us through.

The continuing word of God to us is - **"Be not afraid."** That statement should give our hearts rest, peace, and joy all the days of our lives.

It is my prayer that this book will help you in your walk with the Lord as you strive to maintain the abundant life of joy, righteousness, and peace in the Holy Ghost.

"I Am come that they might have life, and that they might have it more abundantly." John 10:10.

To God be the glory for all the great things He has done and shall continue to do in the wonderful Name of Jesus through the awesome power of the Holy Spirit. Amen

Evangelist Leroy Freeman

FEAR ON THE SEA

❖

"*And the same day, when the even was come, He saith unto them, Let us pass over unto the other side. And when they had sent away the multitude, they took Him even as He was in the ship. And there were also with Him other little ships.*

And there arose a great storm of wind, and the waves beat into the ship, so that it was now full. And He was in the hinder part of the ship asleep on a pillow: and they awake Him, and say unto Him, Master, carest Thou not that we perish?

And He arose, and rebuked the wind, and said unto the sea, Peace, be still. And the wind ceased, and there was a great calm. And He said unto them, Why are ye so fearful? How is it that ye have no faith?

And they feared exceedingly, and said one to another, What manner of man is this, that even the wind and the sea obey Him?" *Mark 4:35-41*

After Jesus finished preaching by the Sea of Galilee, He said to His disciples and to some of the others who were following Him, *"Let us pass over unto the other side."* After He sent the multitudes away, they all boarded ships. While crossing the sea, a great violent, ferocious storm rose up which produced heavy howling winds. Many mighty dashing waves began to beat upon the ship. The little ship seemed to be in great danger. It was being tossed to and fro and was filling up with water. This produced panic and cries as the disciples feared for their lives.

Then they remembered that Jesus was on board in the hinder part of the ship asleep on a pillow. They awakened Him out of His peaceful sleep crying, *"Master, carest Thou not that we perish?"* Immediately, Jesus arose and rebuked the wind, and said unto the sea, *"Peace, Be Still!"*

At the command of Jesus, the storm immediately subsided. The danger fled and there was a great calm. The ship then sailed smoothly on and they were all safe.

Jesus then said to His disciples, *"Why are ye so fearful? How is it that ye have no faith?"* In other words, He was saying, Didn't I tell you that we were going over to the other side? Therefore, we were not going under. No matter how bad it seemed, there was no need for you to fear danger or death.

Even though there was water everywhere on the inside of this little ship, it could not sink because it was upheld by the Word of His Power. Just a little faith in the words of Jesus, about "going over" and making it to the other side, should have soothed all their doubts and calmed all their fears in the midst of the storm.

Beholding everything that had just happened on the sea, the disciples feared exceedingly (or were amazed), and said one to another, *"What manner of man is this, that even the wind and the sea obey Him?"*

What an awesome display of the power of Jesus that was witnessed that day. This was irresistible proof of His Divinity.

From our text, there are two words that characterized the state of the disciples. These two words are - **Fearful** and **Feared**, which comes from the root word **Fear**.

In our text, Jesus let them know that the answer for their fears was Faith. Fear and Faith are the two things we shall look into as we discuss this remarkable subject.

In all things that we encounter in life, God wants our Faith on display and not our Fears. It has been well said, *Fear and Faith cannot keep house together. When one enters, the other must depart.*

> ### God wants our Faith
> ### on display and not our Fears.

2

WHAT IS FEAR?

❖

".....fear hath torment."
I John 4:18

Fear - is an emotion of alarm and agitation or mental
disturbance caused by the expectation, realization, or
perception of instant or future danger.

Someone has well said, "Fear is as old as sin." I agree with
that because before there was sin, there was no mention of
fear. It was only after Adam and Eve sinned, by eating from the
forbidden tree of the knowledge of good and of evil, that we
first hear of fear.

> *"And they heard the voice of the Lord God walking in the Garden*
> *in the cool of the day: and Adam and his wife hid themselves from*
> *the presence of the Lord God amongst the trees of the garden.*

And the Lord God called unto Adam, and said unto him, Where art thou? And he said, I heard Thy voice in the garden, and I was afraid..." Genesis 3:8-10

For mankind, this was the beginning of FEAR in the human race. This fear was caused by disobedience.

Fear Affects All

Every since then fear has become universal, and it comes into everyone's life. We can't outrun, outsmart, or successfully hide from it. For each of us there will be times of fear. We even share fear with all creatures.

I love nature. As I take my walks early in the morning, I am almost always by a body of water in the area. I often come across huge alligators minding their own business close to the banks. I love to rush toward them, as though I want to grab, cuddle, or even wrestle them. It's amazing to see how quickly they can move. As quick as lightning, they disappear and head for deeper waters.

Even though I know how much distance to keep, and that I am no match for the alligators, it's their God given internal fear that makes them run away.

"And the fear of you and the dread of you shall be upon every beast of the earth, and upon every fowl of the air, upon all that moveth upon the earth, and upon all the fishes of the sea; into your hand are they delivered." Genesis 9:2

In humans and in all animals, the purpose of fear is to promote survival. God created both man and animals with the capacity to be afraid for their own good. It is fear that alerts us to danger.

If we couldn't be afraid, we wouldn't survive long. Without fear we would constantly be putting ourselves into dangerous situations like walking into oncoming traffic, stepping off rooftops, trying to catch bullets, or carelessly trying to track down and pet ferocious animals. It's fear that helps us to be careful and cautious.

Characteristics of Fear

We all experience fear every now and then. Listed below are some of the most common sensations associated with fears:

- *Breathing speeds up*
- *The heart races*
- *Dry mouth*
- *Sinking feeling in the stomach*
- *Tightened muscles*
- *Trembling and faintness*

These are some of the characteristics of being afraid. These physical responses are intended to help you survive a dangerous situation by preparing you to either run for your life or fight for your life. That's what it means by either FIGHT or FLIGHT.

We all experience fear in different ways. **Fear is a battle fought in the arena of the mind and it may be caused by a real danger or an imagined one.** The danger may be immediate, as when a person fears an onrushing wild animal, or hears a loud bump or a bang in the darkness of the night; or fear can be distant, as when a test is to be taken, or there's a court date appearance. This anticipated fear is often called **anxiety.**

Even though fear is a normal part of life, living with chronic fear can be both physically and emotionally distressing. Prolonged fear or anxiety can affect the physiological functions of the body, resulting in heart and digestive disorders.

This built in capacity for fear makes fools of two kinds of people:

1. *The one who is afraid of Nothing*
2. *The one who is afraid of Everything*

No-Fear

Only a fool is fearless. The attitude of many who pretend to be fearless, proudly display the No-Fear symbol. With the tough-guy attitude, they don't seem to fear anything – danger, disease, death, hell, or the grave. They boldly say, "I'm tough. I'm not scared." Many even display a bumper sticker that says, "Hell is afraid I'll take over." This mentality is a sad state of error.

Many foolishly feel that they don't need Jesus and that they are alright all by themselves.

"Jesus answered and said unto them, Ye do err, not knowing the Scriptures, nor the power of God." Matthew 22:29

One day I was watching a television show featuring the great Houdini. He was one of the greatest escape artists that ever lived. I heard him say on that program to a group of people, "I have escaped from every bondage imaginable and I will escape death also. Somehow, I will find a way to get back from the grave."

Houdini died and there hasn't been a word from him since. He failed to realize that apart from Jesus Christ, there are no exit signs beyond death's door.

A person with No-Fear doesn't prepare for what's ahead. When I was studying the Martial Arts, it was the fear of losing a match that caused me to prepare to be the best that I could be before I stepped into the ring for competition. Without that fear, I would not have trained as I should have and I would not have gotten far.

A wise student studies and prepares before taking an important exam.

"A prudent man forseeth the evil, and hideth (prepareth) himself: but the simple (unprepared) pass on, and are punished." Proverbs 22:3

Constant Fear

There is also the person who is afraid of everything. They are held captive to extreme, persistent, and unreasonable fears that are often symptoms of mental disorders, demon possession, and demonic oppression. For these tough cases, medical science is doing all it can to keep these disorders under control.

In the Word of God, the disciples faced a father with a little boy who had a mental disorder. This disorder was caused by demon possession which often tried to kill the child. The disciples could not figure out why they could not help this distressed father who came to them for help. Even though the disciples could not help, Jesus was able to bring this child healing and deliverance.

"And when He was come into the house, His disciples asked Him privately, Why could not we cast him out? And He said unto them, This kind can come forth by nothing, but by prayer and fasting." Mark 9:29

I believe that seasons of prayer and fasting by us believers, dependent on the power of the Holy Spirit, will produce the same results as Jesus for those tough cases of demonic possession and oppression.

There are some who are so filled with fear that they go through life running from things that aren't even after them. They become prisoners to their fears. This type of fear paralyzes and destroys one's life. In the face of fear, they have a flight mentality. It's easier for them to run from the fear, contemplate suicide, or other seemingly easier ungodly alternatives, than to face the fear or deal with it in the proper righteous way.

The man of Gadara was possessed by demons and was constantly being tormented. He lived naked in a graveyard. Day and night he was constantly crying and cutting himself with stones. Those around him tried to help this man, but all of their efforts failed.

> *"...immediately there met Him out of the tombs a man with an unclean spirit, who had his dwelling among the tombs; and no man could bind him, no, not with chains:*
>
> *Because that he had been often bound with fetters and chains, and the chains had been plucked asunder by him, and the fetters broken in pieces: neither could any man tame him."*   Mark 5:2-4

One day Jesus came by, filled with power and the Holy Ghost, and cast the demons out of this man. Jesus set him free. This man was then found sitting, clothed, and in his right mind *(Mark 5:1-20)*. After this encounter with Jesus, there were no more extreme, persistent, unreasonable fears, and outbreaks of violence. Jesus changed his life. The man then wanted to follow Jesus, but Jesus said:

> *"Go home to thy friends, and tell them how great things the Lord hath done for thee, and hath had compassion on thee."* Mark 5:19

Jesus is still a deliverer today. He still sets the captives (fearful and tormented) free *(Luke 4:18)*. Jesus is the answer for every fear and torment of the devil.

"How God Anointed Jesus of Nazareth with the Holy Ghost and with power: who went about doing good, and healing all that were oppressed of the devil; for God was with Him." Acts 10:38

Fear Paralyzes Potential

Fear can also paralyze one's potential. Because of fear, many miss doing useful things. The attitude is: What will others think? What if I fail? What if I mess up?

Fear even causes many Christians to do nothing for the Kingdom of God. There was a man who buried his God given talent in the ground. When questioned by the Master, this is what he said,

"...I was afraid, and went and hid Thy talent in the earth...." Matt. 25:25

What was his excuse? He said, "I was afraid!" His talent was taken away from him and he was called a wicked and slothful servant.

Don't cover up fear with excuses, apologies, self-judgment, or with mood-altering chemicals. These are not good hiding places for times of fear. The one thing worse than a quitter, is a person that is afraid to start. It's better to start and fail, than to never start at all.

Don't let fear paralyze you into uselessness. Sure, there are things you face that are frightening, but don't run and hide from your fear. Turn and face it. Even if it's a slow walk, walk toward it.

There are things you can't change. There are things you will not agree with or like, but don't let that stop or control you. Vow to trust God, face the fear, and seek to overcome it. Even if you should fail, God can turn failure around for your good and His glory.

Fear of the Future is a waste of the Present.

❧ 3 ❧

HEALTHY AND
UNHEALTHY FEARS

❖

".....within were fears."
2 Corinthians 7:5

Fear is a small word with very large consequences. As we have seen, the capacity for fear is within us for self-preservation, which activates our bodies and minds to prepare us to deal with threats. Fear is double-edged - it can save and it can destroy. There are unhealthy and healthy fears.

Unhealthy Fear

Unhealthy fears serve only to make us unhappy and to paralyze us. Everyone knows what it is like to be afraid. We all have things that we are afraid of. As young children, most of us had one or some of these fears:

- *Fear of Harmless Insects and Reptiles*
- *Fear of Darkness*
- *Fear of Being Alone*
- *Fear of Strangers*
- *Fear of Heights*
- *Fear of Closed Spaces*
- *Fear of Bodies of Water*

I remember as a little boy I was terrified of going to a place called Juno Beach, Florida. I loved the ocean, but in order to get to the park area for the picnic, we had to cross a little wooden bridge. I was terrified that I would fall through the little cracks in the bridge and into the water below. For many years as a child, before going to the beach, the fear of this little bridge paralyzed me and kept me up most of the night and robbed me of my joy of going to the beach. It took much persuading each time, for me to cross that bridge.

I shed many tears as family members and friends laughed at me for my fear of this little bridge. It was a happy day in my life when I finally conquered my fear. Years later as I have gone back to that little bridge, I laugh to think how terrified I was of it.

Unhealthy fear is being afraid of something that cannot actually harm us. If we let them, these unhealthy fears will work around the clock, inventing and even magnifying dangers in our minds.

As we mature, most of our childhood fears disappear or

become dormant, but we acquire new unhealthy fears, even ones we can do nothing to avoid.

Such as:

- *Fear of What Others Think About Us*
- *Fear of Rejection*
- *Fear of Speaking In Front of Others*
- *Fear of Getting Older*
- *Fear of Losing Loved Ones*
- *Fear of Disease or Terminal Illness*
- *Fear of Death*
- *Fear of God*

We must refuse to let unhealthy fears control and consume us. We must refuse to let them rob us of our joy and the abundant life of peace.

Healthy fear

Healthy fear is an awareness and respect for that which is dangerous in life. Healthy fears stand guard to inform us of real dangers and offer us guidance and constructive steps in order to avoid the fear.

- **Fire** *is useful for good, but it is to be feared, because it can burn, destroy, and even kill.*
- **Drugs** *and* **alcohol** *in certain instances are useful and good, but they are to be feared, because they can result in dependence, disease, and destroyed lives.*
- **Smoking** *is to be feared, because the use of tobacco could result in emphysema, lung cancer, and premature death.*
- **Speeding** *is to be feared, because it could result in traffic tickets, accidents, or even death.*
- **Violence** *is to be feared, because it breeds more violence and also causes punishment and even death.*
- **Promiscuous sex** *is to be feared, because it violates God's*

law of marriage and causes, guilt, shame, sexually transmitted diseases, and even death.

We must be mindful of healthy fears and let them help us. We must avoid those unhealthy fears which can ruin and even destroy us.

> ## "I sought the Lord and He heard me, and delivered me from ALL my FEARS."
> ## Psalm 34:4

4

END-TIME FEARS

❖

"Men's hearts failing them for FEAR, and looking after those things which are coming on the earth…"
Luke 21:26.

Jesus said that in the last days, because of the signs of the times and the things that would be coming upon this earth, there will be much fear.

A recent article shows the relationship between fear and heart failure.

"Study: *Intense Fear and Panic Attacks --*
Really Can Make Your Blood Clot

Sayings about FEAR like, 'The blood froze in my veins' or 'My blood curdled' really are more than just common figures of speech, say researchers who have found that intense fear and panic attacks really can make your blood clot.

These blood samples were then measured, based on that which the researchers concluded - that anxiety patients showed a much more highly activated coagulation system than the healthy control group.

The increased coagulation tendency could, said Franziska G., be the 'missing link' that explains why anxiety patients have a statistically higher risk of dying from heart disease by a factor of 3 or 4." Source-ANI

The financial crisis or recession of 2008 caught many people by surprise and was global in its effect. It caused much fear and panic throughout the world. Fear took a tremendous toll psychologically, economically, domestically, physically, and politically, both nationally and world-wide.

Some of the negative results of this financial crisis included the following:

- *Loss of Jobs*
- *Loss of Medical Benefits*
- *Loss of Homes and Declining Values*
- *Loss or Evaporated Retirement Funds*

With things slipping out of control, the governments of the world had summits in an effort to try to sort it all out. They were at their "wits end" (all wisdom is swallowed up) in trying to find a solution. It was said among them, *"It will not be a quick fix."*

".....at their wit's end."
Psalm 107:27

With the fear and panic of the 2008 financial crisis, and especially with the loss of much that had been accumulated, many were physically sick. In addition to physical sickness, fear began to create overwhelming anxiety, causing many to take their lives and the lives of others as well.

World Headlines and Articles

To illustrate the heavy fear hanging in the air because of the 2008 financial crisis, here are a few headlines and articles from different newspapers and web sites.

- *Last Updated: October 12, 2008: 6:40 PM ET* **Week of Fear** - *World rushes to a fix - World leaders scramble for solutions.*

- *Last Updated: October 13, 2008: 5:50 PM ETAs -* **Economy Drop, Violence and Fear Soar**

- *An out-of-work money manager loses a fortune and wipes out his family in a murder-suicide.*

- *A 90-year-old widow shoots herself in the chest as authorities arrive to evict her from her home of 38 years.*

- *In Massachusetts, a housewife who had hidden her family's mounting financial crisis from her husband sends a note to the mortgage company warning: "By the time you foreclose on my house, I'll be dead." Then Carlene B. shot herself to death, leaving an insurance policy and a suicide note on a table.*

- *In Los Angeles, California, last week, a former money manager fatally shot his wife, three sons, and his mother-in-law before killing himself.*

- *Karthik R., 45, left a suicide note saying he was in financial trouble and contemplated killing just himself. But he said he **decided to kill his entire family** because that was more* *honorable, police said.*

• *Across the country, authorities are becoming concerned and they are urging people to get help. In some places, mental-health hot lines are jammed, counseling services are in high demand, and domestic-violence shelters are full. With nowhere else to turn, many people are calling suicide-prevention hot lines. The Samaritans of New York have seen calls rise more than 16 percent in the past year, many of them money-related. The Switchboard of Miami has recorded more than 500 foreclosure-related calls this year.*

• *"A lot of people are telling us they are losing everything. They're losing their homes, they're going into foreclosure, they've lost their jobs," said Virginia C., Executive director of a suicide resource center in southwest Florida's Lee County.*

• *PANIC IN THE STREETS, FEAR IN THE AIR!*

• *Recession fears deepen global rout – Japan's Nikkei plunges 9.6% to hit five-year low. European shares, U.S. futures tumble. Fear and panic trump good economic news as loonie markets pounded. "This is now about market psychology. There's extreme fear and panic out there." Right now, said Burleton, "the focus is on the doom and gloom and nobody can predict a bottom to this. We may see further bouts of panic before we get to somewhat more stable ground."*

• *ANALYSTS: Markets stuck between fear and panic - PARIS -- Emerging from the wreckage of a historically bad week of trading, dealers from Tokyo to London and New York say the financial turmoil has left markets in an irrational state of fear. Some dealers buried their faces in their hands, unable to watch as index indicators steadily fell Friday morning in scenes that were replayed around the world as each market opened.*

• *"I have never seen anything like this and I hope I never go through anything like this again," said Valerie P., commenting on the clash of the stock fall and the credit freeze. "It's been a long week in the history of the financial markets," said Joshua R. a strategist for City Index in London. "What is happening now is not just history repeating. If you map out every single event along the way, we are setting a whole new precedent."*

I believe that these present days in which we are living are just as Jesus said, *"the beginning of sorrows" (Matthew 24:8).* We may as well brace ourselves, because I believe that once one crisis is over, there will be another and then another of greater sorrow. This world has much more to go through for rejecting the King of kings and the Lord of lords, the Lord Jesus Christ.

God Is In Control

As bad as things may seem, God is still in control. He is upholding all things by the Word of His power and working all things after the counsel of His own will. As He has taken care of Israel throughout the centuries, He will take care of His body of believers in this twenty-first century. Therefore, we need not fear end-time fears. God will come through for us and meet our needs according to His riches in glory by Christ Jesus.

> *"This know also, that in the last days perilous times shall come.....But evil men and seducers shall wax worse and worse, deceiving, and being deceived." II Timothy 3:1,13*

> "These things I have spoken unto
> you, that in Me ye might have
> peace. In the world ye shall have
> tribulation, but be of good cheer,
> I have overcome the world."
> John 16:33

5

BIBLICAL CASES OF FEAR

❖

"When your fear cometh as desolation, and your destruction cometh as a whirlwind.....for that they hated knowledge, and did not choose the fear of the Lord." Proverbs 1:27,29

There are many words that are associated with fear. Let's look at five.

1. FRIGHT – sudden, intense fear, as of something immediately threatening.

When the three ladies came to the tomb early Sunday morning after the Crucifixion of Jesus, they saw that the stone was rolled away. And upon entering the sepulcher, they saw a young man (an angel) sitting and clothed in a long white garment; and they were affrighted.

"And entering into the sepulcher, they saw a young man sitting on the right side, clothed in a long white garment; and they were affrighted.

And he saith unto them, Be not affrighted: Ye seek Jesus of Nazareth, which was crucified: He is risen; He is not here: behold the place where they laid Him.

And they went out quickly, and fled from the sepulcher; for they trembled and were amazed: neither said they anything to any man; for they were afraid. " Mark 16:5,6,8

Their sight of the angel, caused sudden intense fear.

2. STARTLE – fear that shocks momentarily and causes a quick involuntary movement or start.

Prayer was made without ceasing to get Peter released from jail. When the prayer was answered and Peter was miraculously released, he appeared at the door of the Prayer Meeting and they were astonished or startled. Peter had to tell them to hold their peace, to calm them down.

"But Peter continued knocking: and when they had opened the door, and saw him, they were astonished.

But he, beckoning unto them with the hand to hold their peace, declared unto them how the Lord had brought him out of the prison." Acts 12:1-17

3. PANIC – strong, sudden fear, often groundless and frequently results in loss of self control, and mindless actions.

A great host of Syrians came up against God's people in Samaria and besieged it. Just before the Syrians attacked the city, the Lord made them hear a great noise.

"For the Lord had made the host of the Syrians to hear a noise of chariots, and a noise of horses, even the noise of a great host: and they said one to another, Lo, the king of Israel hath hired against us the kings of the Hittites, and the kings of the Egyptians, to

come upon us.

Wherefore they arose and fled in the twilight, and left their tents, and their horses, and their asses, even the camp as it was, and fled for their life." 2 Kings 7:7

Instead of the Syrians checking it out to see if it really was a legitimate army coming against them, panic took over and off they sped leaving everything. They left their tents, horses, donkeys, silver, gold, weapons, and even pots on the fire. What panic! What mindless action for a well trained army!

4. DISMAY – a sudden or complete loss of courage or confidence in the face of trouble or danger.

The Philistines gathered themselves together to fight with Israel. They came with thirty thousand chariots, six thousand horsemen, and with people as many as the sand which is on the sea shore.

"When the men of Israel saw that they were in a strait, (for the people were distressed), then the people did hide themselves in caves, and in thickets, and in rocks, and in high places, and in pits.

And some of the Hebrews went over Jordan to the land of Gad and Gilead. As for Saul, he was yet in Gilgal, and all the people followed him trembling." 1 Samuel 13:6,7

With such a multitude against them, Israel was without hope or courage. They were dismayed.

5. TERROR – violent, paralyzing fear, usually in the presence of great danger.

Highly trained soldiers were stationed at the tomb of Jesus to make sure that nobody would disturb His dead body. All was well for two days, but suddenly on that third day things changed. Terror overtook those soldiers.

"And, behold, there was a great earthquake: for the angel of the Lord descended from heaven, and came and rolled back the stone from the door, and sat upon it.

His countenance was like lightning, and his raiment white as snow: And for fear of him the keepers did shake, and became as dead men." Matthew 28:2-4

Other Descriptions of Fear

There are many other words that describe fear. Some of them are – phobia, timidity, care, apprehension, alarm, trepidation, dread, horror, and consternation.

There are also many phrases or slangs that describe fear. Some of them are:
- *Heebie-jeebies*
- *Cold Sweat*
- *The Creeps*
- *Jumping out of one's skin*
- *Shivering in one's boots*
- *Throwing up one's hands*
- *Scaring the daylights out of*
- *Trembling like a leaf*
- *Making one's teeth chatter*
- *Making one's heart stand still*

The Word of God says, *"Fear hath torment." 1 John 4:18*

Elijah's Fearful Experience

Fear comes to every life. Elijah was one of the most powerful prophets that lived. He was a man of great courage and was mighty in prayer. On one occasion, Elijah was used of God to call fire down from heaven.

"And it came to pass at the time of the offering of the evening sacrifice, that Elijah the prophet came near, and said, Lord God of Abraham, Isaac, and of Israel, let it be known this day that Thou art God in Israel, and that I am Thy servant, and that I have done all these things at Thy Word.

Hear me, O Lord, hear me that this people may know that Thou art the Lord God, and that Thou has turned their heart back again.

Then the fire of the Lord fell, and consumed the burnt sacrifice, and the wood, and the stones, and the dust, and licked up the water that was in the trench." 1 Kings 18:36-38

On another occasion Elijah was used to raise the dead.

"And the Lord heard the voice of Elijah; and the soul of the child came into him again, and he revived." 1 Kings 17:22

As great as this man of God was, fear still drove him to despair. When he was threatened by Jezebel for having killed her prophets, he ran for his life. Under a juniper tree Elijah was so filled with fear, he moaned and requested to die.

"But he himself went a day's journey into the wilderness and came and sat down under a juniper tree: and he requested for himself that he might die; and said, It is enough; now, O Lord, take away my life; for I am not better than my fathers." 1 Kings 19:4.

It was not Elijah's time to die, because His earthly ministry was not over. **God still had much work for him to do, but God could not use him in that fearful state.** Therefore, the Lord came to him, reassured him, strengthened him, and renewed his faith.

God calmed every fear that he had. Then Elijah was able to get up, run on, and finish his ministry in triumph and victory.

> *"And it came to pass, as they still went on, and talked, that, behold, there appeared a chariot of fire, and horses of fire, and parted them both asunder; and Elijah went up by a whirlwind into heaven."* **2 Kings 2:11**

God knows our frame. He remembers that we are but dust. In times of fear, He will come to us and say,

"FEAR NOT. For I Am with you!"

In the midst of all our fears, we must not panic, but trust God to either fix us or fix the situation we are facing.

"Fear Not" - the most often repeated phrase in the Bible.

FACING OUR FEARS

❖

"Man that is born of a woman is of a few days and full of trouble." Job 14:1

In each life, there will always be problems, stress, dissatisfaction, discomfort, and pain. These troubles often produce fears. To help overcome fear, you must first look at the fear and listen to what it is saying and what it is threatening you with. Call it out and be determined to face it.

Our response in the presence of fear is very important. We can't control many of the things that produce fear, but we are in charge of our responses.

As we go through life, there will be many unhealthy fears that come against our lives with the sole intention of driving us to panic. These fears must be mastered, because fears have a way of producing the thing that it is afraid of.

For example, even though Job was a perfect, and an upright man, one that feared God and avoided evil, he still carried certain fears around with him. It seems that what troubled him was the fear of having all of his livestock gone, his children killed, his body diseased beyond recognition, his wife telling him to give up "curse God and die", and then having his best friends accuse Him of being a hypocrite. I know this is so because Job said it himself.

> *"For the thing which I greatly feared is come upon me, and that which I was afraid of is come unto me." Job 3:25*

Job's fears came to pass. He was forced to face them. In facing them, he got to experience the hand of God like he had never known before. At the end of his many months of trial, God commended Job and brought him out with more than what he had before his terrible ordeal.

> *"I have heard of Thee by the hearing of the ear: but now mine eye seeth Thee. ..... And the Lord turned the captivity of Job, when he prayed for his friends: also the Lord gave Job twice as much as he had before." Job 42:5,10*

I too have had many fears in my life that I have been forced to face. If I could have, I would have avoided them all. But God allowed them to come and challenge my life so that they might be conquered. **God wants His Power to reign supreme in our lives and not our fears.** When there is a certain fear, God often allows circumstances to be arranged so that we can face the fear and learn to fear only Him.

> *"Fear thou not; for I am with thee: be not dismayed: for I am thy God: I will strengthen thee; yea, I will help thee; yea I will uphold thee with the right hand of My righteousness." Isaiah 41:10*

There are many unreal, imagined, and unreasonable fears that plague us all. We must reject these fears and be determined to face them. We must sort out our thoughts and allow only those that are sane, sensible, wholesome, and truthful to stay in our minds, if we are to enjoy good mental health and peace of mind.

We must learn the Word of God, strive to keep our minds stayed on Him, and cast out everything else that is contrary to what God says.

"Casting down imaginations, and every high thing that exalteth itself against the knowledge of God, and bringing into captivity every thought to the obedience of Christ." II Corinthians 10:5

"Yea though I walk through the valley of the shadow of death, I will fear no evil. For Thou art with me..."

Psalm 23:4

THE FREEING
FEAR OF THE LORD

"The fear of the Lord is the beginning of wisdom."
Proverbs 9:10

There are many definitions for Fear. The most important definition is the one which helps us overcome all other types of fear.

Fear - extreme reverence or awe,
as toward a supreme power.

This is the type of fear which acknowledges the power of God and bows in awe and reverence before Him.

At one time in my life, I feared God with the fear of bondage. All I saw in Him was a mean God that wanted to cramp my style and take all the fun out of my life. Therefore, I tried to stay at a distance from Him. I was doing a good job at keeping my distance, but somehow He would not leave me alone. The Lord kept showing up in my life by sending me messages through His followers that He loved me.

One day His great love penetrated my sinful heart. I saw for the first time that what Jesus did on Calvary's Cross was on my behalf. The precious blood that He shed was for me, so that I might be saved and have a right relationship with God. Yes, Jesus loved me and wanted me to spend all eternity with Him.

"For God so loved the world, that He gave his only begotten Son, that whosoever believeth in Him should not perish, but have everlasting life."   John 3:16

One day I could not hold out any longer. I repented and received Jesus Christ as my Lord and Savior. Amazingly, when the Lord walked into my life, He cast out all my fear of being in His presence, and of one day going to Hell.

"There is therefore now no condemnation to them which are in Christ Jesus..." Romans 8:1

Now, I love walking and talking daily with Him. Because I now know He lives and He lives in me, I can face tomorrow. Now, I rejoice in having the righteousness of Jesus Christ and the hope of Heaven. His great love has conquered the fear of Hell and the Lake of Fire that tormented me for years.

"There is no fear in love; but perfect love casteth out fear." 1 John 4:18

One of life's greatest discoveries is a thing called the *"freeing fear of the Lord."* This is the spiritual place of seeing only God, His awesome power, and knowing that He has everything under control. This freeing fear of the Lord is a powerful thing in the life of a believer. This freeing fear of the Lord controlled Paul's attitude as he faced prison, hardships, and even death.

"None of these things move me, neither count I my life dear unto myself, so that I might finish my course with joy......

For I am ready not to be bound only, but also to die at Jerusalem for the Name of the Lord Jesus." Acts 20:24; 21:13

The fear of bondage and even the fear of death had to take a backseat to Paul's faith in God. The fear and reverence of God teaches us that He is the only One whom we should fear.

"And fear not them which kill the body, but are not able to kill the soul: but rather fear Him (God)...." Matthew 10:28

"For God hath not given us the spirit of fear; but of power, and of love, and of a sound mind." 2 Timothy 1:7

Solomon said, ***"Fear God, and keep His commandments: for this is the whole duty of man." Ecclesiastes 12:13***

Our fear of God and reverence for God invites us to choose what is right, not because we are terrified of His wrath, but it's deeper than that. Our fear of Him includes the love covenant relationship that we have with Him. This love relationship should cause us to want to always please the One we've come to love.

"For the love of Christ constraineth us....."
2 Corinthians 5:14

It's not my fear of Him, but my love for Him, that constrains or holds me back from the wrong that I am constantly tempted to do. Because I have been made a partaker of His divine nature, my constant desire is to please the One that has done so much for me. This is proof that I have been changed internally. This freeing fear of the Lord has done more for me than I could have ever imagined.

At one time I didn't understand this freeing fear of the Lord, but now I cherish it. Through an understanding of His great love for me, my life now is sweet and my joy is complete in Him. It provides great comfort to know that nothing will ever separate me from God's great love.

"...for He hath said, I will never leave thee, nor forsake thee. So that we may boldly say, the Lord is my helper, and I will not fear what man shall do unto me." Hebrews 13:5,6

"Stand fast therefore in the liberty wherewith Christ hath made us free, and be not entangled again with the yoke of bondage." Galatians 5:1

I have been delivered from the fear of death, because of the freeing fear of the Lord.

"...He also Himself likewise took part of the same; that through death He might destroy him that had the power of death, that is, the devil; and deliver them who through fear of death were all their lifetime subject to bondage." Hebrews 2:14,15

When we experience the freeing fear of the Lord, we are immediately led to life's great discovery, that the only One whom we need to fear comes to us in love, and tells us not to be afraid. Therefore, **when fear comes with its torment, the realization and the awareness of God's perfect love for us should cast out all fears.**

Knowing God's great love for us should cause us to trust Him and help relieve our fears.

"...as I was with Moses, so I will be with thee: I will not fail thee, nor forsake thee. Have not I commanded thee? Be strong and of a good courage; be not afraid, neither be thou dismayed: for the Lord thy God is with thee whithersoever thou goest." Joshua 1:5, 9

"Then had the churches rest...and were edified; and walking in the fear of the Lord, and in the comfort of the Holy Ghost..."
Acts 9:31

MY PERSONAL FEAR

"And I was with you in weakness, and in fear,
and in much trembling."   *I Corinthians 2:3*

Phobia – a persistent, abnormal, or illogical fear of a specific thing or situation. A strong fear or dislike.

Growing up I was a middle child in a family of eight. I was addicted to sugar and suffered with severe acne. This caused me to became very reclusive and as a result I became a shy loner and as often as I could, I withdrew from others.

In those times, in my little world of solitude and seclusion, I felt so much comfort and peace. All I needed was a book and silence and I was happy.

Even though I loved people and was liked by many, I did not enjoy social encounters. In social settings, somehow I would experience brain freeze and have nothing to say. I tried and tried, but my brain would not function in the art of conversation. Once the "**how are you doing**" was said, I was done with conversation.

When I was forced to attend social settings you could always find me, I was the one in the back, over in the corner trying to hide. In order to function socially, I would drink a fifth of wine just to be able to communicate and feel comfortable about speaking.

When I met my girlfriend Patricia, whom I later married, she was very popular and outgoing. We were total opposites. I was shy and she was a great communicator. A few minutes with her and she would have your whole life story. When we met, she was too young to realize the seriousness of my social phobia. We survived the dating years with most of those years being away from the crowd. Later, we were married.

Called to Preach

The Lord saved me at twenty-one years of age. Six months later I felt the call to preach the Gospel. I was excited at first, but quickly dismissed the thought because I was terrified of public speaking. I said, *"Preach? Not me Lord! Stand before people? Not me! There must be some type of mistake, Father."* It was no mistake, it was the Spirit of God. The Lord had spoken. He wanted me to go in His Name, stand before people, and preach the Gospel.

It's amazing how God can take foolish things to confound

the wise, and how He can take weak things and use them to confound the things that are mighty. I know it's true, because it happened in my life.

Many don't believe me and are shocked when I tell my testimony of shyness, especially when I let them know that deep down on the inside, much of the shyness remains. To do what I do and have done over the years in ministry is an awesome testimony to the power of God.

This social phobia that I thought would be my biggest hindrance in carrying the Gospel of the Lord Jesus Christ, has actually turned out to be one of my biggest blessings in ministry. It's the fear or the phobia of social shyness that makes me much more dependent on the Spirit of God. This phobia that I have makes me prepare, prepare, and over prepare in order to face my fear each time.

Because of Jesus and the power of His Holy Spirit, I have been able to face my fear each time He has called me to deliver His Word. When the phone rings or I'm invited to preach, it would be so easy to say, *"No thanks. My schedule won't allow it."* But over and over again (when I'm led of God), it's always, *"Yes, I'll be there, I'll stand and speak. I'll say a few words for my Lord and Savior Jesus Christ."*

As a result of my willingness to forego the fear of my social phobia, God continues to empower me to stand and speak in public, sit and counsel others, lead meetings, and even relax at social functions.

One of my biggest challenges was being asked to lead a KAIROS International Prison Ministry team of twenty-six men (clergy and laymen) from many different denominations into a maximum security prison for a weekend of ministry. I feared all of the social contact that would be involved in putting this all together. I tried to get out of it and said, "No" six times before finally saying "Yes." My answer of "Yes" was followed by the continuous urging of the Lord. I could hear Him say, "What's the problem? It's a work of the Holy Spirit. I just need a vessel to work through. Do it." I faced my fear and it was amazing what the Spirit of God accomplished in all of our lives that glorious weekend of ministry. I'll never be the same.

When I am led to go and share God's Word, I prepare to the best of my ability. Then I rely upon the strength of the Lord God and leave the results with Him.

> *"I will go in the strength of the Lord God."*
> **Psalm 71:16**

Every time I have stood in His name and through His power, God has never failed me.

> *"...as I was with Moses, so I will be with thee: I will not fail thee, nor forsake thee.*
>
> *Have not I commanded thee? Be strong and of good courage; be not afraid; neither be thou dismayed: for the Lord thy God is with thee whithersoever thou goest." Joshua 1:5,9*

God has no respect of persons. Whatever fear that you are faced with, the Lord can help you to overcome it. If you are willing, He can and will use your fear, and even help you to defeat your fear in order to make you a blessing to others. Through the power of God, there is no fear that can't be faced and overcome.

What He's done for me, He can and will do for any and all who will trust Him.

> *"For there is no respect of persons with God."*
> *Romans 2:11*

❖

9

THE ANTIDOTE FOR FEAR

❖

"So then Faith cometh by hearing, and hearing by the Word of God." Romans 10:17

We can rest assured that any fear we may have is covered by one or more of the promises of God. *The promises given in the Word of God are the best antidote for fear.* Exposure to the Word of God builds faith, and when faith comes, fear must leave.

Fear and faith are opposites. They cannot keep house together. When one enters, the other must depart.

The battleground is the mind. We must keep our minds stayed on the Lord, remembering that with Jesus we are safe.

"Thou wilt keep him in perfect peace, whose mind is stayed on Thee: because he trusteth in Thee." Isaiah 26:3

The storms of life will come. At times, fierce winds are going to be howling all around us. The gates of hell will constantly threaten to engulf us. It's okay to come trembling to the Savior. He has bidden us to come and call on His great Name.

"Let us therefore come boldly to the Throne of Grace, that we may obtain mercy, and find grace to help in the time of need." Hebrews 4:16

God knows all about our troubles. He cares and He understands.

"O Lord, Thou hast searched me, and known me. Thou knowest my downsitting and mine uprising, Thou understandest my thoughts afar off. Thou compasseth my path and my lying down, and art acquainted with all my ways." Psalm 139:1-3

Jesus has been through all that we go through.

"For we have not an High Priest which cannot be touched with the feeling of our infirmities; but was in all points tempted like as we are, yet without sin." Hebrews 4:15

When we call on Him, He will hear our faintest cry and He will answer by and by. He will rebuke the fear that is threatening us and comfort us on every side.

Through Him:
- *We can face foes and danger*
- *We have power to bear up under trials*

- *We can triumph in persecutions*
- *We have power to withstand sickness and disease*

This is the mighty message and plan of the Gospel of the Lord Jesus Christ. Not one word of His promises has ever failed.

".....according to all that He promised: there hath not failed one word of all His good promise, which He promised......"
I Kings 8:56

"For all the promises of God in Him are yea, and in Him Amen, unto the glory of God by us." 2 Corinthians 1:20

This knowledge of Him and His Word should calm our fears and inspire our hearts, minds, and souls with boldness and holy courage.

"...the righteous are as bold as a lion." Proverbs 28:1

There will be fears, but we must give our fears to the Lord in prayer. This is what the Psalmist did when he was troubled, and it worked.

"I sought the Lord, and He heard me, and delivered me from all my fears." Psalm 34:4

As a Child of God, why should we fear? God has been good to us. He has done so much (for us not to trust Him). His will for our lives is awesome. Jesus came to deliver us from a lifetime of bondage to the spirit of fear.

"For God hath not given us the spirit of fear; but of power, and of love, and of a sound mind." 2 Timothy 1:7

If we stand in awe of Him and walk close to Him, the fears that have bombarded our minds will be brought unto subjection of His Mighty Power. We have been given power to cast down troubling thoughts and fears, but we must use it.

"Casting down imaginations and every high thing that exalteth itself against the knowledge of God, and bringing into captivity every thought to the obedience of Christ.."
2 Corinthians 10:5

There are many mysteries in life that we do not understand. Still we must trust God. Through it all, He always has our best interest at heart. Time and time again I have seen dreaded evils and fears pass away as I trusted and depended on the power of God.

The song says, *"Twas grace that taught my heart to fear, and grace my fears relieved; How precious did that grace appear the hour I first believed."*

The song also says, *"Thro' many dangers, toils and snares I have already come; 'Tis grace hath brought me safe thus far, and grace will lead me home!"*

If we are acquainted with God, we can be at peace, and thereby good will come to us. Those who fear are the ones who look only at their circumstances, and not unto God. Someone has well said, **"Glance at the problems, but stare at the promises."**

None of us will ever outgrow the spiritual warfare against fear. We must simply learn to fight the good fight of faith. According to Scripture, the devil is a defeated foe who knows who we are and Who we have on the inside.

"And the seventy returned again with joy, saying, Lord, even the devils are subject unto us through Thy Name."
Luke 10:17

"Ye are of God, little children, and have overcome them: because greater is He (JESUS) that is in you, than he (the forces of Satan) that is in the world." 1 John 4:4

The truth of the matter is – it's the devil who should be trembling because of us believers, and not the other way around.

Remember when the children of Israel were walking in obedience to God and on the move toward the Promise Land, it was the enemy that was trembling and afraid.

Rahab said, *"I know that the Lord hath given you the land and that your terror is fallen upon us, and that all the inhabitants of the land faint because of you.*

And as soon as we had heard these things, our hearts did melt, neither did there remain anymore courage in any man, because of you: for the Lord your God, He is God in Heaven above, and in earth beneath." Joshua 2:9,11

The same is true today. Concerning our God, *"the devil (demons) fear and tremble." James 2:19*

That's why Paul said, *"And in nothing terrified by your adversaries: which is to them an evident token of perdition, but to you of salvation, and that of God. For unto you it is given in the behalf of Christ not only to believe on Him, but also to suffer for His sake." Philippians 1:28,29*

We are King's kids. We have nothing to fear but fear itself. Let us REST on the promises of God.

"Now unto Him that is able to do exceeding abundantly above all that we ask or think, according to the power that worketh in us....." Ephesians 3:20

Let us prepare ourselves spiritually by praying and feeding on the Word of God. Let's be determined to put every fear under our feet. If we don't, we will be forced to face the fear in order to show that God is well able to bring us through it.

If we stand in awe of God, aware of His presence and aware of His power, this should release us from the bondage of the terror of our fears.

"And I say unto you my friends, Be not afraid of them that kill the body, and after that have no more that they can do. But I will forewarn you whom ye shall fear: Fear Him, which after he hath killed hath power to cast into hell; yea, I say unto you, Fear Him." Luke 12:4,5

Trust is meaningless if there is nothing to fear. That's why fears are allowed to challenge us, because they are a part of our growth process into His image. Watching His power in the midst of fear teaches us deeper trust in God. As He provided reassurance to the Psalmists, He will do the same for us.

"I sought the Lord, and He heard me, and He delivered me from ALL my fears." Psalm 34:4

The song says, *"What have I to dread, what have I to fear, leaning on the everlasting arms. I have blessed peace with my Lord so dear, leaning on the everlasting arms.*

Leaning on Jesus - Leaning on Jesus - Safe and secure from all alarms."

God wants us to express our fears and then TRUST Him.

"What time I am afraid, I will Trust in Thee."
Psalm 56:3

SCRIPTURES
FOR TIMES OF FEAR

❖

The cure for fear is faith. Let's fill our hearts and minds with the Word of God so that we will be ready in the times of trouble and fear. Here are some verses that will help you to trust God in times of fear.

"Be not afraid of sudden fear, neither of the desolation of the wicked, when it cometh. For the Lord shall be thy confidence...." Proverbs 3:25,26

"Ye are of God little children and have overcome them because greater is He (Jesus) that is within you, than he (the devil) that is within the world." 1 John 4:4

"The Lord is my Light and my Salvation; whom shall I fear? The Lord is the Strength of my life; of whom shall I be afraid? Though an host should encamp against me, my heart shall not fear: though war should rise against me, in this will I be confident." Psalm 27:1,3

"Yea, though I walk through the valley of the shadow of death, I will fear no evil: For Thou art with me." Psalm 23:4

"I sought the Lord, and He heard me, and delivered me from All my fears." Psalm 34:4

"When the enemy shall come in like a flood, the Spirit of the Lord shall lift up a standard against him." Isaiah 59:19

"There is no fear in love; but perfect love casteth out fear: because fear hath torment. He that feareth is not made perfect in love." 1 John 4:18

"God is with us. ....neither fear ye their fear, nor be afraid." Isaiah 8:10,12

"Fear thou not: for I am with thee: be not dismayed, for I am thy God: I will strengthen thee: yea, I will help thee; yea, I will uphold thee with the right hand of my righteousness." Isaiah 41:10

"Peace I leave with you, My peace I give unto you: not as the world giveth, give I unto you. Let not your heart be troubled, neither let it be afraid." John 14:27

"The fear of man bringeth a snare: but whoso putteth his trust in the Lord shall be safe." Proverbs 29:25

"Have not I commanded thee? Be strong and of a good courage; be not afraid, neither be thou dismayed: for the Lord thy God is with thee whithersoever thou goest." Joshua 1:9

"By humility and the fear of the Lord are riches, and honor, and life." Proverbs 22:4

"In the fear of the Lord is strong confidence: and His children shall have a place of refuge." Proverbs 14:26

"The angel of the Lord encampeth round about them that fear Him, and delivereth them." Psalm 34:3

*"...fear was on every side: while they
took counsel together against me,
they devised to take away my life.
But I trusted in Thee, O Lord:
I said, Thou art my God."*

Psalm 31:13,14

11

PRAYER OF FAITH
FOR TIMES OF FEAR

❖

*"Call unto Me, and I will answer thee,
and show thee great and mighty things,
which thou knowest not."*

Jeremiah 33:3

❖

Father in the precious Name of Jesus Christ, I thank You for Your great love. Forgive me for the wrong that I have done and the sin knowingly or unknowingly that I have committed.

Lord, I realize that we are not to be fearful or afraid, but that we are to trust You. At this time, I confess that I am fearful of what I am facing. I ask that You take this fear out of my mind, heart, and life right now. Strengthen me and help me to trust You and be ALL that You would have me to be.

I rebuke the hand of the enemy that comes to make me afraid. I come against him through the shed blood of Jesus Christ, who loves me and lives within me. For truly Greater is He (Jesus) that is within me, than he that is in the world. This is what I believe and Lord help me continue to confess this in the times of all my fears.

Now Lord, You have not given me the spirit of fear, but of power, love, and a sound mind. Therefore, I thank You for victory, deliverance, and power. I refuse to wait until the battle is over, but I shall shout right now!

Victory today is mine. Victory today is mine. Hallelujah! In Jesus Name! Amen

❖

12

QUIPS & QUOTES
ABOUT FEAR

"Both fear and faith sail into the harbor of your mind, but only faith should be allowed to Anchor." [1]

"Fear tends to produce the thing that it's afraid of." [1]

"The greatness of our fears shows us the littleness of our faith." [1]

"While fear slows down our thinking process, it greatly improves our footwork." [1]

Babe Ruth said, *"Never let the fear of striking out get in your way."*

You gain strength, courage, and confidence
with each fear that you face and overcome.
Each victory will help you to win other victories.

"It is easy to be brave from a safe distance." [1]

"Courage is not the absence of fear,
but doing what you are afraid to do."

What an amazing verse by Mrs. C. D. Martin as she penned the words of His Eye Is On The Sparrow.

"Let not your heart be troubled, His tender word I hear,
And resting on His goodness, I lose my doubts and fears;
Tho' by the path He leadeth, But one step I may see: His
eye is on the sparrow, And I know He watches me."

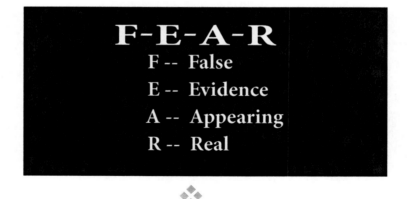

F-E-A-R
F -- False
E -- Evidence
A -- Appearing
R -- Real

[1]*MAC'S Giant Book Of Quips & Quotes*, E.C. McKenzie, Baker Book House, Grand Rapids, Michigan, Copyright 1980

❧13❧

WORRY

❖

"Therefore, I say unto you: take no thought for your life, what ye shall eat, or what ye shall drink; nor yet for your body, what ye shall put on. Is not the life more than meat, and the body than raiment?

Therefore, take no thought, saying, What shall we eat? Or, what shall we drink? Or, Wherewithal shall we be clothed? For after all these things do the Gentiles seek: for your Heavenly Father knoweth that ye have need of all these things.

But seek ye first the Kingdom of God and His Righteousness; and all these things shall be added unto you. Take therefore no thought for the morrow; for the morrow shall take thought for the things of itself. Sufficient unto the day is the evil thereof."
 Matthew 6:25, 31-34 KJV

The Living Bible reads: *"So My counsel is this: don't worry about things – food, drink, and clothes. For you already have life and a body and they are far more important than what to eat and wear. So don't worry at all about having enough food and clothing.*

Why be like the heathen? For they take pride in all these things and are deeply concerned about them. But your Heavenly Father already knows perfectly well that you need them, and He will give them to you if you give Him first place in your life and live as He wants you to.

So don't be anxious about tomorrow. God will take care of your tomorrow too. Live One Day At A Time." Matthew 6:25, 31-34 *Living Bible*

In these verses Jesus is teaching about worry. In His earthly ministry, Jesus spent a lot time teaching His disciples to trust God rather than worry about their own needs.

What is worry?

Worry means to feel uneasy about; to cause to feel anxious, distressed, or troubled. Worry is nagging concern which divides and distracts the mind, by drawing a troubled person's mind in different directions. Worry is a form of fear that attacks our well-being through many different areas.

Much worry is about:
- *The Future*
- *Death*
- *Failure*
- *Accomplishments*

- *Acceptance*
- *Having daily food, clothing, shelter*
- *Money for obligations*
- *Safety*
- *Security*
- *Protection from hurt, harm, danger*
- *Disease, illness, disability*

As you can see, the list goes on and on.

No disciple of Jesus can afford the luxury of worry. Worry is not only a sin against the power and the ability of God, but is a sin against ourselves. Worry is a foolish and destructive habit that can kill – like a slow poison. Thousands have shortened their lives by worry, and millions more have made their lives bitter by dropping this unhealthy habit into their souls every day.

Concerning the basic necessities of life, God has given us a promise that if we seek first the Kingdom of God and His righteousness all these things shall be added unto us.

This promise is conditional. If we fail to pay attention to the condition, we can't expect the performance of the promise. If we fail to do our part, (deep down on the inside) it robs us of our confidence in the Lord to do His part, and this produces worry.

"...If our heart condemn us not, then have we confidence in God." I John 3:21

Through our seeking first the kingdom of God and His righteousness, God has promised to make sure that all of our needs are met according to His riches in glory by Christ Jesus.

"But my God shall supply all your need according to His riches in glory by Christ Jesus." Philippians 4:19

If we live in obedience to God and His Word, He can never be accused of non-support concerning one of His children.

David said, *"I have been young, and now am old; yet have I not seen the righteous forsaken, nor His seed begging bread." Psalm 37:25*

The opposite is true when you decide to run your own life. Look at what God says about that:

"But ye have set at nought all My counsel, and would none of My reproof. I also will laugh at your calamity; I will mock when your fear cometh." Proverbs 1:25, 26

Through this foolish mistake of living without depending on the Lord, you have the monumental task of trying to take care of yourself against everything that will come against you. That is not an easy road.

Many are either finding out or have found out that money, good looks, great caution, excellent health care, stocks, bonds, and bodyguards cannot guarantee a long, happy, fulfilled, and satisfied life. Many that have an abundance of all the so-called nice securities are still filled with WORRY.

Only a true disciple of Jesus Christ has the power of complete freedom from worry. Here is the scenario:

- *God Is our loving Heavenly Father*
- *The Lord Jesus Christ Is our Savior and Friend*
- *The Holy Spirit Is our Comforter and Strength*

The Triune God is on our side.

"If God be for us, who (or what) can be against us?" Romans 8:31

Therefore, the believer doesn't need to worry about anything, because we have a great convoy through life – the Father, the Son, and the Holy Spirit. Our Great God has All-Power in His hands and He has made that power available to each of His children. We must only Ask, Seek, and Knock, through prayer.

Here is God's instruction from His Word.

"Be careful for nothing (don't worry about anything); but in everything by prayer and supplication with thanksgiving let your requests be made known unto God." Philippians 4:6

Here is a poem that blessed me as it speaks about the foolishness of not trusting God. We must do the former of this poem and not the latter.

His Will
"It is His will that I should cast my care on Him each day;
He also bids me not to cast my confidence away.
But oh! How foolishly I act when taken unaware,
I cast away my confidence and carry all my care!"
James Seward

"Cast not away therefore your confidence, which hath great recompense of reward. For ye have need of patience, that, after ye have done the will of God, ye might receive the promise." Hebrews 10:35, 36

There is no need to
nervously pace
the deck of the ship of life
when the Great Pilot
is at the wheel.

❖

$\wp 14\wp$

WHY PEOPLE WORRY

❖

"Then Daniel...was astonied (dazed) for one hour; and his thoughts troubled him." Daniel 4:19

Normal, sensible concern is an important attribute of the mature person. This is the type of concern that Paul had for Titus.

"I had no rest in my spirit, because I found not Titus my brother." II Corinthians 2:13

Senseless worry is different from normal, sensible concern. Senseless worry can never help us, but it can harm us by disturbing one's ability to function properly. Not only is worry spiritually unhealthy, but it is also physically unhealthy. Worrying about a thing does more damage to those who worry than the actual thing itself.

Worry and health

Medical Science agrees that the strain and stress of needless worry and anxiety produces stomach ulcers and other physical problems. Modern medical research has also proven that worry breaks down resistance to disease.

More than that, worry can actually disease the nervous system by constricting the vessels that carry blood, particularly to the digestive organs and the heart. It has great affect in destroying the effectiveness of the human body.

If you add to this the toll of unhappiness, sleepless nights, and days void of internal sunshine that worry causes, you then have a glimpse of the work that this monster of worry does.

Much time and energy is wasted worrying, wondering about, and trying to prepare for what might happen. This is a major trick of the enemy who is out to steal, kill, and destroy lives. I've found out over the years that many of the things the devil causes us to worry about never come to pass.

Worry is like a rocking chair.
It will give you something to do,
but it won't get you anywhere.

Many are constantly tormented in the mind and just want a break from the voice in the head that is forever giving dire warnings, predicting possible disaster, and making it nearly impossible to simply be in the present moment.

Sometimes it's hard to put a finger on any one cause for worry.

It may be:
- *Something from childhood, as a deep emotional scar*
- *Past sin that hasn't been confessed or forgiven*

- *Uncertain possibilities of the future*
- *Possibility of failure*
- *Harsh criticism*
- *A big problem that's threatening and getting closer*

Satan is a master at using things to trouble our minds and distract us in order stop us from being effective light-bearing Christians. The enemy of our souls would love to make us miserable with worry, than let us live lives of joy and peace within.

God wants His peace to reign and rule in our lives.

Worry is an inside job.
Let's keep it unemployed.

Said the robin to the sparrow, *"I should really like to know, Why these anxious human beings rush about and worry so."*

Said the sparrow to the robin, *"Friend, I think that it must be, That they have NO Heavenly Father, such as cares for you and me."*

∽15∾

WORRY *vs.* FAITH

❖

You only worry about things that you have never given completely over to God. If you really trust God, there is no need to worry.

You have two choices to make about the things that trouble you:

1. *Try to solve them on your own*
2. *Give them to God*

You can't give your worries up for a little while and then grab them back to worry about them again. It's like this – have you ever tried to watch a seed grow into a plant by digging it up every day to see how it is doing? No, No, No! It doesn't work that way. You have to leave the seed in the soil and then the miracle will take place. Give your worries to God and leave them there. Rest your case in His strong loving hands. Let Him take total charge and He will fix it for you!

"For the eyes of the Lord run to and fro throughout the whole earth, to show Himself strong in the behalf of them whose heart is perfect toward Him..." *2 Chronicles 16:9*

Time and time again our basic necessities and well-being are going to be challenged and threatened. God often times let situations come into our lives that we can't handle by ourselves. These things are not to be stressed out and worried over, but they are designed to bring about (in us) greater levels of trust in God. According to Scripture, we should rejoice in the midst of them.

"My brethren, count it all joy when ye fall into divers temptations" (tests or trials).... *James 1:2*

To rejoice rather than worry is a chance to prove to ourselves, the devil, and those around us how faithful God is.

"There hath no temptation taken you but such as is common to man: but God is faithful, who will not suffer you to be tempted above that ye are able; but will with the temptation also make a way to escape, that ye may be able to bear it." *I Corinthians 10:13*

Why worry?

If the problem is so big that you can't think of an answer or a solution, it will be more amazing and miraculous to see how God solves it. When we trust Him to meet our needs, it gives God a chance to show Himself strong on our behalf.

Many of us can testify to the fact that most of the things that the devil cause us to worry about never come to pass. Yet, this same thought pattern of worry, that has paralyzed many yesterday, is doing the same thing today.

The battleground is the mind. The best way to fight off the fiery darts of worry is to memorize and fill your heart and mind with Scripture.

"Thou wilt keep him in perfect peace, whose mind is stayed on Thee: because he trusteth in Thee."
Jeremiah 26:3

Satan wants control of your mind by filling it with worry and the cares of this life. God says, Don't let the enemy have control of your mind. Fill your mind with My Word. It is the perfect antidote for worry. God's Word will produce comfort, peace, and confidence when facing life's crises. That's why the Psalmist said:

"Oh how love I Thy law! It is my meditation all the day."
Psalm 119:97

"Thy words were found and I did eat them, and Thy Word was unto me the joy and rejoicing of my heart."
Jeremiah 15:16

"This book of the law (the Bible) shalt not depart out of thy mouth; but thou shalt meditate therein day and night, that thou mayest observe to do according to all that is written therein: for then thou shalt make thy way prosperous, and then thou shalt have good success." Joshua 1:8

Many people will tell you that they can never remember Scriptures, yet they know addresses, phone numbers, television show times, recipes from scratch, sports statistics, lyrics to songs, and countless other memory things. If you really want to, you can learn to memorize Scripture. Learning them is done through constant repetition. With God's help it can be done.

"I can do all things through Christ which strengtheneth me." Philippians 4:13

If we fill our hearts and minds with God's Word, it will become a part of us, and it will leave no room for worry. The antidote for worry is faith.

How do we get faith?

"Faith cometh by hearing, and hearing by the Word of God." Romans 10:13

Speaking God's Word in faith is the tactic to be used when worry comes to attack our minds. As you recite the Word of God, worry must depart. When worry comes back, speak the Word again and again if you must, and worry must flee. This is what daily spiritual warfare is all about.

".....Resist the devil, and he will flee from you." James 4:7

Sister Freeman and I often discuss how through the years, in the midst of disappointments, trials, problems, and other worries of life, we have held on to one of the greatest promises in Scripture.

"And we know that all things work together for good to them that love God, to them that are the called according to His purpose." Romans 8:28

Instead of being depressed, discouraged, defeated, and filled with worry, Sis. Freeman and I have used God's Word to hurdle us higher. Through the reliance of Scripture, we have learned to maintain a positive outlook on life. No, all things have not been joyous, but we have learned to obey God and count it all joy anyhow. Because of that, many think we have had it easy and haven't gone through much in life. We've had our share of distresses but it hasn't shown, because of the way the Lord has allowed us to go through each test and trial.

Each day we strive to walk *"in the fear of the Lord, and in the comfort of the Holy Ghost...."* Acts 9:31

The Spirit filled life in Christ is the sweetest life on this earth.
- *Only the disciple of Jesus has One who guards better than armies.*
- *Only the disciple of Jesus has security stronger than castles.*

Whatever we need for living, His strong hands will provide for us as the need arises.

In my life, there have been a lot of LMD's (last minute deliverances) by the hand of God. He has never been too late. In Him I find no fault. His ways are sometimes difficult to understand, but in time He makes it all plain. Oh, how I love the Lord! What great wonders He constantly performs.

"Blessed be the Lord, who daily loadeth us with benefits..." Psalm 68:19

As we live for Him, work for Him, and are faithful and obedient to Him, He will supply all our needs. We have an ironclad guarantee of His faithfulness – *"All these things SHALL be added unto you."* Matthew 6:33

You can't prevent the birds of worry and care from flying over your head, but you can prevent them from building a nest in your hair.

∽16∾

TWO AWFUL ETERNITIES

❖

I read a saying called "Two Awful Eternities" that has blessed me over the years. This chapter is based on that saying.

There are two days we should never Worry about; two days which should be kept free from fear and apprehension. One of these days is YESTERDAY.

Yesterday

Yesterday there were cares, hurts, aches, pains, mistakes, faults, and blunders. But yesterday has passed forever beyond our control. All the money in the world cannot bring it back.

We cannot erase a single word that we have said. We cannot undo a single deed that we have done. We are dead to yesterday. We must let it go.

....."*but this one thing I do, forgetting those things which are behind, and reaching forth unto those things which are before...*" *Philippians 3:13*

Tomorrow

The other day that we should not worry about is TOMORROW.

Tomorrow will have its own share of possible successes. Only God knows about tomorrow. Tomorrow is beyond our immediate control. Tomorrow's sun will rise either in splendor or behind a mask of clouds – but it will rise. Until it does, we have no stake in tomorrow, it is yet unborn. Rest assured –when tomorrow comes, God's grace will be with it, sufficient for the tasks, the trials, and any troubles that it may bring.

"My grace is sufficient for thee: for My strength is made perfect in weakness." *2 Corinthians 12:9*

Today

That leaves only one day – Today. Today comes only once in a lifetime. Once spent it cannot be brought back at any price. It will never return. Today is the golden tomorrow that you dreamed of yesterday, and so will it be till the end of time.

Today is our day of opportunity. Any man or woman can fight the battles of just one day. However, when we let the devil pile on the burdens of those two awful eternities of yesterday and tomorrow, is when we are liable to break down. Worrying about those other two days of yesterday and tomorrow poisons our whole system. It Kills! That's why Jesus said that we are to live one day at a time.

Therefore, don't worry about tomorrow. It will take care of itself. You have enough to worry about today.

Those that don't know God may worry about tomorrow, but we believers should trust Him for all of our needs, wants, and wishes. **God will provide for our needs as they occur.**

"Lord, for tomorrow and it's needs, I do not pray; But cleanse me, keep me, guide me, use me Lord - Just For Today!"

Do not let this day escape misused or abused. Today is the day to rejoice. Today is the day to give, to serve, to worship, to pray, and to work. Today is the day to care, to be reconciled, to forgive, to trust, to love, to speak a kind word, to forget old wrongs, to share the Gospel, to obey the Bible, to appreciate loved ones, and be glad.

"This is the day which the Lord hath made; we will rejoice and be glad in it." Psalm 118:24

Today, we shall have bread. Today, we shall ride out the storm. Today, He shall make ways and open doors. Today, He shall exceed our every expectation. Today, He will provide.

"Casting all your care upon Him, for He careth for you." 1 Peter 5:7

"Many are the afflictions of the righteous: But the Lord delivereth him out of them all." Psalm 34:19

In Jesus there is Pardon for the Past! For the believer, the guilty past is gone. No Worry!

"As far as the east is from the west, so far hath He removed our transgressions from us." Psalm 103:12

In Jesus there is Power for the Present! The believer can now walk right, talk right, and live right. There should be no worries about our needs being met, staying saved, or whether we will make Heaven or not.

"Behold...I give you power over all the power of the enemy....." Luke 10:19

In Jesus there is Peace, Hope, Victory, Security, and Assurance for the Future. Our future is out of this world.

"Let not your heart be troubled:...I go to prepare a place for you. And if I go and prepare a place for you I will come again, and receive you unto myself; that where I am, there you may be also." John 14:1-3

In Christ, we are safe and secure from all alarms!

Remember: The first priority in our lives should be to "seek first the Kingdom of God and His righteousness." He has promised to take responsibility for the rest.

> # Do not be afraid of TOMORROW, for God is already there.

❧ 17 ❧

UNSAVED SHOULD WORRY

❖

Those that are unsaved should worry, because there is great eternal danger in living without Jesus, and being outside the sheepfold of salvation.

One of the purposes of the Holy Spirit is to create worry (conviction) in the life of the unsaved.

"And when He the Spirit of Truth is come He will reprove the world (cause great concern) of sin, righteousness, and of judgment." John 16:8

This worry that is caused by the Holy Spirit is the goodness of God attempting to lead the unsaved to repentance.

"The Lord...is longsuffering to us-ward, not willing that any should perish, but that all should come to repentance." 2 Peter 3:9

While in an unsaved state, there were always the temporal things to worry about, but what I constantly worried about most was my soul. I constantly worried about the fact that I was a sinner with no Savior. I worried knowing that my righteousness was as filthy rags before God. I worried knowing that I would have to face the Righteous Judge on judgment day and I knew I was not ready.

Therefore, before I met Jesus, there was much worry and constant fear in my heart because of my soul's condition. I could not escape this worry and it caused my soul to constantly cry out like Paul:

"O wretched man that I am? Who shall deliver me from the body of this death?" Romans 7:24

One Friday night, it happened. The burdens of my heart and the worries that troubled my soul were rolled away. I found myself singing the song:

"What a wonderful change in my life has been wrought, since Jesus came into my heart! I have light in my soul for which long I have sought, since Jesus came into my heart!"

Since that miraculous encounter with Jesus Christ, my biggest worry was now gone forever.

"There is therefore now no condemnation to them which are in Christ Jesus, who walk not after the flesh, but after the Spirit." Romans 8:1

God troubles the mind of the unsaved for their own good. The only cure to silence the guilt, shame, and condemnation of the heart is to surrender to the Lord Jesus Christ.

".....the riches of His goodness and forbearance and longsuffering; not knowing that the goodness of God leadeth thee to repentance." **Romans 2:4**

"Today if you will hear His voice, harden not your hearts."

Hebrews 4:7

⚓18⚓

CASTING CARES ON HIM

❖

What joy to be invited to come to the King of kings and the Lord of lords. If you've never acquainted yourself with the depths of God's love, then His call to you is to live in His love. Instead of being fretful, restless, and always looking for that illusive "something more" you can learn to turn your confidence toward God and cast your cares on Him. You then can learn to be calm in the midst of life's demands. Here is His invitation.

"Come unto Me all ye that labor and are heavy laden and I will give you rest...And ye shall find rest unto your souls."
Matthew 11:28,29

"...Him that cometh to Me, I will in no wise cast out."
John 6:37

There is hope today, whereby the biggest worry can be taken care of. You can enter into the peace of God. Those who come to Him and cast their cares on Him will never be cast out.

"Therefore being justified by faith, we have peace with God through our Lord and Savior Jesus Christ."
Romans 5:1

Even though we have peace with God, that does not mean that we will escape life's dangers and dilemmas, but it does mean that we can have the ability to live with tranquility in the midst of them. Though troubles may remain, the confusion, apprehension, and despair will begin to fade away as we learn to trust God more and more.

Through God's power we can:
- *Show poise under pressure*
- *Be unshaken by life's alarms*
- *Have peace in the midst of problems*
- *Radiate peace wherever we go*
- *Be untroubled in a troubled world*

Paul and Silas were thrown in jail. Instead of being discouraged about it, they prayed and sang praises to God. God showed up and He performed a miracle by bringing them deliverance. As a result, a whole household was saved.   Acts 16:23-31

God can and wants to use you in the same way, to show forth His power. God will take care of you. There is no problem you have that is too big for Him. Whatever it is that troubles you, turn it over to the Lord and TRUST Him.

"....and he that believeth on Him shall not be confounded (disappointed)." 1 Peter 2:6

"There hath no temptation (trial, test, worry) that hath taken you but such as is common to man: but God is faithful, who will not suffer you to be tempted above that ye are able; But will with the temptation also make a way of escape, that ye may be able to bear it." I Corinthians 10:13

Today, don't worry, but be happy. God will take care of you.

"Rejoice in the Lord always and again I say, REJOICE!!!" Philippians 4:4

May you experience daily FREEDOM from FEAR and WORRY and walk in Total Victory through our Lord and Savior Jesus Christ and the power of His Holy Spirit. Amen

> *"If ye abide in Me, and My words abide in you, ye shall ask what ye will, and it shall be done unto you."*
>
> *John 15:7*

19

PRAYER OF FAITH
FOR WORRY

❖

Father in the Precious Name of Jesus Christ, I know that it is a sin to worry and not trust You. Forgive me of this sin and cleanse me from all iniquity. Lord, I am Your child. This situation that I am facing is too big for me to handle. But I know that with You "all things are possible." You can help me where no one else can help.

Here are my worries. Take them now. I give them to you as a child gives his father a broken toy for him to fix. I ask that You work out my fears and worries whether they are real or imaginary. Deliver me from these burdens. Through the power of Thy Holy Spirit, take control of my life and give me peace in the midst of this storm. I thank You in advance for what you are doing in my life right now.

Now Lord, help me as I pray each day and read my Bible. Open my understanding to what the Scriptures say, so that I'll never doubt You again. Even if I should come to you again with this same worry, in Your love and mercy I know You'll welcome me as if it were my first time.

Thanks for being so kind, loving, and patient with me. I thank You for blessing me right now. Help me to continue to confess and believe that I don't have any trouble; all I need is FAITH in God. In Jesus Name. Amen

❖

QUIPS & QUOTES
ABOUT WORRY

❖

*"Every tomorrow has two handles. We can take hold of it
by the handle of Anxiety or the handle of Faith."* [1]

Don't take tomorrow to bed with you.

*Instead of counting their blessings,
many magnify their problems.*

"Worry often gives a small thing a very big shadow." [1]

"Worry never robs tomorrow of its sorrows;
it only saps today of its' strength." [1]

Worry that comes from sin must be taken care of
by honest repentance, forgiveness, and restitution.

"Worry is the advance interest you
pay on troubles that seldom come." [1]

"Worry is like a rocking chair, it will give you
something to do, but it won't get you anywhere." [1]

"Blessed is the man who is too busy to worry in the
daytime and too sleepy to worry at night." [1]

❖

[1]*MAC'S Giant Book Of Quips & Quotes*, E.C. McKenzie, Baker Book House,
Grand Rapids, Michigan, Copyright 1980

❧21❧

JESUS - LORD OF THE STORMS

❖

"When Jesus therefore perceived that they would come and take Him by force, to make Him a king, He departed again into a mountain Himself alone.

And when even was now come, His disciples went down unto the sea, And entered into a ship, and went over the sea toward Capernaum. And it was now dark, and Jesus was not come to them.

And the sea arose by reason of a great wind that blew. So when they had rowed about five and twenty or thirty furlongs, they see Jesus walking on the sea, and drawing nigh unto the ship: and they were afraid. But he saith unto them, It is I; be not afraid. Then they willingly received Him into the ship: and immediately the ship was at the land whither they went." John 6:15-21

The thing that God truly desires to have from each of us is a relationship. Adam and Eve in the beginning had a close relationship with God.

Their relationship was severed when they disobeyed God and ate from the Tree of the Knowledge of Good and of Evil. The fall of man in the Garden of Eden put a great distance between God and man.

When the sin gap was created by man, there was no way that man in his own self or power could get back what he had lost. If it had not been for the compassion and the grace of God, mankind would have been lost forever.

God came to man's rescue after man's fall, and gave man a way to once again find favor with Himself. That way was through sacrifice. Not just any type of covering or sacrifice would do. Adam and Eve tried to cover themselves with fig leaves, but that would not do. It had to be a blood sacrifice. God gave them coats of skin that came from innocent animals blood (Genesis 3:21).

The blood of those innocent animals, pointed to the supreme sacrifice that Jesus Christ would one day make on Calvary's Cross.

> *"But now once in the end of the world hath He appeared to put away sin by the sacrifice of Himself."* Hebrews 9:26

> *Neither by the blood of goats and calves, but by His own blood He entered in once into the Holy Place, having obtained eternal redemption for us."* Hebrews 9:12

God's love for us and His desire to have a close relationship with us caused Him to give His only begotten Son, the Lord Jesus Christ on our behalf. God gave Jesus even while we were yet in our sins.

"But God commendeth His love toward us, in that, while we were yet sinners, Christ died for us." **Romans 5:8**

Once we receive Jesus as Savior, our sins are forgiven and we are then, born-again. We are born into the family of God, which restores our relationship with God through Christ.

"For He hath made Him to be sin for us, who knew no sin; that we might be made the righteousness of God in Him." II Corinthians 5:21

All our sins are then cast into the sea of God's forgetfulness, and we are given a brand new start.

After we come to faith in Christ, God wants us to grow in our relationship with Him. We are commanded to *"grow in grace and in the knowledge of our Lord and Savior Jesus Christ."* *2 Peter 3:18*

As we begin to grow in Him, life takes on a new meaning. The new meaning should be one of getting to know Jesus more and then setting out to make Him known. This process of knowing the Lord more comes about in many different ways. **One of the ways that God uses to cause us to know Him more is through lessons or trials.**

These lessons or trials are something that we don't like to hear, but it is the truth. The Scriptures point out over and over again that God uses trials to deepen our faith in Him.

A series of miracles took place to give the disciples a closer look at Jesus and who He really was.

In John chapter 6, there was a multitude following Jesus around. They had seen Him work physical miracles on those that were sick. Now, they had just seen Him feed five thousand men, not counting the women and children, with five barley loaves and two little fish.

This made such an impression on the mob, that they said, this is what we need, a Prophet like Moses. He'll heal us and feed us. Let's make Him a king and no doubt He can mobilize us, lead us, and eventually, we can then overtake the Romans.

Their thoughts were only on the physical. Jesus did not come here to set up a physical kingdom the first time that He was here. He came to set up a spiritual kingdom, and they had missed what Jesus was really trying to do.

To get his disciples away from that type of thinking and the error of this mob mentality, Jesus constrained them or strongly urged them to go to Capernaum.

> *"And straightway Jesus constrained His disciples to get into a ship, and to go before Him unto the other side, while He sent the multitudes away."* Matthew 14:22

Now, Capernaum was about six to seven miles away. The disciples got in the little ship and off they went.

After the multitude was gone, Jesus departed into the mountain alone to commune with His Father, by spending time in prayer. Nothing got in the way of the prayer life of Jesus - not preaching, not teaching, nor serving. He was often alone in secret prayer with the Father.

He said, *"Men ought always to pray..."* Luke 18:1

The Disciples on the sea

The disciples obeyed. They manned the oars, and started to row. At first, all was well out on the sea. Then it got dark. They encountered a storm and the sea became very rough. The wind was howling and the waves were crashing against them. They were seemingly in big trouble.

I read that even today on the Lake of Galilee, when those winds and waves kick up, they keep the motor boats at the dock. They dare not go out there in that sea in the time of a storm. Can you imagine being in that little boat in a storm like that?

I've been in rough waters at night in a little boat, and it was not fun. A few years before my salvation, I went out into the ocean one night with my boss for a boat ride in his little boat. It got dark and it seemed like we were the only ones in the ocean. The winds picked up and the water became very choppy.

To get back to the shore we had to come through the inlet. The waters were so rough and treacherous that I didn't think we were going to make it. We were the only ones out there and there was no help in sight.

Being unsaved at the time, I was terrified and afraid of death. I said to myself, "What was I thinking, by getting in this little boat!" I prayed that night and made all kinds of promises to God. I thank God we made it. Then I quickly forgot my promises I made to God.

Now, back to the disciples. They had been rowing the boat for hours, yet they had made very little progress against the fierce storm. Their limbs were bone tired. They were no farther than the middle of the lake and still they were about three miles from shore. The disciples were tired and frustrated. They were having a difficult time.

I'm sure there were questions such as - Where is Jesus? Is He sleeping somewhere, while we are out here rowing? Why would He send us out here like this?

The disciples were right about their assessment of the situation. Indeed, it was Jesus that had put them in that situation. It was

Jesus that told them to go to Capernaum. It was Jesus who orchestrated this whole event.

However, the question is, why did Jesus send them into the sea like that? I believe that Jesus deliberately sent them into the sea to face that storm to teach them an important lesson.

Through this event of the storm and the sea, God would give them a clearer picture of Who Jesus really was and is. Jesus was more than a man. They had to know His divinity in order to carry out His mission of evangelism.

As we also go forth in daily missions of evangelism, we too must know who Jesus really is. God still uses stormy encounters of life in order to give us clearer pictures of Himself and His ways. Therefore, there will be storms in our lives.

Life's Storms

There are some myths in our day about life's storms. Many believe that obedience to God produces smooth sailing. Yes, obedience does bring blessings into our lives, but obedience does not necessarily produce smooth sailing. We believers will still have our storms.

There are two types of storms.
1. *Storms of Correction*
2. *Storms of Perfection.*

Storms of Correction

Some storms happen as a result of our personal sins. When we yield to temptation, it gets us in trouble with God and this can cause storms. These storms come to help cleanse us from the error of our ways. These are storms of Correction.

Remember the man who was lame for thirty eight years?

Jesus said, *"Behold thou art made whole, sin no more, lest a worse thing come upon you."* John 5:14

This man's infirmity seems to have happened because of something he had done - some personal sin or disobedience. This was a storm of correction.

Storms of Perfection

There are some storms which we are called to go through which are not a result of something that one has done wrong. These are storms of Perfection.

Remember in John 9:1-3, the man that was blind from birth? The disciples asked, *"Master who did sin that this man was born blind?"* Jesus said, *"Neither hath this man sinned nor his parents."* The reason was so that the works of God might be made manifest in his life. This man's blindness would be used to bring God glory. This was a storm of Perfection.

There will also be some that think the storms of life are there because one's faith is not strong enough to move or end it. Beloved, that is not always the case.

The Word of God reveals that the Apostle Paul had great faith. Yet, he was in many storms *(II Corinthians 11:23-28)*. For one particular storm Paul sought the Lord three times to get him out of it and deliver him.

But God said, *"My grace is sufficient for thee. My strength is made perfect in your weakness."* II Corinthians 12:7-10

Once this was made known to Paul by God, Paul gladly accepted the will of God and rejoiced in all that he was called to suffer for the cause of Christ.

"Most gladly therefore will I rather glory in my infirmities, that the power of Christ may rest upon me. Therefore I take pleasure in infirmities, in reproaches, in necessities, in persecutions, in distresses for Christ's sake: for when I am weak, then am I strong." II Corinthians 12:9,10

Beloved, attached to the Christian life is persecution, suffering, and spiritual warfare. It's all a part of the Christian call. That's what taking up the Cross and following Jesus is all about. What they did to the Master, they will also do to His servants.

Now, the disciples sea trip was Jesus' idea. The Bible says, "He constrained" or sent them. Notice, this storm came because they were IN the will of God.

Storms of life

All of us will face storms. Sometimes life gets tough, sometimes things can get messy fast, and sometimes there seems to be no end as to how bad it can get.

We can't forget the recession of 2008 and how it brought with it many worldwide crises. It brought many crises such as housing, energy, rising oil prices, cutbacks, downsizing, disappearing paychecks, and faded American Dreams for many.

There are also other storms that we have to contend with. There is:

- *Disease*
- *Disability*
- *Collapse of loving relationships*
- *Loved ones taken over by addictions and evil habits*
- *Growing older and all the complications it brings*

There are winds of change on every turn. In our own strength, we seem powerless to make any headway against these storms.

When the seas are raging, and it looks like the ship of our lives are about to sink in the midst of the storms, oftentimes it causes fear and worry as life seems to be unraveling.

Then there is the cry, *"Where are You Jesus? Don't You care? Can't You see what I'm going through?"*

Let's look at the hand of God in this text. Did Jesus really leave the disciples? The answer is NO. His eyes were on them all the time. Miles away, in the black darkness, He saw them struggling with the storm that He had raised up for them. In the midst of their fear, confusion, and even terror, they didn't realize that Jesus was interceding and praying for them. His eyes were on them all the time (Mark 6:48).

In the fourth watch of the night, it was not too early and it was not a moment too late. Here comes Jesus walking on the water. Suddenly, out of the darkness they see Someone. It's a faint figure in the distance, effortlessly approaching them. How could a man walk on the surface of the water as if it was dry ground? Would he not sink and drown?

Suddenly someone cried out, *"It is a ghost."* The disciples were terrified, and every trace of courage vanished. They were filled with so much fear that it made them forget about the wind and the waves.

Often times God shows up in unexpected ways. The thing we think is a curse can turn out to be our biggest and best blessing.

The disciples, after seeing what appeared to be a ghost, heard a voice saying, *"It is I, be not afraid."* It was Jesus. It was Jesus. He had not abandoned them. He had come to them.

Right in front of them, they witnessed the miracle of Jesus exerting His full power over nature. He exercised power over the law of gravity and power over the law of liquidity. These forces were fully subject unto Him. Jesus had created these laws of the universe, and of course He could override and overrule them anytime He wanted to.

Jesus identified Himself as I Am, in a sense the very name of God. This encounter strengthened their faith. The disciples saw Jesus like they had never seen Him before.

When Jesus got into the boat the wind ceased. Not only that, but they were at their destination immediately. What an amazing night, the disciples had that night.

The next day, I don't think it was the storm that stuck out in their minds, nor their heroic effort to get to other side. But I think it was Jesus and Who He really was that filled their thoughts. The encounter they had in the midst of the storm, pointed them in the right direction as to Who Jesus really was.

Jesus often demonstrates the reality of His claims. He piles signs upon signs to prove who He claims to be. He is the Lord of all storms. He rules over all creation, time, and space. I've seen His mighty hand time and time again in my life.

We all encounter frequent storms in life. God is sovereign over all that happens in our lives. We are not alone at any time in our Christian lives. The Lord is always with us through His Spirit.

> "*...for He hath said, I will never leave thee, nor forsake thee.*" *Hebrews 13:5*

If you are currently experiencing some difficulties or troubles in your life, there is no need to fear or worry. Jesus has His eyes on you. He is actively praying for you. He is interceding on your behalf right now. Do you know that?

".....He ever liveth to make intercession for them."
Hebrews 7:25

Jesus Christ is entered into "Heaven itself, now to appear in the presence of God for us." Hebrews 9:24

For each storm of life that you encounter, perhaps there is something you need to learn. Remember, it's God who sets up the classroom. It is God who sends the lesson.

Then, He prays for your success of the lesson and for your Christian perseverance through that lesson.

Jesus told Peter, *"Simon, Simon, behold, Satan hath desired to have you, that he may sift you as wheat: But I have prayed for thee; that thou faith fail not: and when thou art converted, strengthen thy brethren."* Luke 22:31

After the arrest of Jesus, Peter failed by denying Jesus three times. This was the result of that denial.

"And he went out and wept bitterly." Matthew 26:75

God did not leave him in that state. Jesus came to him and restored him.

"He saith unto him the third time, Simon, son of Jonas, lovest thou Me?

And Peter said unto Him, Lord, Thou knowest all things; Thou knowest that I love Thee. Jesus saith unto him, Feed my sheep." John 21:17

On the Day of Pentecost Peter did just that, he fed the sheep as Jesus had commanded. God used him mightily as he preached the Word of God and three thousand lives were changed from death to life.

"Then they that gladly received his word were baptized: and the same day there were added unto them about three thousand souls." Acts 2:41

Jesus is actively praying for us in every situation that we face, that our faith will not fail, that we will stand firm, and that we will endure and persevere to the end.

In order to be effective in our walk and witness, we need to be rock solid as to Who Jesus is. We must know that He loves us, that each and every event that occurs in our lives is allowed by the hands of an All-Wise providence, and that the events allowed are good for us.

When facing our trials and tribulations, we must say to ourselves, if God brings an event or storm to me, and it bear upon me, He has a purpose for me in it. Not only is He watching over me in it, but He's praying for me in it. What a Great Deliverer God is. God cares not only for my salvation, but for everything about me.

Of all the promises Jesus gave to us about Heaven, Eternal Life, the Rapture, etc., probably among the most meaningful are those where He says,

"I will never leave thee." Hebrews 13:5

"Lo I am with you always." Matthew 28:20

"I will not leave you comfortless, I will come to you." John 14:18

There is never a need to fear or worry because we are never alone at any moment of the trial or difficulty. God does not promise that we can avoid the storms and that He will prevent unfair or terrible things from happening to us. But He does provide assurance that when the worst does happen, we are not alone. He will help us and guide us through each event.

David said of the Lord, *"Yea though I walk through the valley of the shadow of death, I will fear no evil. For Thou art with me." Psalm 23:4*

My counsel to those in the midst of a storm is -- God knows the load you bear. God knows what opposition you are fighting against right now.

> *"Thou knowest my downsitting and mine uprising, Thou understandest my thoughts afar off. Thou compassest my path and my lying down, and art acquainted with all my ways."* **Psalm 139:2,3**

The Lord of Storms

In our text, Jesus calmed the storm. At His command, the waves and the winds lay down at His feet like little puppies.

What is your storm today? Jesus can handle it. He can calm your storm. He is the Lord of all storms.

God knows what He is doing. He never makes mistakes. Call on Him and in His time, the winds will cease, and there will be peace. *Sometimes He calms the storm and sometimes He let the storm continue to rage, but He calms us in the storm.*

The Lord can bring peace to the storm that's raging in your mind and heart right now. Jesus says, "It is I, do not be afraid. My eyes are upon you. I Am praying for you. You are going to make it through this. I will provide."

There are no pointless trials. If Jesus sent us into a storm, His authority is reigning over it even though it may be raining on us.

Your storm may be caused by your sin or your failure, but God is still able to make something positive out of it. He can walk right over the top of the storm. He is bigger than any of our problems. We can face any enemy on the outside, because Jesus is on the inside.

> *"Ye are of God, little children and have overcome them: because greater is HE that is in you, than he that is in the*

world." I John 4:4

When the going gets rough and the love of God seems furthest away, do not be fearful. Do not be afraid. The love of Christ rides with you. His love will bear you up and sustain you through each and every circumstance.

God is sovereign and He controls all. He's the Master of the sea. Billows His will obey. He rules over the winds, the sea, storms, nations, kings, rulers, wicked men and over all their schemes. **If you're unsaved, He wants to be your Savior.** Be saved today.

Remember: If you are born again, God does not always use the sunshine to teach us, often times He uses storms. None of us can dodge storms. We will all have our times on life's stormy seas. **These trials or storms are not designed to sink our boat, but they are to enhance our navigation skills.** As children of God, we are never alone. No matter what the test, we are to REJOICE. God is up to something. He's doing something special in our lives.

There is no need to fear or worry. There is One who stands by us and will never leave us. His Name is Jesus. He has already proved His love for us. For while we were yet sinners, Christ died for us. Now that He arose and lives again, there is nothing that He won't do for us. He is our Salvation and our Mighty Deliverer. When we come to Him and Him alone, He will help us overcome the insurmountable circumstances that test our lives.

"Those that come to God must believe that He IS, and that He is a Rewarder of them that diligently seek Him."
Hebrews 11:6

Amen

"In our lives there is bound to come some pain, surely as there are storms and falling rain; Just believe that the One who holds storms will bring the sun."   Unknown

"God left the world unfinished for man to work his skill upon. He left electricity still in the cloud, the oil still in the earth.

How often we look upon God as our last and feeblest resource. We go to Him because we have nowhere else to go.

And then we learn that the storms of life have driven us, not upon the rocks, but into the desired haven."   George MacDonald

May God richly bless you as you walk with Him.   Amen

More Than Conquerors

The Leroy Freeman Evangelistic Association, Inc./DBA/More Than Conquerors is a non-profit, evangelistic, mission-minded ministry dedicated to the purpose of:

- *Lifting up the Name of Jesus*
- *Winning Souls*
- *Edifying the Body of Christ*
- *Destroying the Works of the Devil*

Your prayers and love gifts are encouraged and will be greatly appreciated as we ever seek to know Jesus more and make Him known.

I pray that you have received a blessing from this book. To share your testimony with me, your prayer request, or if you would like more information about this ministry, Write Me:

MORE THAN CONQUERORS
Evangelist Leroy Freeman
P. O. Box 221076
West Palm Beach, FL 33422 USA
Off (561) 684-2193
Cell (561) 329-0173
Fax (561) 684-1109
E-mail: ministries@mtcm.com
Web site: **www.mtcm.com**

Pray for us! God Bless You!

Do you know someone whereby fearful and worrisome thoughts dominate their thinking?

Do you know someone that feels anxious most of the time?

Do you know someone whereby fear keeps them from moving forward?

This book will make a great gift for them.

Get additional copies Today!

Available CD's by Evangelist Leroy Freeman

Jesus - The Messiah *CD*

Suffering then glory is what Isaiah 53 is all about. Follow along verse by verse as we look at the vicarious sufferings of the Lord Jesus Christ and the glory that follows. What an encouragement this chapter is to our lives as we strive to follow in His footsteps.

Victory Over Trials

We were not meant to live in the Agony of Defeat. God wants us to experience the Thrill of Victory, even though our days may be filled with trouble and trials. From this CD get greater insight about TRIALS.

7 Churches 7 Messages
CD

Follow the history of the church from these two chapters of Revelation 2 & 3. These are some of the last words of Jesus spoken to the early body of believers and His messages are still very relevant today. **What type of Church is your church where you worship?**

Jesus - Lord
Of The Storms *CD*

None of us are exempt from the Storms of life. There are Storms of Correction and Storms of Perfection. Find out about them on this CD. Also hear the horrific tragedy that inspired the song: Precious Lord Take My Hand.

Psalm 23 *CD*

This is one of the greatest chapters in all of the Word of God. Each verse is explained and shows the tender care of a good shepherd toward his sheep. This symbolizes God's love, care, provisions, and protection of His believers. Your heart will rejoice as you listen to all of the great God given benefits found in this Psalm that's available to us today.

CD's

$7.00 each

+ shipping and handling
Write me or visit our web site
and order your copies.
www.mtcm.com

About the author

Evangelist Leroy Freeman is an anointed preacher and teacher of the Word of God, who has been walking with the Lord for over 30 years. He believes in the simplicity of the Gospel and ministers in a unique way, often times using simple visual illustrations of many different Bible truths, painting unforgettable pictures in the mind. This unique style of ministry ministers to both the sheep (mature) and especially the lambs (young). He is ever striving to prepare everyone for the soon return of the Lord Jesus Christ.

Over the years, apart from doing personal ministry, he has supported and assisted other local and world-wide ministries as they too advance the Gospel of the Lord Jesus Christ.

He is an associate minister of Christ Evangelical in West Palm Beach, Florida where the Pastor is Minister Allen McClinton. He is also an active volunteer of KAIROS International Prison Ministry, a Men's Ministry leader, and is involved in other local organizations.

He currently resides in West Palm Beach, Florida with his lovely wife Patricia A. Freeman and has been married for over 32 years. He has three beautiful children - LeRoy Jr., Angel, and Gabriel and a growing number of adorable grandchildren.

To find out more about Evangelist Freeman and the work that God is using him to do visit his web site:

www.mtcm.com

Printed in the United States
136389LV00005B/1/P